READ TO DEATH

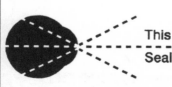

A READ 'EM AND EAT MYSTERY

READ TO DEATH

TERRIE FARLEY MORAN

WHEELER PUBLISHING
A part of Gale, Cengage Learning

GALE
CENGAGE Learning®

Farmington Hills, Mich • San Francisco • New York • Waterville, Maine
Meriden, Conn • Mason, Ohio • Chicago

LIBRARY OF CONGRESS CATALOGING-IN-PUBLICATION DATA

Names: Moran, Terrie Farley, author.
Title: Read to death / by Terrie Farley Moran.
Description: Large print edition. | Waterville, Maine : Wheeler Publishing, 2017. |
    Series: Wheeler Publishing large print cozy mystery | Series: A Read 'em and eat
    mystery
Identifiers: LCCN 2017004706| ISBN 9781432838249 (softcover) | ISBN 1432838245
    (softcover)
Subjects: LCSH: Large type books. | GSAFD: Mystery fiction.
Classification: LCC PS3613.O6826 R43 2017 | DDC 813/.6—dc23
LC record available at https://lccn.loc.gov/2017004706

Published in 2017 by arrangement with The Berkley Publishing Group, an imprint of Penguin Publishing Group, a division of Penguin Random House LLC

Printed in Mexico
1 2 3 4 5 6 7 21 20 19 18 17

Robert Adam Moran:
best son ever

CHAPTER ONE

In the parking lot of the Read 'Em and Eat Café and Book Corner, I stood by the side of a sky blue van with oversized white letters advertising the "Gulf Coast Cab and Van" etched on the center door panel. I mentally counted the members of the Cool Reads/Warm Climate Book Club as they settled in. All six were present. My BFF and business partner, Bridgy Mayfield, was busily stowing thermoses of sweet tea and pastry boxes in the carrier right behind the driver.

Oscar Frieland sat in the driver's seat, his bony knees sticking out of a pair of khaki shorts; one cuff was ripped, leaving a strip of cloth dangling. His thin gray hair stuck out in every direction. Thick black eyebrows looked as though they hadn't been trimmed in decades. A number of wiry brow hairs were inching toward his receding hairline. He had a plump red pillow stuffed behind his back, pushing him toward the steering wheel. Oscar eyed the pastry boxes. "Hey, missy, you got any of those Robert Frost fruity things stuck away in there for later? Sure do love 'em."

A few rows back, well into her seventies but still quite perky, Blondie Quinlin said, "Oscar, you never met a sweet you didn't want to nibble."

"True enough. And that especially goes for your sweet cheeks."

His mischievous reply caused the women on the van to laugh uproariously, except for Blondie's seatmate, Augusta Maddox, who boomed, "Mind your manners, Oscar. All ladies here, you know."

Oscar ignored Augusta and turned back to Bridgy. "So, what's in the boxes?"

Bridgy smiled. "Miguel made his wonderful Miss Marple Scones with a delicious sweet orange sauce to give our snowbird members a final taste of Florida before they head up north."

"But no fruit?" Oscar was insistent.

Rather than remind him that orange was indeed a fruit, Bridgy sighed and got out of the van, rolling her eyes at me. "Sassy, I'll run inside and pack up a few Apple and Blueberry Tartlets, rather than listen to Oscar teasing me about them all day."

I pushed an unruly lock of auburn hair out of my eyes and reached into the wide turquoise messenger bag slung over my shoulder and across my chest. I pulled out a set of colorful visitor's guides to the Edison and Ford Winter Estates and was about to step on the bus when I heard a familiar voice. "Wait. Don't leave. I told you I want to tag along. Here I am."

Bridgy's aunt Ophelia, owner of the Treasure Trove, an upscale consignment shop a few doors from the Read 'Em and Eat, was hurrying toward the van. Her left hand was squashing a wide-brimmed straw hat firmly on the crown of her head, and she was waving her right arm in wide circles, as if anyone could miss her dashing along the asphalt in a chartreuse dress cinched with a bright green belt that matched her strappy high-heeled sandals.

She stopped in front of me and dropped her hand onto her ample, heaving chest. "Darlin', I had so much to do. Cancel two appointments. Reschedule a delivery. There's no way I was going to miss this trip with all of your charming book club ladies. I was afraid you'd leave without me, even though I know I told Bridgy . . ."

I tuned Ophie out completely and focused on counting the visitor's guides. I clambered into the van and began passing the guides to the four snowbirds who, along with townies Blondie and Augusta, had been attending the book club all winter.

Oscar didn't seem to notice that his plaid shirt was misbuttoned. He reached for the longer hem, grabbed at the fabric and began polishing the lenses of his sunglasses. He glanced at Ophie. "Hey girl, come if you're coming."

Ophie stood stock-still until she realized that Oscar had no intention of helping her climb into the van. Then she pulled herself up two high steps, settled into a seat and gave a honey cheerful "Hi y'all" to the other occupants.

"Didn't take you to be one who's interested in the history of these parts." Augusta's rumbling baritone filled the van, floated out the door and caught the ear of a man walking across the parking lot. He stopped and checked the sky for dark clouds accompanying what he thought was thunder. Seeing none, he continued on his way.

"Gracious me! Of course I'm interested." Ophie took off the straw hat and began fluffing her hair, which I considered to be oat colored but she constantly referred to as "natural blond." "At one time brilliant men such as Thomas Alva Edison and Henry

Ford agreed that Fort Myers was the finest place to live, leastwise in the winter months. Why then, their reasons pique my curiosity."

"When we decided to read *The Florida Life of Thomas Edison* as our final book of the season, I thought, *ho hum.* But it turned out to be fascinating." First-time snowbird Tammy Rushing was pleased that most of her fellow clubbies um-hummed in agreement. "It's great to know the history of a place. I loved learning about the Calusa Indians when Margo and I toured the Mound House. I expect today we'll all find out a lot about the history of the area in a timeline much closer than the two thousand years ago when the shell mound was built."

Her seatmate Margo Wellington replied, "I'm sure you Americans know a lot more about Edison and Ford than we do. They both are icons down here. In Canada we know who they are, what they did. We appreciate their achievements, but we don't glorify them the way you seem to. In Fort Myers, everyplace I turn there is an Edison something or other. Even the big mall is named after him."

Sonja Ferraro was stuffing a sweater into her massive imitation alligator tote. She paused, glanced at the ceiling for a few seconds as if making a decision and then turned catty-corner in her seat and looked directly at Margo. "Speak for yourself. I grew up in Windsor, right across the river from Detroit. You can bet we learned everything there was to know about Henry Ford. Jobs at the Ford plant kept our families going for generations. And we learned plenty about Edison, too."

Margo dismissed her with a hand flap. "No need to get snippy. I only meant . . . Oh, why am I bothering? I don't have to explain myself." And she turned to gaze out the window.

Tammy offered a rueful smile, as if silently apologizing to all for her friend's rudeness, and popped her sunglasses on top of her head. The wire rim got caught in a tuft of hair, and Tammy grimaced.

While Tammy was struggling to untangle, Margo pointed to the glasses. "That's why I wear plastic frames. You paid what? I'm guessing more than a hundred dollars for a first-class highlight process resulting in those blond and silver streaks. Every time those glasses pull out a few strands, the symmetry of the shading is damaged. Although with all the red in your hair, I'm not sure why your hairdresser didn't recommend gold tones."

Tammy pushed her hair back into place and turned her attention to me as I reminded everyone to fasten their seat belts.

"It's going to be a bumpy ride. Remember that movie with Bette Davis? What was the name?" Ophie looked to Blondie Quinlin for help, but it was the much younger Sonja who chimed in.

"*All About Eve.* And it's a bumpy night, not ride. 'Fasten your seat belts. It's going to be a bumpy night.' I love the old black-and-white movies."

I interrupted before the conversation wandered too far afield and someone whipped out a cell phone to look up the day's schedule on TCM.

"We're going to have a busy morning. We'll visit both the Edison and the Ford houses, and then Edison's laboratory — a fascinating place. Those of you who like gardening will be amazed at the variety of plant life Edison cultivated. Not to mention his dozens of experiments to grow a plant that could be used as rubber for tires. After World War One and the rise of the automobile and the airplane, Edison and his friends, Henry Ford and Harvey Firestone, wanted to develop a replacement for rubber, which was a major import product. They wanted to be sure the United States had its own supply."

I felt my face flush when Margo let out an exaggerated sigh. "I thought that section about trying to develop rubber plants was the most boring part of the book."

Quick to the rescue, Oscar leaned out of his seat and reminded me, "Don't forget the tree."

I flashed him a grateful smile. "Somewhere around 1925 Edison had a banyan tree planted on the property, and today it covers somewhere around half an acre. I seem to recall it is the largest banyan in the nation, maybe the world. You'll want to take pictures. No one back home will believe it."

"And they have a weird swimming pool tucked off in a corner." Augusta Maddox's voice thundered through the van again. "You would think with the houses built right on the Caloosahatchee, they'd jump into the river to cool off, like we jump into the Gulf of Mexico. Rich folks. Humph." She shook her head.

Bridgy stepped up into the van with a big pastry box, which she stowed behind Oscar's seat.

He eyed the package. "Fruit?"

"Fruit," Bridgy answered.

"Okay, then. You and Sassy get into your seats. Snap your belts. This train is leaving

14

the station." Oscar hit a button on the dashboard that slid the wide door closed. He turned the key in the ignition and said, "I'm putting the air conditioner on low. Let me know if anyone is too hot or too cold." And he pulled the van into the traffic on Estero Boulevard.

Traffic was light on the San Carlos Bridge, and it didn't take long before we were on the mainland and the van was rolling along McGregor Boulevard.

"I never get tired of looking at the magnificent royal palms that line this street. Why, some must be one hundred feet high. Do you think Edison planted them?" Ophelia asked.

I was searching for an answer, mentally going through all the material I'd prepared for the excursion, when Oscar chimed in. "McGregor Boulevard was nothing but a dirt road when Edison showed up in 1885. Wasn't even McGregor Boulevard. There was a time it was known as Riverside Drive. Caloosahatchee is right there." He waved vaguely to his left. "Of course now houses block our view. There was a time you could see the river while you were riding on this road. I'm guessing that's what attracted Edison. Pure country."

Remembering my notes, I interjected,

"Edison started by planting a few hundred royal palms on the road to beautify his ride into what used to be known as downtown. You know, where the hotel was. It's mentioned in the book."

"And didn't the road lead to Punta Rassa where the boats landed?" Tammy didn't sound quite sure.

Blondie nodded vigorously, her curls tapping against her forehead. "Punta Rassa was the major port for these parts. Back in those days this was cattle country. Edison was here before the railroad came over this way. Quite a trip he made each year."

Angeline Drefke laughed. "My husband and I drove down from Pennsylvania. We took our time, stopped along the way, and I was still bushed when we got here. But we had such a wonderful winter, it was well worth the trip. When I was reading how the Edison family traveled, I was totally worn-out from imagining what they endured and how long it took."

"We sure had an easier time of it than folks did more'n a hundred years ago. I'll give you that." Oscar made a smooth right turn into the parking lot of the Edison and Ford Winter Estates complex. "Course we only come from the beach, not from some faraway place like New Jersey." He growled

16

a laugh as he pulled into a space between two vans, one a bit bigger than his own.

The clubbies climbed out of the van and were getting ready for their tour. A few were rearranging their hats. Tammy Rushing was rubbing sunscreen on her nose and cheekbones. Blondie Quinlin shook her head. "Should have thought of that sooner, honey. Takes time to seep in, you know. You can borrow my hat if it gets too sunny, but Edison was one for planting trees, so we'll have lots of shade."

Ophie got her bearings quickly and did a little spin on her spiky heels. "There's acres and acres of land here. Imagine living like this? Such luxury."

"You're one who ought to know, given the prices you charge for them trinkets you sell." Augusta waggled an accusing finger.

Ophie reared back for a few seconds and then leaned toward Augusta. "I'll have you know . . ."

"Time to get moving. Our guide will be wondering where we are." I pushed expertly between Augusta and Ophie all the while sincerely hoping that I wasn't going to have to stay between them for the rest of the morning.

CHAPTER TWO

Bridgy and I herded our charges across the parking lot toward a buxom mid-fiftyish woman wearing a broad-brimmed straw hat. She introduced herself as Ivy, our tour guide.

"Right on time. I love that in a group. Welcome to the Edison and Ford Winter Estates."

I introduced the book club members, and Ivy handed each of them a set of earphones attached to a small box. "I am going to walk you around the estate and tell you lots of stories. When we are done, you'll have some time to wander on your own, and you can listen to the guided tour on tape as a refresher. That way we can enjoy our time together, but you can be sure not to miss out on any facts. We get so many tourists here that the audio tours are available in French, German and Spanish. These are English. Anyone need another language?"

Margo pushed her sunglasses to the top of her head. "Some of my neighbors at home in Quebec would appreciate the French language tape. Though I'll wager most Canadians take the English tape just as I will, thank you."

Sonja grabbed a headset and stuffed it in her alligator bag. "Probably won't need it, but better safe than sorry." She turned to Bridgy. "I have a perfect memory. I won't forget anything. No 'refresher' on tape for me."

Bridgy nudged Sonja to follow along in the direction Ivy and I were leading the group.

"How big is this place, anyway?" Ophie swiveled her head, looking for clear boundaries.

Ivy gave an expansive smile as she turned to be sure the entire group heard her answer. "The museum covers twenty acres on both sides of McGregor Boulevard. We'll be crossing to the west side so we can visit Seminole Lodge — that's the Edison home — then we'll walk a few feet next door to The Mangoes, the Henry Ford estate."

"How many years was Edison here before Ford came along?" Blondie Quinlin was a woman who liked her facts to be as exact as possible.

"Well, Edison came to Punta Rassa by boat from Cedar Key in 1885. Then he traveled upriver. Liked what he saw and bought this land from one of the Summerlins — you know, the cattle barons."

Sonja interrupted. "You mean like Summerlin Road? Where the outlets are?"

Bridgy and I exchanged a smile. If Sonja had such a great memory, how could she have forgotten that the Summerlins were a founding family of the area? And the story of the sale of the house was right in the beginning of the book the clubbies read for today's outing.

Ivy continued as if Sonja hadn't spoken. "It was well after 1900 when Henry Ford came for his first visit, and right before America entered the first World War he bought The Mangoes and began wintering here with his family."

Augusta Maddox poked Blondie with her elbow. "That's about what the book told us." Ivy never missed her stride when Sonja spoke, but Augusta's booming voice startled her for a few seconds. She recovered quickly.

"I have arranged for a table and chairs to be set up under the banyan tree for a small refreshment break after we visit the houses and before our trip to the laboratory. Now, are we all set? Any questions?"

Ivy gave me a tight smile. "Seems like an interested group. Let's go." And she led the Cool Reads/Warm Climate Book Club across McGregor Boulevard.

A while later we were standing on the porch of Seminole Lodge. Augusta pointed to the long, narrow swimming pool near the riverbank and thundered, "Who would be so foolish? There's the pool." She swung her arm a few degrees. "And there's the Caloosahatchee. Where'd you rather swim? I'd take the river any day."

Ivy moved quickly as if to block the staircase before she realized that Augusta wasn't planning on rushing off to dive in for an immediate swim. She grabbed my arm. "Er, perhaps while I show The Mangoes to the ladies, you could walk back to pick up the refreshments. We can meet at the banyan."

Bridgy and I went off to the parking lot to get the sweet tea and pastries. Along the way we bantered about how uptight Ivy seemed to be. I thought she took her job very seriously, but Bridgy was of the opinion that Ivy was bossy.

"She's one of those people who thinks that whatever she's saying is much more important than what anyone else has to say."

The door to the van was open, and Oscar

was sitting on the steps. He stood, rolled the battered magazine he'd been reading and thrust it into his back pocket. Judging by the red trim, it was an issue of *Time.*

"Snack time, is it? Good thing. I was getting a mite peckish. Let me help you carry the provisions. Then I'll help you eat them."

"Sure, we could use the extra hands." Bridgy handed him a box of pastries and a jug of tea and then divided the rest of the packages with me.

Oscar set his jug on the ground so he could close and lock the van door. Then he followed along behind us. "Where did you stash the ladies?"

"Ivy took them to Seminole Lodge. We're meeting them under the banyan tree."

"I suppose the tourists will be having their pictures taken with Edison's statue so that they can go home and brag about how they hung out with old Tom under the largest banyan tree in North America." Oscar shook his head. "It's amazing what some people think is important."

"Well, you have to admit that the man himself was important. Think how much he and his friends contributed to Fort Myers and the surrounding area. They brought money and visitors, who in turn brought money, and some even became settlers." I thought it best to encourage Oscar to get all his complaining out of the way before we joined the book club members.

"Edison did his most famous work in New Jersey, but around here folks act like he invented the lightbulb while fishing off that old pier that juts out into the Caloosa-hatchee. You know, the one right behind the house."

Bridgy ducked under one of the outer reaches of the banyan tree. "At least he planted this tree giving us a lovely shady spot to rest while we nosh."

A life-sized statue of Thomas Edison was nestled amidst the hundreds of prop roots that had grown into sturdy trunks and continued to increase the size of the original banyan. Ivy was describing how the tree had expanded over the years and now covered the better part of an acre. Margo and Tammy ignored her and were taking turns standing next to Edison and snapping self-ies with their phones.

Oscar nudged me. "See, I told you. Pic-tures. Watch me rile 'em."

He stepped closer to the statue. "Ah, Edi-son groupies, are ye? Must be Jersey girls."

Tammy laughed. "I wish. Jersey has gor-geous beaches. I always seem to live inland. Insert exaggerated sigh here. Guess that's why I vacation in places as lovely as Fort Myers Beach. Trying to enjoy the water while I can."

Bridgy waved them over to a long wooden table. "Time to eat."

Oscar double-timed it and sat in the nearest chair.

"Where are your manners, Oscar? Make sure them women have a seat," Augusta Maddox ordered.

Oscar turned to Margo and Tammy, who were walking behind him. "Come along you Jersey girls. Grab a seat."

Margo practically stamped her foot. "I'm from Canada. Westmount. Near Montreal. I only come to America in the winter. I fly to the beaches in Florida." She shook her head and shrugged her shoulders as if asserting her French Canadian roots. "I don't think I would care for the American northeast."

Oscar stood. He pulled out chairs for Margo and Tammy and then moved and stood near the center of the table, where he could be sure to be seen and heard.

"Like Frankie Valli, I'm a Jersey boy through and through. Born in New Brunswick, not far from Edison's compound in Menlo Park. I'd like to stand up for my home state and say that Thomas Edison is more closely identified with New Jersey than he'll ever be with Florida, Seminole Lodge or no Seminole Lodge." And he gave Ivy a wide, slightly evil grin as he walked to take a seat.

Watching Ivy turn purple, I grabbed the topic and gave it a quick detour. "How many of you saw *Jersey Boys*? Bridgy and I saw it at the Barbara B. Mann Performing Arts Hall in Fort Myers a few years ago. What a terrific show."

Ivy relaxed and raised her hand, as did Angeline.

Sonja said, "People were dancing in the aisles when I saw it. That's one show I'd love to see again."

"Of course it was outstanding. Who made better music than the Four Seasons?" Angeline Drefke crossed her arms and nodded her head. There was no need for her to say, "That settles that." Her body language told all. But she was alone in her opinion.

"The Beatles!"

"The Eagles!"

"Bon Jovi!"

"Wait one minute now. Y'all are ignoring our fine southern music. Don't be forgetting Lynyrd Skynyrd." Aunt Ophie stood up half singing, half humming "Sweet Home Alabama." Then she began clapping. In less than a minute, most of the group was swaying and clapping along with her.

Bridgy decided to begin serving tea while everyone was in a festive mood. I followed along, putting out plates of snacks. I centered a plate piled high with Miss Marple Scones and put two bowls of orange icing on either side, with deep scooping spoons alongside the bowls.

Very gingerly, I set Miguel's famous Question Mark Cookies on a plate. He'd packed the cookies so carefully that the chocolate frosting trimmed with white icing hadn't smeared at all.

Unpacking the Robert Frost fruit tartlets, I toyed with the idea of putting them as far away from Oscar as possible, but there was no sense agitating him. If we were lucky, he'd be busy eating until Ivy started the tour again. I divided the tartlets onto two plates, placing one at each end of the table.

I didn't realize how parched I'd become until I pulled out the chair next to Bridgy and sat down. I took a big gulp of sweet tea and felt refreshed with the first swallow.

Ophie fanned a fly away from her scone, took a bite and blotted her mouth with a napkin. No lipstick was disturbed by the dabbing. "I didn't read the book y'all read, but I am sure Miss Ivy here can tell me how this land came to be owned by, who, exactly?

The City of Fort Myers? The Edison heirs?"

Ivy gave a sly glance at Oscar. While brushing imaginary specks from her fingertips, she preened silently until she had everyone's attention. Her smile said she was happy to be back in charge.

"Well, having read Ms. Albion's book, I know you are all aware that Thomas Edison died in 1931. However, his second wife and then widow, Mina Edison, remained very active in the Fort Myers community even after she remarried."

It was amazing how much noise Oscar could make getting out of his chair.

"I'll see you all back at the van." Then he looked directly at Ivy. "How long would you say, an hour?"

Ivy sucked in her cheeks looking more and more like an angry fish. "Maybe a bit longer."

I got the impression she would make the second half of our tour last as long as she could in the hopes it would annoy Oscar.

Ivy slipped back into her tour guide demeanor. "Let me see . . . The question was about the ownership of the estates. Shortly before her death in 1947, Mina Edison turned her Fort Myers property over to the City of Fort Myers, which immediately opened it for community tours. Two decades later the town purchased The Mangoes and added it to the public grounds."

Ophie raised her hand. "So our tax dollars support this entire place?"

Ivy shook her head. "No. There was a planned renovation, but as the project grew and grew, it seemed wisest to create a nonprofit corporation to run the estates. More than a dozen years ago the Thomas Edison and Henry Ford Winter Estates, Inc., came to be. And I'm sure you would agree, they've done a superb job of what I like to call renovation without modernization."

She looked around, expecting agreement, and everyone nodded and smiled. Well, nearly everyone. Augusta was captivated by a large white butterfly as it danced from one branch to another of the old banyan tree.

Ivy pursed her lips. "Well, I guess we're done here." She caught my eye and pointed to Bridgy. "You two can clean up. I'll lead the tour on to our next venture. We'll meet you in the laboratory."

She double clapped her hands in a rhythm that sounded eerily like the clicker that Sister Mairéad used to demand immediate silence and obedience when I was in second grade. The clubbies recognized the sound of a directive. They stood.

Ivy walked purposefully and signaled with a wave for the ladies to fall in behind her. As we watched them head off to the laboratory, I was grateful she didn't make them march to the cadence of *hup two three four, hup two three four.*

I had a feeling my day would greatly improve as soon as this outing was finished.

CHAPTER THREE

Bridgy and I piled all the trash in a sturdy bag. I ate the last Question Mark Cookie, and we were able to fit all the remaining scones and tartlets in one box. Two of the tea jugs were empty, and the third was only half full. All in all, our bundles were much lighter as we walked back to the van. I was grateful that the clubbies' appetites and our food estimates were in sync. I suppose that's one of the perks of being in the restaurant business. I was mentally patting myself on the back for guesstimating so accurately when Bridgy said, "Sassy, did you hear me? I asked how long you think the book club meeting will last once we get back to the Read 'Em and Eat."

"Oh, I don't think the ladies will want to chitchat too long. After all, we've been together for hours. They probably won't be up for an in-depth conversation. Think third grade book report: *I like this book. Mr. Edi-*

son was a smart man. He didn't like the cold winter so he came to Fort Myers. That was when the cowboys lived here. The End."

We were still laughing when we got to the van. Oscar was nowhere to be seen. We were deciding whether or not to leave the bags and jugs when he came up behind us.

"Took a little stroll to walk off those fruit thingies. Wouldn't you know, I ran into an old fishing buddy and got to gabbing. Reminded me of some stories I'd like to tell the ladies on the drive home." He unlocked the van and took the pastry box out of Bridgy's hand. "Now that I got my exercise, I believe I have room for more fruit." He shook the box. "Have any extras?"

We left him to eat another tartlet or two and went off to find Ivy and her charges. The clubbies were remarkably chipper, filled with enthusiasm.

Sonja positively bubbled. "I had no idea Edison's lab was so . . . so scientific. I mean, they call it a botanic research laboratory, so I thought it would be, well, all about making flowers prettier. You know, stuff like that."

Angeline picked up the thought. "Ivy told us this place was designated by the American Chemical Society as a National Historic Chemical Landmark only a few years ago.

31

It's not only about flowers. It's really systematic. Wait 'til you see."

And see we did. Even though I'd carefully read *The Florida Life of Thomas Edison,* I still didn't get how Edison's mind worked. Where did his wisdom come from? What prompted him to decide America needed to find a way to grow its own rubber for tires and such? How did he have the gumption to plow ahead and try to accomplish it? I guess for a man with more than a thousand patents, it all came naturally.

I followed the presentation carefully, but even after Ivy explained Edison's ideas and the process he followed, I couldn't fathom how he picked the goldenrod as the most likely plant to produce rubber. The conversation got more and more animated. And I had never seen the Cool Read/ Warm Climate Club members so energized.

As soon as we'd taken leave of Ivy and were walking back to the van, Tammy Rushing said, "I'm so glad that we took this tour. It really brought the book to life. Don't you think?"

Everyone had a lot to say. Even the usually unsocial Augusta Maddox contributed, "Old as I am, I'm not old enough to have been alive when Mr. Edison lived hereabouts. Wish I had met him. Would have been an honor."

I think she was pleased to see much younger heads nod all around her.

We were still chatting away as everyone climbed into the van. Oscar interrupted with a loud whistle followed by his "buckle up" speech, and he smiled broadly at the resounding clicks of latch plates locking into latches.

He nodded. "Now we can get under way. I'll have you ladies back on the island quicker than young Edison could telegraph the Gettysburg Address."

He pulled smoothly out of the parking lot and turned south on McGregor Boulevard.

Angeline guffawed. "You weren't on the tour. You didn't read the book. How do you know that as a teenager Thomas Edison started out as a telegraph operator?"

"Everyone in these parts acts like Thomas Edison is as much a product of Florida as big, ripe oranges. Well, I'll tell you, he was rich and famous long before he ever set foot in Fort Myers. Bothers me no end that this town places such a claim on him."

I could see that this was a touchy subject for Oscar, but before I could think of a way to steer the conversation in another direction, Sonja and Angeline exchanged a glance, and Sonja asked, "What's got you

33

so riled? You should be honored that you live in a place where such a famous man, and his famous friends, for that matter, spent a lot of time and did some magical things."

"Missy, I told you, I'm a Jersey boy from the start, and that is where Edison did his finest work. Menlo Park, West Orange, Newark. Those are the places where the real magic happened."

Bridgy flashed me her round-eyed look. The look that said, "Fix this now before there's a fight and our day is ruined."

Oscar continued. "Not only born there. I spent a good part of my working life there, too."

I jumped in. "Oscar, I don't remember you ever saying. What did you do for a living up north? Drive a bus, maybe, or a cab?"

"Nothing so boring. Oh, not that driving you nice ladies is in any way boring. Accept my apologies. It's that I was younger in my Jersey days, and I craved action. Headed for the bright lights."

"Broadway?" Bridgy asked.

"No, princess, the real bright lights. Atlantic City. Once the casinos opened, I knew that was where I had to be."

Happy to have the conversation off Edison and onto anything else, I decided to push Oscar further into his past. "What did you do in Atlantic City?"

A broad smile, steeped in memory, crossed his face. "I started as a busboy at the Brighton. Real classy place. Always treated their staff well. While I was going to school they let me work around my classes. Even promoted me to waiter. I can't say nothing bad about the Brighton. 'Course when I was done with my schooling they had no room for me as a croupier, so I had to move along."

Ophie was visibly impressed. "A croupier? Not a dealer? And you expertly wielded one of those long sticks? What are they called?"

Oscar beamed. He had the rapt attention of everyone in the van, including me. "Stick works, although some folks call it a rake. We used it to 'rake' in the money. Dice and chips, too. You don't strike me as a gambler, but you sure could be the fancy lady on a high roller's arm."

Ophie flushed with pleasure. "Whenever we went on a cruise, my first husband, Mr. McLennon, enjoyed a turn around the casino floor, as you say, with me on his arm. We both liked the atmosphere, but he wasn't what I'd call a gambler."

Angeline Drefke nearly shouted, "You have no idea how lucky you are, Ophie. I

35

come from Johnsonburg, Pennsylvania, out past the Appalachians. Right by Allegheny National Forest." She paused for a few seconds so we could each check the GPS she imagined was implanted in our brains. Then she continued. "We went to Atlantic City, and my first husband became a torment and stayed a torment 'til I finally tossed him right out the door with the clothes on his back and the change in his pocket."

She looked around with such fierce pride in her eyes, I almost blurted out, "Atta girl," but thought better of it. Just as well. Angeline was far from finished.

"That first trip he told me would be a vacation at the beach. He said maybe we'd take a peek at a casino. We left home early, took our time, stopped for lunch at Hershey and got to the hotel by dinnertime. Our last happy meal. That night we went to the casino at Resorts, and, to my horror, I quickly found out he loved the tables more than he ever loved me.

"Next thing I knew we were going to Atlantic City every chance we had. It's at least a six-hour drive, but he put the pedal to the metal. Not so much as a bathroom stop, much less a leisurely trip. He often had us there in under five and a half hours.

Couldn't care less about my safety or comfort."

Except for Oscar, who was focused on the traffic ahead, which had slowed down to a crawl, everyone in the van seemed to be holding her breath. I know I was.

Angeline's voice cracked. "Looking back I'm amazed he didn't total the car and us with it."

Tammy reached over, rested her hand on Angeline's shoulder and said, "Thank goodness that didn't happen." She hesitated, then asked, "Where was he getting the money to play?"

Angeline reached up and patted Tammy's hand. "When I asked about the money, he'd tell me that he won more than he lost, but . . . I knew that wasn't true. When I started gathering papers to file for divorce, I found out he mortgaged our house to the hilt and borrowed against our retirement fund. That was the end." Then she brightened. "Second husband is a dreamboat. Most of you have met him . . ."

The instant response was a general "nice man" and "such a gentleman" buzzing throughout the van.

Angeline finished in triumph. "And he has never so much as played bingo at church."

Sonja clapped Angeline on the back and

shouted, "Good for you," which started the rest of us cheering, mostly in relief that the story had a happy ending.

As the noise died down, Oscar said, "I still say some of you gals look familiar. I'm inclined to think there are a few former chorus girls in this van. Who's willing to show off her high kicks when we get back to the Read 'Em and Eat?"

Amidst the general laughter, Ophie said, "I will, if you will."

Margo Wellington had her face pressed to the side window and was staring at the traffic in front of us. "I see the problem. A car broke down up the road. The tow truck is hitching it up right now. This snarl should clear in a jiffy."

Between Angeline's story and Oscar's jokes, I'd completely forgotten that we were creeping along at two miles an hour.

Tammy said, "I love the beach in Atlantic City. I wonder if folks still ride bikes on the boardwalk in the early morning. Oscar, I never was a chorus girl." She slapped her thigh. "Don't quite have the legs for it."

Oscar said, "Are you sure about that? What with all the bike riding . . ."

Tammy giggled. "I'm sure." She turned to Margo. "What about you? Have you ever vacationed in Atlantic City?"

"No. I told you. I only come to the United States to head south for the sunshine and balmy breezes."

"You should really try the Jersey Shore in the summer. Sassy and I went there all the time when we lived in Brooklyn." As though she was the New Jersey Division of Travel and Tourism, Bridgy signaled for me to add my two cents.

"The Shore is great fun. Seaside Heights is my favorite. They have an outstanding boardwalk, too."

"Okay, ladies, hold on to your hats, the boulevard is finally clear. We're going to sail down the road and across the bridge." Oscar hit the gas.

In no time at all we pulled into the parking lot of the Read 'Em and Eat and tumbled out of the van.

Sonja lifted both hands, one holding her ever-present alligator tote filled with visors, sunscreen, protein bars and water bottles. In her other hand she was holding several bags from the museum gift shop. "I know I overbought, but I couldn't help myself. Twice I left the gift shop, and twice I turned right around and went back for one more thing. I'll put my things in my car and meet you inside."

"Brilliant." Tammy looked around. "I'm

going to put my stuff in my trunk. Why drag it all inside when we'll have to drag it out again?"

While the clubbies scattered around the parking lot, Bridgy bundled up our supplies, left two iced tea jugs at my feet and headed into the café with Ophie. I settled up with Oscar, picked up the jugs and followed along straight to the kitchen.

A few minutes later, carrying a fresh pitcher of lemonade, I came into the dining room and was pleased that the clubbies were organizing themselves for what I hoped would be a brief meeting. I grabbed a sleeve of paper cups from under the counter and set the lemonade and cups on the Dashiell Hammett table, next to the book club circle.

Bridgy came out of the kitchen and started poking around by the register. I held the sleeve of cups over my head. "Don't worry, I have them."

Bridgy shook her head. "No. I'm looking for my sunglasses. I don't know what I did with them. First time I wore my brand-new Ray-Bans."

Was it only two weeks ago that I told her not to spend so much money on sunglasses? Who listens to me? Not Bridgy, that's for sure. "Maybe you left them in the van."

She glanced through the plate glass window. "Right. And Oscar is still in the parking lot." She flew out the door.

I was serving lemonade to the clubbies when Ophie came out of the kitchen, carrying a small bag. She looked at me. "Hope y'all don't mind, but I helped myself to a container of *Old Man and the Sea* chowder. With some greens and tomato, it will make a nice dinner. Enjoy your meeting."

Ophie gave a wide good-bye arm circle to the group, but when she opened the door, she stopped dead still. She stuck her head out the door, looked back at me and barked, "Sassy, get over here."

I nearly knocked over a chair and ran to the door, thinking, *Please, don't let her be having a heart attack.*

Ophie put her finger to her lips and whispered. "Listen. Is that . . . ?"

"Help me. Please. Someone, help me."

It was Bridgy. I pushed past Ophie and ran out the door.

CHAPTER FOUR

The van. Bridgy said she was going to look in the van for her sunglasses, but I didn't see her, or Oscar, for that matter. Then I heard her again. "Someone. Anyone. Please. I think he's dead."

I ran to the van. Oscar was lying across the middle row of seats. Bridgy was kneeling at his side, her face soaked with tears. She looked at me and said, "He's dead. I'm so sorry."

I patted my pockets but couldn't find my phone. I heard Ophie coming behind me, her spiked heels tap-tapping on the pavement. I yelled, "Call 911," and when I heard her gasp, I reassured, "It's not Bridgy. It's Oscar."

It didn't take more than a glance to see that Oscar was, indeed, dead. His jaw was slack and his eyes opened and unfocused. The pallor of his skin looked ghostly. Heart attack, I thought. Then I saw the pair of scissors protruding from his neck. Oh dear Lord.

There was nothing I could do for Oscar, so I turned my attention to Bridgy. Her sunglasses were lying on the floor. I picked them up and held out my hand. "Come on. Ophie called for help. Let's go inside and wait."

Bridgy started sobbing. "We can't leave him alone."

I heard the wisdom in her words. There would be an inquiry. We certainly would be questioned.

"Listen, you go to the café with Ophie, and I'll wait here until the, uh, ambulance comes." In truth I had no idea what Ophie said when she called or who would respond first, but I was hoping for an ambulance. I was positive an emergency medical technician should take a look at Bridgy, so I hoped one was on the way.

I handed her out of the van into Ophie's waiting arms. Of all the big ole bear hugs I'd seen Ophie give Bridgy through the years, this was the most heartfelt. Ophie stroked Bridgy's hair and crooned, "It will all be fine, baby girl. You wait and see. Let's get your face cleaned up and maybe a soothing cup of tea. I have some chamomile in the Treasure Trove. Let's walk over."

I realized Ophie was right. The café, with the clubbies sitting in the book nook and waiting to begin a meeting, was the wrong place to bring Bridgy. I watched as Ophie loosened the hug, wrapped her arm solidly around Bridgy's shoulders and began leading her off to the Treasure Trove.

Bridgy looked back at me. "I don't want to leave you alone with . . . Oscar."

As the sound of sirens came closer, I reassured her, "Don't you worry. I'm going to stand outside the van. Hear those sirens? Help is on the way."

A white car with "SHERIFF LEE COUNTY" stenciled in green across the front and back doors pulled up beside the van. Deputy Ryan Mantoni jumped from the driver's seat. He grabbed me by both arms and stared into my eyes. "Are you all right? Where's Bridgy? Who's hurt? When we heard the address . . ."

Behind him, Lieutenant Frank Anthony was speaking into his shoulder radio. I didn't know if I should wait to tell them both at once. Past experience had taught me that the lieutenant was a stickler for getting information exactly as he wanted it.

"It's Oscar Frieland, the van driver. He drove a group of us to the Edison and Ford Winter Estates. He's in there." I pointed to

44

the van. "And he's dead."

Ryan immediately moved toward the van until I continued. "He's been murdered."

That stopped him. "How could you possibly . . . ? Never mind." He climbed into the van and came right out again. He leaned past me. "Loo, we got a homicide."

Ryan and Frank locked eyes and did that telepathic thing they do. Ryan took me by the arm and began steering me to the front door of the Read 'Em and Eat. "Sassy, it's going to be a long day. Why don't we go inside for a glass of sweet tea and a piece of buttermilk pie?"

We hadn't quite reached the door when it opened and Miguel came out. He sensed trouble immediately. "*¡Dios mío!* What is wrong? Are you hurt? Where is Bridgy?"

I was too frazzled to answer. Ryan said, "Oscar had an, er, accident. Sassy is fine." Then he looked at me. "If she's not with Miguel and she's not with you, where *is* Bridgy?"

I head-butted toward the Treasure Trove. "She's with Ophie." No point in getting into anything else for the moment. All I wanted was to sit down and have a drink. I thought wine would be nice. Fat chance.

As we walked in, the chatter from the book corner ceased instantly. I wondered if

I looked bad enough to stun the clubbies or if they picked up on how solicitous Ryan was being. Whichever, their curiosity was piqued. Ryan led me to the Emily Dickinson table and pulled out a chair. Grateful, I sat, or rather, buckled onto the chair. He leaned in and asked if he could get me anything. If it wasn't for Oscar's murder I would have thought the scene comical. Here was Ryan offering to serve me in my own café.

Miguel told the clubbies there had been a slight mishap and they were free to conduct their meeting without me, or they could go home and we could reschedule. A couple of the members glanced my way, but when they saw no obvious signs of injury, the ladies started talking among themselves.

Ryan, who had followed Miguel across the room, straightened to his tallest. "Excuse me . . . did you ladies all go on the trip to the Edison and Ford estates?"

"It was a book club field trip. We always have one before the snowbirds go home. We were all there. Together. What's your point? Did that Ivy person complain about us? I'd have to say we were better mannered than she was." Augusta stood up and rested her hands on the rope belt that held up her ancient jeans, ready to take on Ivy in any argument.

Ryan raised his hands defensively. "Miss Augusta, I don't know anything about how your trip went, and I don't know anyone named Ivy."

Augusta sat down and flashed a small but triumphant smile.

Ryan continued. "There's been a problem, so I am going to need you to stay here for a while."

"Problem? What sort of problem and how long? I have a hair appointment." Angeline fluffed her salt-and-pepper curls. "I certainly don't want to spend the rest of the week looking like this. Do you know how hard it is to reschedule an appointment with Nancy over at Creative Hair? She is always booked solid."

Ryan deflated slightly. Even watching him from behind I could see that the gentleman in him wanted to tell her she looked lovely, but the deputy wrestled for control and won. "Sorry, ma'am, but . . ."

"We all have errands. I'm sure this won't take too long." Blondie Quinlin tried a peaceful approach.

The door opened, and Frank Anthony walked in. Ryan took a giant step backward. "All these ladies were on the outing."

Glancing out the window, I saw several additional sheriffs' cars and an ambulance in the parking lot. Oscar's van was the epicenter of boundless activity. I raised my hand, because I was sure that if I spoke prematurely, Frank would accuse me of speaking out of turn, an accusation he'd made a time or two in the past. Of course still other times he blamed me for withholding information. Honestly, I couldn't win with that man. To avoid even the appearance of conflict, I wanted to give him complete information as quickly as possible, even if I did look like a schoolgirl in need of a hall pass.

He bobbed his head, which I presumed was permission to speak.

"Bridgy and Ophie were also on the trip with us."

He crossed his arms, never a good sign. "Where are they now?" His voice sounded like I'd let Bonnie and Clyde escape after still another bank robbery.

And I answered, completely forgetting that the clubbies had no idea what had happened. "At the Treasure Trove. You see, Bridgy found the body —"

The entire book club jumped from their chairs. Everyone started speaking at once, with noisy versions of "Body?" "What?" "Who?" "That can't be." It was their unique adaptation of "Liar, liar pants on fire." I wanted to throw a pitcher of lemonade on them. That would quench their curiosity.

Frank Anthony ignored them for the moment and instructed me to put the "Closed" sign on the door and to lock it for good measure, then he crossed the room with a powerful stride until he was nose to nose with the clubbies. He held up one hand, silencing them instantly. It occurred to me that I could have used him at some of the more rambunctious book club meetings.

"Ladies, there has been an incident in the parking lot. The driver of your tour van is being . . . cared for. I am sorry to inconvenience you, but it is imperative that you all remain here until my deputies have an opportunity to speak with you."

I was more than a little surprised he didn't get the same back talk that Ryan was subjected to a few minutes earlier.

There was a knock on the door. I stood, but Ryan waved me back into my chair and opened the door to a deputy I didn't recognize. He stepped inside and spoke in hushed tones. "Tell the boss we've set up a perimeter. The medical examiner is on the scene, and the DOA will be transported to the county morgue as soon as the photographer is done."

It sounded like I was living in an episode

of *Major Crimes.* If only Flynn and Provenza would come out of the kitchen squabbling while they chomped on purloined *Cubano* sandwiches. Then I'd know I'd hit the play button on the DVR and fallen asleep on the couch.

Ryan nodded. "You better stay here for now. Control the door. Don't let anyone in or out without the lieutenant's say-so."

Miguel came out of the kitchen. "I straightened the kitchen. I have two apple pies in the oven. I can take them out in a few minutes. Then the kitchen will be ready."

"Ready?"

He read my blank stare correctly. "*Chica*, Ryan and Lieutenant Anthony are going to want to talk to all of us . . ."

"Us? You weren't even on the trip."

"But I was here. Whatever went on, it happened right here after you got back from the museum. So they will want to talk to all of us. They will want privacy, and we have only the kitchen to offer. Unless you want them to use that cubbyhole you and Bridgy insist on calling an office."

I envisioned the oversized desk and chair cramped into the tiny room, maybe five square feet larger than the desk. Then I saw all the papers scattered on top of the desk

50

and the ever-present array of tanks and shorts that Bridgy and I left hanging on wall hooks in case we needed a quick change after a kitchen mishap. And if I remembered correctly, there was something I kept forgetting to bring home tucked in the well of the desk — a denim laundry bag holding a few odds and ends of dirty clothes. Okay. I'd rather not have Lieutenant Judgmental conduct his interviews in the office.

I stood and grabbed the back of my chair. "You're right. Let's bring a couple of chairs into the kitchen."

Miguel grabbed a chair under each arm and followed me through the swinging door. As always, the kitchen was immaculate. I marveled at Miguel's ability to prepare such tasty food while keeping the kitchen in tip-top shape. I shuddered at the thought of how it had looked when Miguel had an accident a while back and Aunt Ophie filled in for him. Oh, the food was delicious, but the kitchen looked as though an F3 category tornado spun through every twenty minutes or so. Miguel opened the oven, and the aroma of apples and cinnamon filled the room. He placed the pies on cooling trays and turned off the oven.

Ryan pushed the door open. "Lieutenant is looking for you two. Oh, do I smell fresh pie? Um-um."

Miguel knew Ryan was one of his biggest fans. "Perhaps when your work is done, there will be time for pie."

Ryan widened his eyes. "Sounds as good as the pie smells. Sassy, Lieutenant Anthony wants to talk to you first."

My interrogation was about to begin.

CHAPTER FIVE

Miguel took my arm, and we approached the lieutenant together.

"We can put some chairs in the kitchen so you will have privacy for your interviews. Will you require anything else? A table? Perhaps some lemon water and cups?" Miguel was always a cordial host, no matter how trying the circumstances.

"All good suggestions. Ryan will give you a hand."

Miguel picked up one end of the Robert Frost table, and Ryan grabbed the other. Frank Anthony and I followed them into the kitchen. Miguel filled a pitcher with ice, lemon slices and water. He set it on the counter next to a tray of glasses, then he excused himself, saying he would wait in the dining room.

At least with Ryan in the room I felt like I had a friend nearby, but that was short-lived. The lieutenant asked Ryan who was on the door. Ryan answered, "Doyle."

Frank Anthony thought for a moment. "New, but competent. He should be able to handle this group. Leave him on the door and go to the Treasure Trove. Bring Bridgy and Miss Ophelia here."

As I watched Ryan leave, I could only imagine what Bridgy and Ophie would think when they saw the commotion in the parking lot. Then I realized that after seeing Oscar's body, nothing was likely to shake Bridgy. Ophie was another matter entirely.

Frank indicated that I should sit down. I countered by offering a glass of water, which he declined. I poured myself a glass and sat at the table. The lieutenant stood over me for what seemed like eons. Finally, he sat opposite me.

I half expected some flippant remark about me attracting murder like honey draws flies, but he was direct and to the point.

"Tell me exactly what happened. How you found the body."

When I said I wasn't sure what he wanted to know, he said, "Start at the beginning."

Where was the beginning? I organized my thoughts and found a place I thought would work. I told him how Oscar teased us about Thomas Edison really being from New

Jersey and entertained us with stories about Atlantic City on a slow ride home due to the car breakdown on McGregor. I even mentioned Angeline Drefke's tale of marital woes. That caught Frank's attention.

"Let me be clear. This woman's husband ruined their life by gambling in the same place Oscar used to work."

I sighed. "Well, in the same city where Oscar worked. Atlantic City. Oscar and Angeline each mentioned a few casinos. You'd have to ask her about that."

He made a note in that small black leather-bound pad he always carried. Come to think of it, Ryan had one, too. Must be standard-issue. Oh, he was asking another question.

"What happened when you pulled into the parking lot? Who got out of the van first?"

"Everyone sort of tumbled out. Someone suggested that the ladies store their things in their cars so as not to have to lug them into the café and out again."

"Who? Whose idea was that?"

I thought for a few seconds. "Margo. No. It was Tammy. Oh, not really. She was responding to Sonja, who said . . . I remember exactly. Sonja said: 'I'll put my things in my car and meet you inside.' Everyone thought she was brilliant, and they scattered around the parking lot and then, I guess they drifted in here."

"You guess?"

"I was settling up with Oscar . . ." I could see everything clearly. Bridgy was carrying the remnants of our snacks to the café. The clubbies were laughing back and forth across the parking lot while they stowed their gear in car trunks and backseats. And Oscar and I were alone in the van. He was sitting in the driver's seat, and I was standing on the bottom step counting out his payment and adding in a hefty tip. My stomach lurched. I may have been the last person to see him alive.

Frank slid my glass of water right across Frost's fruit poems that were laminated on the tabletop. It landed next to my hand. I took a long drink followed by a deep breath. The panic didn't subside.

"This may have been my fault . . ."

"How's that?"

"I paid Oscar in cash. Right out there in the parking lot for all the world to see. For any thief to see. Did he have the money I gave him?"

Frank scribbled on his pad. "We'll find out." And he began to ask me detailed questions about everything I'd told him right up to when I finished paying Oscar and went to the café. "When you got inside, who did you see? Were all the ladies present?"

"There were some clubbies . . ." He raised an eyebrow of enquiry. "Book club members already seated in the book nook. I don't remember who exactly. I went into the kitchen to get them a pitcher of lemonade. Bridgy, Ophie and Miguel were all in the kitchen. Ophie was deciding what to take home for dinner. That I do remember."

"And then," Frank prompted.

"I fixed the lemonade and brought it to the clubbies."

"Were all the ladies here?"

"Yes. They were sitting and chatting. Waiting for me to start the formal meeting, I guess."

He changed direction. "If you were in here with your book club members, how is it you were outside next to the van when Ryan and I pulled up?"

"Bridgy's sunglasses." I explained how Bridgy went looking for her glasses and Ophie heard her call for help. "So I ran out to see what happened."

He made me repeat at least three times what I saw and heard when I got to the van. It was like having a jackhammer rat-a-tat-tat inside my brain. After I repeated my story for the final time, we sat quietly for a few seconds. I was hanging on to my composure by a thread. My brain was tired, too tired to keep answering Frank's questions.

Suddenly, he seemed to relax and tilted his chair back, raising the front legs right off the floor. I took it to mean that my ordeal was over. The inquisition was done. Then he dropped forward. The chair legs banged on the floor, startling me from my fugue state. "Tell me again. What did Bridgy say?"

"She said, 'He's dead. I'm so sorry.' Oh." For the first time I realized how he was hearing what Bridgy said. "No. No. She wasn't saying she was sorry because she'd . . . done anything. She was sorry he was dead."

Frank persisted. "But she didn't say, 'I'm sorry he's dead.' According to you, she said, 'He's dead. I'm so sorry.' Correct?"

I tapped my fingers on the tabletop and began tracing the picture of a carefree Robert Frost smiling at me from the cover of an ancient issue of *Life* magazine. There was no way around it. I hung my head. "Yes. That's what Bridgy said."

Finally, the lieutenant thanked me for my time and stood up. Rather than dismissing me, he walked me into the dining room and pointed to the Emily Dickinson table. Ophie was sitting at Robert Louis Stevenson. Bridgy was leaning against the counter near the register, with Ryan by her side. I wondered if he was guarding her. When she wasn't dabbing at her reddened eyes, Bridgy was shredding a tissue.

Frank asked Bridgy to come into the kitchen and told Ryan to join them. Just before he went through the kitchen door, he told Doyle, who had moved from the doorway and was standing by the clubbies, to call for another deputy to come into the café.

I sat quietly for a few moments, straining to hear whatever I could from the kitchen, but except for the occasional unintelligible rumble of Frank Anthony's baritone, there was nothing to hear.

I hadn't noticed Miguel sitting in the book nook. He poured a glass of lemonade and set it in front of me. I smiled my thanks and looked at the kitchen door. "I'm worried about Bridgy."

He patted my hand. "*Chica,* I promise, all will be fine."

There was a knock on the door. I half rose from my seat, ready to answer it, or at least tell whoever that we were closed, but Deputy Doyle was Johnny-on-the-spot. He opened the door, and a female deputy about my age came in. She looked familiar. Then I remembered Bridgy and I met Deputy Wei, a soft-spoken Asian woman, when we first came to Fort Myers Beach. In fact, we met her the day we moved into our first apartment in the Beausoleil near the northern tip of the island. I was glad to see a familiar face. I couldn't hear what the deputies said to each other, but he went back to stand near the clubbies, and she stood by the door.

Clearly, we were under guard. It wasn't a great feeling. I supposed the lieutenant sat me here, all alone, for a reason. Still, I was debating moving over to sit with Ophie when Ryan opened the kitchen door, looked at Wei and waved her into the kitchen.

I took the opportunity to move over to Ophie. As I pulled out a chair, I looked at the deputy, but he remained motionless, his face immobile. Apparently, he hadn't been told to keep us apart.

"How was Bridgy? I mean before Ryan went to get you."

Ophie shook her head. "The poor lamb. She was trembling, not that I blame her. And she kept saying how sorry she was."

"Sorry Oscar was dead?" I had my fingers crossed.

"No. Just sorry. Y'all have to admit this is

a sorry mess we're in."

"Bridgy's in the sorriest mess. She keeps apologizing as if she had something to do with . . ."

Ophie's sharp intake of breath told me she got my point. "She has trouble swatting at flies. Bridgy'd never hurt a living thing."

"We know that. How do we convince the law?"

The kitchen door opened. Deputy Wei had Bridgy by the arm and walked her into the alcove leading to the restrooms. Bridgy never glanced in our direction. The dazed look on her face told me all I needed to know.

Ophie whispered, "That poor child needs our help."

Not our help, I thought. Bridgy needed a lawyer. And she needed one right away. How long could the deputies keep badgering her? Her interview with Frank was already much longer than mine had been. And since they'd given her an escort to the bathroom, Bridgy was likely to be under the deputy's watchful eyes for a while yet to come.

I pulled out my cell phone and hit speed dial. Cady Stanton, reporter for the *Fort Myers Beach News,* answered on the second ring. "Hey, Sassy, how was your tour of the

Edison and Ford estates?"

"Forget about that. Why aren't you here? There's been a murder and Bridgy is a suspect and where are you? We need help. Bridgy needs a lawyer. Shouldn't you be covering this for the paper?"

"I'm off today. I'm on the mainland hacking my way through the golf fund-raiser for Pastor John's church. Thank goodness it's a scramble. Golf's not my best sport. But I don't look so bad when we play best ball. If only they'd have a soccer fund-raiser. Now there I would shine."

I lost patience. "Cady, about Bridgy . . ."

My tone brought him back to reality. "Who could suspect Bridgy of doing anything wrong? Murder? Don't be silly."

"Frank Anthony." I tossed the right name at him. Cady wasn't a fan.

"I'm playing with Owen Reston. Do you want me to ask him to come by and talk to Bridgy? You know he doesn't really do criminal."

Owen was an Afghanistan war vet and an attorney who served as counsel to some of the veteran support groups on the island. He may not be well versed in criminal law, but I was desperate.

"Bring him, if he'll come. Someone has to stop the lieutenant. He's badgering Bridgy and making her sick." I knew I was poking Cady with the "Frank Anthony" stick, but I needed to get help quickly. I clicked off the phone and watched Deputy Wei guiding Bridgy out of the restroom alcove. They were heading toward the kitchen again. Bridgy was ashen and looked as weak legged as a newborn calf. I'd had enough.

"Deputy Wei, Bridgy's lawyer is on his way. He's directed that there be no further questions until he arrives."

Wei looked confused for a moment and waved Doyle to stand by Bridgy while she went inside, I guess to confer with the lieutenant. In two seconds she was back with Frank at her heels.

He stood over me, arms crossed, never a reassuring pose. "Who's the lawyer?"

"Owen. Owen Reston."

He nodded. "If Miss Mayfield needed an attorney, we would have advised her of such. Still, leave it to you to stick your nose in where it doesn't belong."

Miss Mayfield? Bridgy was in deeper trouble than I thought.

CHAPTER SIX

I sat perfectly still, and when Frank realized I wasn't going to respond, he executed a sharp left turn and walked over to Ophie. "Miss Ophelia, if you'd be so kind." And he indicated the kitchen door. Ophie and I locked eyes as I silently wished her luck. She slumped off to the kitchen as if she were heading to the gallows. There was no bounce in her step, no *click-click-click* of her spike heels on the tile floor. But right before she walked through the kitchen doorway, she seemed to recover her gumption. With as bright a smile as she could muster, Ophie turned back and gave the entire room a wink and a wave.

As soon as they disappeared into the kitchen, I walked over to Bridgy and put my arm around her. Deputy Wei stepped back to give us some fake privacy, but I knew she could hear anything we had to say.

"How about a cup of tea?"

Bridgy attempted a smile. "In case you hadn't noticed, the kitchen's kind of busy."

"I know. I already survived my interrogation." I grimaced to let her know we were all together in this. "We have the electric kettle behind the counter. I can make you a cuppa in minutes."

During the breakfast rush we kept the electric kettle full and hot for the tea drinkers. Bridgy always insisted there was nothing worse than a restaurant where the staff instantly topped off coffee cups while the tea drinkers waited endlessly for a refill. And our tea-drinking customers agreed. We got a lot of compliments about tea refills.

Bridgy brightened and rewarded me with a grin. "Sounds like exactly what I need."

I nodded, relieved at signs of a spark in her. I looked at our discreet guardian. "Deputy, would you like a cup?"

She smiled her thanks but shook her head "no." As I went behind the counter, I sneaked a look at the clubbies. They had stopped chattering among themselves. Margo seemed engrossed in whatever app she was fiddling with on her cell phone. Angeline Drefke was staring at the door as if at any moment Nancy from Creative Hair would come rushing in, with a comb in one hand and a blow-dryer in the other, her leopard-print hairdresser smock flying behind her. Augusta crossed her arms on the table and rested her head, eyes closed. Everyone else looked tired as well. I made a snap decision. Lee County Sheriff's Department notwithstanding, I was taking back my café. I stepped over to the book nook. "Ladies, does anyone want a cup of tea?"

There were a few yeses, more nos and some whining from Angeline Drefke about her hair appointment. I filled the kettle at the tiny counter sink and plugged it in. I set mugs on a tray and decided that everyone could use the caffeine boost from a nice English breakfast tea. I took milk and a lemon from the under-the-counter fridge. I sliced the lemon, put milk in a small pitcher and refilled a sweetener bowl with the usual white, yellow and pink packets. The kettle beeped to let me know the water was ready. I was pouring boiling water over the tea bag in each mug when I heard a knock at the door.

Deputy Wei looked outside and began rapidly waving her hand back and forth. "No press. Absolutely no press."

I was so excited my hand shook the kettle and I nearly burned my arm. It must be Cady. Hopefully he had Owen with him. I set the kettle on its trivet and rushed to Deputy Wei. "That's not the press." I dropped my voice to a whisper. "That's Bridgy's lawyer."

The deputy's dark brown eyes flashed at me. "I've known Cady Stanton for years. When did he pass the Florida state bar exam?" She turned back to the door and resumed waving both hands. "Go away, Cady. No news scoops for you today."

"Tina, don't be like that. I brought Bridgy's lawyer." Cady hooked a thumb over his shoulder at Owen, whose tousled blond hair rested on the collar of his bright red golf shirt.

"Doesn't look like much of a lawyer to me. Who is he? Your cameraman?"

"Tina." Cady started doing that hand-smoothing-his-hair motion that he always did when he was getting frustrated. "Seriously. This is Owen Reston . . ."

I backed up Cady's plea. "He's telling the truth. Owen is Bridgy's lawyer." *At least temporarily,* I thought.

Tina Wei's eyes left "flashing" and moved directly to "thunder and lightning." I'd swear the lightning bolts were shooting directly at me.

She stood facing me and planted her hands on her hips exactly the way Bridgy does when she's about to lose it with me. "You know you're impeding this investigation, right?"

I was not about to back down. "I did what I thought was best for my friend. She's entitled to a lawyer."

"*Suspects* are entitled to a lawyer. Everyone here is being interviewed as witnesses. Once we determine that a person fits the profile of a suspect, we are legally obligated to tell the person she is a suspect and recommend she call a lawyer. That hasn't happened here." She crossed her arms as if she'd settled the issue once and for all.

I decided to let it go. I had a larger argument to win. "Can we open the door now?"

She held up an index finger pointing straight to the ceiling. "Give me a minute." She tapped lightly on the kitchen door. Ryan stuck his head out. They whispered, and Ryan ducked back into the kitchen for thirty seconds or so. Then he came into the dining room. He avoided looking at me as he walked to the front door and turned the lock.

He opened the door but held a hand straight out, almost in Cady's face. "Sorry, I can't let you in. Owen can meet with Bridgy, but he can't talk to anyone else. Unless he's representing all the ladies," Ryan tossed on as an afterthought.

Cady took a half step forward. "Can I at least speak to Sassy? Make sure she's okay?" I had to give Cady an "A" for effort, but Ryan was adamant.

The kitchen door swung open, and Ophie came through, looking a little the worse for wear. As soon as she saw Bridgy, she pulled herself together and sprinted to give her niece another of those big ole bear hugs.

"Oh, my poor, darlin' girl. I so wish it was me found him and not you." The fact that Frank Anthony was standing in the kitchen doorway was not lost on Ophie. She was determined to make him see Bridgy as a victim, not as a potential culprit. She stroked Bridgy's hair. "You are too gentle a flower to suffer from making such a gruesome discovery. Why don't you come back to the Treasure Trove with me? We'll have another cup of chamomile and call your momma. A girl needs her momma at a time like this."

Without daring to look at anyone, Ophie began guiding Bridgy to the door. Frank gave the merest nod of his head toward them, and both Ryan and Deputy Wei stepped between them and the door, stopping them cold. After that display of power, I expected the lieutenant to be at his most officious, but he surprised me by saying, "Ryan, let Stanton in along with Reston."

Ryan stepped back and swung the door wide open. Owen walked directly to Frank, his hand outstretched. I pictured them as gladiators, tall, muscular men ready to do battle. Then they broke the image by shaking hands.

Owen was all business. "I'm going to be representing Bridgy until we decide whether or not she needs . . . different . . . counsel."

Cady leaned down and began whispering in my ear, asking if I was okay, but I shushed him so I could eavesdrop on the conversation between Frank and Owen.

Frank hitched his belt like an old-time cowboy. Instead of answering Owen, he turned to Cady. "Hey, Pulitzer. You're here on my authority. Anything you see or hear is strictly off the record."

Cady bobbed his head in a gesture that covered both thank you and agreement, but Frank had already moved on and was speaking to Owen. "We've finished interviewing your client for now. We will want to speak to her again, probably later today but certainly by the morning. Make sure you're available to accompany her. We can't put this entire investigation on hold because *she*" — he hooked a thumb in my direction

— "decided her friend needs a lawyer."

He made it sound like Bridgy having a lawyer at her side was the most ridiculous thing in the world. Maybe to him, but I was nervous. My mother always warns, "Be ready. Sometimes life acts as though Mercury is in retrograde, even when it isn't." I'm more inclined to go with, "Better safe than sorry."

Oozing with southern charm, Ophie batted her eyelashes at Frank. "If there is nothing else y'all need from us right now, I suppose I can take my niece to the Treasure Trove?"

Generally, when Ophie used her feminine wiles on Frank or Ryan, they would respond playfully. But this situation could not be salvaged by flirtation. All she got back from Frank was a curt nod and a direct order. "Check in with us if you are going to leave the Treasure Trove. I want to know where you are at all times."

I could tell by her expression that Ophie had a coquettish answer on the tip of her tongue, but the look on Frank's face made her swallow it. She nodded meekly and said nothing.

Miguel came across the room at the same time I stood. Two minds on the same path. I asked Bridgy to wait while I packed to-go

71

cups of tea for them to take along.

Miguel approached the lieutenant directly. "If the kitchen is free for a few moments, I would like to prepare a snack bag for Bridgy to take and some fruit and cheese for the book club ladies. It has been a long day," he finished by way of explanation.

Frank mulled for a second or two. "Sure, why not. Ryan will go with you."

I was busy packing up the to-go cups but not too busy to recognize who the intended target was when he finished with, "Of course we'd be done a lot quicker if only people would stop interfering." I knew that dagger was aimed at me, but I was resilient enough not to duck — or to answer back.

We loaded Owen down with a large bag of food. He managed to joke with Miguel. "I hope there is a *Cubano* sandwich tucked in there for me."

"*Sí.* I know you need your strength to help our Bridgy. I feed you only the best. I think you will all enjoy the salads and cookies as well."

Miguel hurried back into the kitchen, with Ryan on his heels.

I handed Ophie the cardboard tray of to-go cups and hugged Bridgy while I whispered, "I'll see you in a few."

Deputy Wei escorted them out the door

and then locked it firmly so the rest of us had no chance of escape.

Miguel came out of the kitchen once more, this time carrying a large fruit and cheese platter and a plate of cookies. Ryan came along behind, chewing on what looked to be a Robert Frost fruit tartlet. The sight of the pastry brought back the memory of Oscar, just a few hours ago, demanding Bridgy bring them along to the Edison and Ford estates. I shivered, although I was far from cold.

The food seemed to cheer the clubbies, or at least it gave them something to occupy their time. I reminded myself to thank Miguel profusely when this ordeal was finally over. He was still serving the fruit and cheese when Ryan announced they wouldn't be detained much longer. Lieutenant Anthony was ready to interview each of them. Ryan emphasized that it shouldn't take long.

He pointed at Angeline. "Perhaps we can get you to your hair appointment on time. Would you come with me, please?"

Angeline preened, "I'd like that."

I looked at the clock over the front door. Unless she was the final appointment on the daily schedule, Angeline wasn't getting her hair done this afternoon. I'm sure she thought feigning that she had a chance to make her appointment would get her out fast no matter where she was going.

Frank Anthony said something I couldn't hear to Tina Wei, and then he went back into the kitchen, ready to interview Angeline.

Tina seemed pleased to be able to tell me that I was finished for now and the lieutenant said I could leave.

Frank Anthony was dismissing me from my own café. I didn't think he had the right, and I said as much. I barely noticed Tina's cheeks redden as I sat back in my chair. I caught Cady shrug and exchange a helpless look with Tina.

Too bad on them all. Much as I wanted to rush over to the Treasure Trove to make sure Bridgy was okay, I refused to let anyone push me out of my own café.

CHAPTER SEVEN

Cady offered to stay with me while I waited for the interviews of the book club members to be over so Miguel and I could lock up for the night. When Bridgy and I were under the gun, it seemed as though we were being grilled for hours. The time the lieutenant spent with each of the clubbies was trifling by comparison. I clocked Angeline's interview at less than ten minutes. Ryan opened the kitchen door, and Angeline came barreling out. She headed for the front door and pulled on the handle. When the door resisted, she grabbed the handle with one hand and the doorknob with the other and shook until the door rattled. I felt Cady slide his chair back, and I put my hand on his arm.

Deputy Wei opened the kitchen door, stuck in her head and asked if Angeline could leave. Then she moved to the front door and turned the lock above the doorknob. "You are free to go."

With her hand still on the knob, Angeline flung the door open so hard I feared the glass would break. I was half out of my chair when Cady grabbed my arm. It was as if we were taking turns keeping each other in our seats. Cady leaned in and said, "It will all be over soon."

Sure, the interviews would be over soon, but then what? Frank Anthony had already warned Bridgy that he'd want to speak with her again — and soon.

I was still fretting about the chaos brewing around us when the kitchen door opened and Ryan escorted Tammy Rushing out of her interview. She came over to say good-bye. "I loved being in the Cool Reads/ Warm Climate Book Club. I hope I get a chance to spend another winter in Fort Myers Beach. Great place for snowbirds." Then she lowered her eyelids for a few seconds, and her demeanor became solemn. "It's a shame that today ended so badly. Does the poor man have any family?"

I turned my palms up and sighed. "I really didn't know him that well. Whenever we rented a van for a group trip, we requested him, because he loves, er, loved to laugh and tease. A trip with Oscar was always fun."

Tammy leaned in to give me a kiss on the

cheek and a pat on the shoulder. "In case I don't see you before I leave for home, I want to say thanks to you and Bridgy for making this winter such a memorable season for me. When I travel it's usually difficult for me to find friends who love books and reading as much as I do. You made it easy."

By the time Deputy Wei unlocked the door for Tammy, Sonja Ferraro was finished speaking to the lieutenant. She came out of the kitchen, looking flustered and exhausted like a woman who'd barely survived the Black Friday sales at the Edison Mall. I couldn't figure out why she was so harried; hers was the quickest interview yet.

She asked if she could sit for a moment. "I need to catch my breath. What a distressing experience. This is my final trip to Fort Myers Beach, I can tell you that."

Cady made a chamber of commerce–ish speech about the wonders of the town and how much better she would feel in the morning, but Sonja wasn't buying it.

"Nope, I'm finished. Next year I'm off to Marco Island for sure. I've taken a couple of day trips there with the Ladies Tennis League for tournaments and such. Once I attended a fund-raiser for the community theater. It's a pretty island, and after today, I'm sure it's a lot safer."

She glared at Cady as if defying him to argue. I got the impression she was disappointed when he said, "We'll miss you," and turned to me and asked for a cup of tea.

I went behind the counter and brought refills for us both. Then I walked to the book nook and asked Augusta and Blondie if they would like to sit with us. Miguel came along carrying the fruit and cheese tray from their table to ours.

Cady glanced at the book nook. "You forgot the cookies. I'll get them."

We all settled in just as Margo Wellington bounded through the kitchen door, gave us a quick smile and a wave and went on her way, leaving us with the impression that she had places to go and people to see.

Ryan called Blondie Quinlin into the kitchen. With only Augusta and Miguel left to be questioned, we could easily be rid of the sheriff's deputies and have the café cleaned up within the hour. My neck and shoulders ached from the tension of the day. Miguel interrupted my fantasy, which involved a deep-tissue massage at one of the hotel spas.

"*Chica,* if you want to check on Bridgy, I can stay. I haven't been spoken to yet, and I can finish closing on my own."

Miguel was always so thoughtful. His offer was tempting. I was worried about Bridgy's reaction to being the center of this investigation, but I refused to leave the café. No way I'd leave and let Frank Anthony think he was in charge. Never mind that for all intents and purposes he was.

I knew Owen could protect Bridgy up to a point, but shouldn't we find a criminal lawyer before she talked to the sheriff's deputies again? No massage for me tonight. I rubbed my neck and wondered if I had aspirin in my purse when Cady came to the rescue. "Why don't I see how things are going at the Treasure Trove? If Bridgy needs you, I can buzz your cell."

Without waiting for an answer, he dashed out the door. I was a little surprised that Deputy Wei let him go, but then I remembered she wasn't too happy to see him arrive.

Augusta was unusually quiet. Miguel offered her more tea, but she shook her head. "No. Can't eat no more. This killing thing, it brings back bad memories."

Miguel and I sat quietly. I was thinking about Augusta's cousin, a sweet woman who had been murdered a while back. I was trying to think of something to say to distract Augusta when Miguel suddenly announced, "I am going to clean the dining room. Once

I get things onto the counter, it will be a breeze to get everything shipshape when the lieutenant is done with my kitchen."

I opened my mouth, but before a sound came out, Miguel said, "No. You sit with Miss Augusta. You've had a long day."

I gave him a grateful smile and pulled my cell phone from my pocket, willing it to ring, but Cady didn't call. I wasn't sure if that was a good sign or a bad sign.

Ryan shepherded Blondie Quinlin out of the kitchen, led her straight to our table and pulled out a chair. Once she was comfortably seated, he offered his arm to Augusta.

"The lieutenant would like to speak with you now, Miss Augusta."

Ryan was always kind and deferential to the older ladies, but I was sure he was being extra gentle with Augusta because he was remembering how difficult it was for her the last time she had to be interviewed about a murder.

I was gratified that, except for Sonja, the ladies were unruffled when they came out of the kitchen. I guess Frank Anthony had been kinder to them than he'd been to me.

I offered Blondie a cup of tea, but she said she preferred something cold. Miguel quickly poured her a glass of lemonade from the pitcher on the counter, and then he

80

continued straightening the dining room. He was moving the chairs from the book nook back to their usual homes — some against the wall, some surrounding tables, when Blondie asked how Bridgy was doing.

"I wish I knew. Cady went to check, but I haven't heard from him." I looked at my silent cell phone. "I guess if she needed me . . ."

"Don't you worry. She's in good hands. Ophie gives the impression that she is all frou-frou and giddy, but she loves that girl and won't let nobody harm her. Aunts love their nieces and nephews. I ought to know. Oh my Lord." Blondie smacked her cheeks with both hands. "Michael. My nephew Michael. You need to meet him."

Now? With all this going on, Blondie wanted to fix me up with her nephew?

I started to demur, but she waved away my objections. "Oh tosh, you are misunderstanding me. No romance intended. Michael, or Mugsy, as everyone calls him — the nickname is a throwback to his boxing days — anyway, he is the head dispatcher at the Gulf Coast Cab and Van."

Blondie leaned back in her chair and folded her arms across her chest. It was strange that her arms-across-the-chest position didn't annoy me the way it did when

Frank Anthony adopted the pose. Instead, I felt she was calmly waiting for me to get her point.

For the first time since Bridgy discovered Oscar's body, I sensed I could help her. Here was something I could do casually, without annoying anyone in the sheriff's office. I would offer my condolences to the cab company. After all, Oscar was murdered at the end of our trip. Wouldn't it be natural for me to talk to Blondie's nephew? I organized the trip; Blondie was on the trip. Oscar worked for Mugsy. A definite connection.

Blondie watched me carefully, and her eyes began to sparkle when she saw the comprehension dawn. She opened her basket weave tote and pulled out a pink cloth purse. Out of that she withdrew a brown plastic loose-leaf binder, opened it and removed a pen. It was like watching a child play with those Russian nesting dolls.

She ripped a blank page out of the binder and began to scribble. "I'm giving you Michael's contact information. If anyone knows more about Oscar than we do, it's Michael."

The kitchen door opened, and as Ryan ushered Miss Augusta to our table, Blondie pushed the paper. It glided across the table and landed at my fingertips. I shoved it in my pocket.

Ryan pulled out a chair for Augusta, but she wasn't having it. "Thanks but no thanks. I been here too long. Blondie, we should get going."

Blondie stood and winked at me. "Don't forget to make that call."

I promised I would take care of it.

The two ladies reached the front door when Miss Augusta turned around and said, "Sassy, tell Bridgy I'm sorry for her trouble."

I promised I would but, if even Augusta, who rarely focused on other people's lives, knew Bridgy was in trouble, we were in deep weeds.

Ryan told Deputies Doyle and Wei that they were no longer needed, and he locked the door behind them. He turned to me.

"Who was she reminding you to call? You're not going to meddle in this investigation, are you?"

"Oh please. According to Deputy Wei I meddled just by getting a lawyer for Bridgy. You have a very low bar when it comes to 'meddling.' If you must know, Blondie would like me to meet her nephew." I ran my fingers through my unruly auburn curls and gave him a look I hoped was girlie-girl.

Let him draw his own conclusions.

Ryan grimaced. "Personally, I hate blind intros, but good luck. I hope he's a nice guy." He turned to Miguel. "You're up."

He and Miguel went into the kitchen, leaving me alone for the first time since I got out of the shower that morning and joined Bridgy for coffee on the patio of the Turret, the nickname we gave to our apartment on the top floor of the Beausoleil, a beachside building on the north end of the island. I wallowed in the silence for a few minutes and then grabbed the electric broom from behind the counter.

I was barely halfway through cleaning the dining room floor when Miguel and Ryan came through the kitchen door carrying the table and chairs the deputies had borrowed from the dining room.

The interviews were over. With Miguel's help, cleanup would be finished in a few minutes, and I could hustle over to the Treasure Trove and see how Bridgy was managing.

Then Frank Anthony came out of the kitchen and asked, "Sassy, do you have a minute?"

As if I could say I didn't.

CHAPTER EIGHT

I was tempted to ask him to wait until I'd finished cleaning the floor, but why prolong the agony? I set the broom aside, and before I could reach the kitchen, Frank stopped me.

"No need for privacy. This isn't an interview, it's more my observation."

I could almost see Ryan's and Miguel's ears perk up. They were curious to find out what Frank observed, while I wasn't sure that I wanted to know what he *thought* he had observed. With my hands clasped behind my back like a schoolgirl in the principal's office, I stood in front of him and waited impatiently.

He raised a hand and ruffled his dark hair. I was always intrigued that when he was out of sorts Frank ruffled his hair; while Cady, in a similar situation, would repeatedly smooth his hair front to back. And they say women are hair obsessed.

Frank's tone was gentler than I was used to. "I know how close you and Bridgy are, and I know you thought you were being helpful when you sent for Owen to represent her. But she discovered the body, which makes her a key witness, vital to our inquiry. I am asking nicely. Please don't jump into this investigation with both feet and no thought."

I opened my mouth to protest, but he held up a hand. "I know you mean well, but for Bridgy's sake, I am telling you to stay out of this." He did one of those military about-face turns and said, "Ryan."

The two of them were gone in a flash. Ryan scarcely had a chance to wave good-bye.

I was livid. I grabbed the electric broom, turned it on and was pushing it around the floor with such ferocity that Miguel came up behind me, took it out of my hand and shut it off.

"*Chica,* he is doing his job. Believe me, he was not put on this earth specifically to annoy you. Just as you were not put on this earth to investigate murders. And yet, he annoys you and you stick your nose in where it doesn't" — when I squinted my eyes at Miguel and pursed my lips, he changed his direction. "Er, you stick your nose in where *he* doesn't think it belongs."

Good editing on Miguel's part.

"Why don't you go find Bridgy, and I will finish up here." He lifted the electric broom. "With the mood you are in, you are using this as a weapon with the floor as your worst enemy." He gave me a soft smile. "Go, *chica*. I can take care of this."

I knew Miguel was right. I really needed to see if Bridgy was okay. I gave him a kiss on the cheek and gathered my things. When I left the Read 'Em and Eat, the parking lot was much less frenetic. Most of the county vehicles were gone, but a large part of the parking lot, including Oscar's van, was surrounded by yellow crime scene tape. I could see several rubber-gloved technicians moving around both inside and outside the van. Two sheriff's deputies stood at either end of the parking lot, keeping a watchful eye on the area. It took me a moment to realize that, under the broad-brimmed Smokey Bear hat, Tina Wei was the deputy nearest me. I waved and started to walk over to the Treasure Trove when I realized I'd better ask about our morning rush, so I turned back.

Before I could ask my question, Tina said, "I know it was a rough day for you. Sorry if I made it rougher. It was just, well, I was

87

surprised to see Cady. Besides, none of us knew you'd called a lawyer."

I shaded my eyes from the sun and decided to put it all behind us. "It was a difficult day for everyone. Especially Bridgy. I'm worrying about tomorrow. I have the Books Before Breakfast Club meeting in the café. Are we going to be able to open in the morning? Or should I call the club members and cancel?"

"What did Lieutenant Anthony say?"

I sighed. I hadn't thought to ask. "He didn't."

Tina asked for my cell phone number and assured me that she would find out the status of both the parking lot and the café. She promised to call me within the hour.

Aunt Ophie unlocked the Treasure Trove door and peeked over my shoulder. "No one followed you, did they?"

I was about to say, "Who? Who would follow me?" when Cady surprised me with a kiss on the cheek and asked, "What happened after I left?"

I nudged him away. "Nothing happened. The interviews went on forever. Then we were finally allowed to leave. Miguel is on cleanup duty, and Tina Wei is going to let me know if the parking lot will be back to normal by the time we open in the morning. Nothing sharpens folks' appetite for breakfast like a wide expanse of yellow crime scene tape blocking off the parking lot. I guess we should be grateful that there isn't a chalk body outline on the ground."

To distract myself from the thought, I looked around the Treasure Trove, which was part consignment shop and part boutique with just enough beachy shtick thrown in to have something to attract every shopper. I noticed that the wide glass jewelry case held several new pieces of shell and wire jewelry made by a handyman named Tom Smallwood who traveled the islands by boat, selling his labor and his wares. A while back he found a human skull on Mound Island. It seems he carried it around with him for months before the sheriff's office found out and took it away. It turned out to be an ancient Calusa Indian skull and now sits in a museum somewhere. As a result, some people around here call him Skully, but he doesn't seem to mind a bit.

Ophie offered me a cup of chamomile tea. "Or would you prefer dandelion? I think I have some lemongrass, and I know I have peppermint . . ."

She was halfway to the back room when I stopped her by saying, "No. No tea, thank you. I'm really looking for Bridgy."

Ophie waved me along behind her. "Well, y'all come on back, then. After we called her momma, I sent Bridgy and Owen into the back room. Cady and I were giving them some privacy to talk about Bridgy's case."

That stopped me. "Bridgy's case? I wanted her to have a lawyer as . . . as a preventative measure. And now there is a case against her? How did that happen? Was Frank Anthony here?"

Even as I asked the question, I knew it wasn't possible. He'd only left the café a few minutes before I had.

Ophie waved my fears off like so much nonsense. "Don't go getting your feathers ruffled. No one is bothering Bridgy. Not if I can help it. We do need to be prepared, and that is what Owen is doing. Preparing her. Y'all know that handsome lieutenant is going to come looking to ask her more questions. It's just a matter of time. Bridgy needs to know how to answer."

"Answer? She tells the truth. She hasn't done anything wrong."

Cady stepped up. "It's not always that simple. Owen is coaching Bridgy how to answer. Things like why did she wait until Oscar was alone to go out to the van?"

"Because that's when she noticed her

sunglasses were missing. Duh. Bridgy going to the van had nothing to do with Oscar."

"Take a breath." Cady could tell I was getting worked up. "*We know* that's why she went outside, but *we don't know* how the lieutenant is going to ask the question. It's not likely that he'll just ask why she went outside. That's what the prep is for. To get her ready to answer whatever questions are asked with the complete truth but in a way that the truth puts Bridgy in a favorable light."

Before I could absorb the intent of his words, Bridgy came bounding out of the back room and fell on me the way Rosie, a part shepherd, part terrier mix we had for most of my years in elementary school, used to do. I could barely get in the front door and there was Rosie jumping on me. Bridgy not only did the same jump-on-me thingy, she had the same look on her face that Rosie had: "I'm so happy you are home. I'm so glad you didn't abandon me."

She squeezed just short of breaking at least a few of my ribs, then Bridgy let go and stretched out to hold me at arm's length. "You are the best friend ever. I owe you a zillion quarts of butter pecan ice cream. Thank you. Thank you."

I was starting to think Ophie had slipped

some happy pills in Bridgy's herb tea when Owen came out of the back room. "Sassy, I'm glad to see you. I've been getting all of Bridgy's thank-yous, but I keep telling her the reason I'm here is because you sent for me."

"Well, like Bridgy, I'm grateful you came to help." I'd watched enough courtroom dramas on television to know that I shouldn't ask about what he and Bridgy had discussed. So, with us all thinking about lawyer/client confidentiality, the conversation fell flat in a hurry.

Ophie came to the rescue by offering tea and steering us into the back room. We crowded around an antique French Provincial coffee table that she used to both impress and entertain her more upscale clients. Before I had a chance to admire the inlay design, Ophie threw a length of thick quilt on the table and covered it with a strip of green oilcloth. I was willing to bet that her clients never had to deal with balancing their teacups on the lumpy, bumpy combination of quilt and oilcloth, but, then again, we weren't clients.

I asked Cady and Owen how their golf game went.

"To be honest" — Cady blushed ever so slightly — "I was glad to get your call. Even playing scramble, I was the worst player of the foursome."

Bridgy asked who completed their foursome.

"Mark Clamenta and some friend of his from the VVA."

As soon as he mentioned Mark's name, I stole a glance at Ophie. We all met Mark some time ago, but I suspected she and Mark had become friendlier in recent months. She never said, so I was never going to ask. Still, at the mention of his name, she lowered her eyelids and controlled a smile so that it stayed teeny, almost unnoticeable.

Bridgy raised a questioning brow. "VVA?"

Owen answered, "Vietnam Veterans of America. When they came home, a lot of the Vietnam vets didn't feel comfortable in the American Legion or the VFW, you know, the Veterans of Foreign Wars. They felt that their war was different from the wars that came before, so finally, in the late 1970s, they formed their own organization."

Cady chimed in, "My editor is a member. They do a lot of great work both for the vets and in the community at large. We give them a lot of press."

I was relieved he didn't add his usual, "You'd know that if you read the *Fort Myers*

Beach News." Cady's job as a reporter depended on readership, and he wasn't above reminding me that I had a responsibility to read the news.

As we finished our tea, I could see Bridgy was fading fast. "Owen, I was wondering . . . would it be all right if Bridgy and I went home? It's been such a long day."

He grinned. "I'm sure it has. If you should hear from Lieutenant Anthony, Bridgy has my cell number. I put it in her phone. Here, let me put it in yours."

As Owen handed my phone back to me, it rang. It was Tina Wei with good news. I hung up and said, "The parking lot will be cleared within two hours. No remnants of the crime when we come to work tomorrow."

It was the first sign that we were on our way back to normal.

Ophie refused my offer to help tidy up, so we said our good-byes. We walked across the parking lot, avoiding the yellow-taped area. An unfamiliar deputy was now standing where I'd seen Tina earlier.

When we got to Bridgy's shiny red Escort ZX2, she handed me the keys. "I can't."

I wasn't the least bit surprised. She curled up in the passenger's seat, and right before she closed her eyes, she asked, "Can I bor-

row a pair of your Winnie the Pooh footie
pajamas? I need to feel snuggly tonight."

CHAPTER NINE

The café was busier than usual the next morning, with every table occupied, and within five minutes after we opened, there was a line of customers outside the door. Some folks came for breakfast. Many more came for gossip but were willing to order breakfast as a side benefit. Bridgy and I could have used roller skates to speed around the dining room.

At one point we nearly collided at the end of the service counter.

"We could really use an extra pair of hands today."

Bridgy shook her head. "Remember how that turned out the one time we tried? Ugh."

"I remember, but the Books Before Breakfast Club will be here soon. I don't like to leave them on their own, but with this crowd I've barely been able to save empty chairs in the book nook. One of the men sitting at Ernest Hemingway commandeered a chair from the nook to pile up his beach towels and laptop."

Behind me I heard the front door open, and in waltzed Ophie wearing a frilly little French maid apron over a 1950-ish magenta circle skirt topped by a white lace bolero jacket over a shimmery pale plum shell. Today's spiky, strappy high heels were white with a blush of lavender. Obviously, Ophie had dressed for the crowd.

"I thought y'all might need some help this morning. I woke up, and when I checked the messages on the Treasure Trove phone line, why, half the island wants an appointment today to look over my wares."

I blinked; did she actually puff out her chest on the word "wares"?

She came right to the counter. "If my telephone was ringing off the hook, I knew you would be overwhelmed for the breakfast rush. The Treasure Trove doesn't open 'til later in the morning, so here I am."

Ophie to the rescue. I remembered the time Miguel broke his leg and Ophie drove all night from her home in north Florida to be here to help with the breakfast rush. Now she lived only a few blocks away, but the offer was no less meaningful.

"You, my adorable aunt, are a lifesaver." Bridgy and Ophie did a brief version of their

97

big ole bear hug. "Sassy has the Books Before Breakfast Club meeting in . . ." — she looked at the large-faced round clock over the front door — "in about ten minutes. And I do love your apron."

Ophie beamed. "I took extra care knowing folks would be looking us over." She pointed to the copies of the *Fort Myers Beach News* piled by the cash register. "The witness list is in the newspaper for everyone to see. I can tell y'all, we're going to be very popular 'til the fussin' dies down."

Only Ophie would think being witness in a murder investigation was a surefire path to the Miss Popularity crown. We'd been so busy, I never even thought to look at the newspaper. I hoped Cady had kept his word and hadn't crossed his personal friendships with his professional duties. He was always scrupulous, but he did have unusual access yesterday. While Bridgy and Ophie were deciding who would serve which tables, I picked up a paper, but before I could open it, Jocelyn Kendall, pastor's wife and general irritant, came through the café door.

"It's absurdly crowded in here this morning. I hope you saved our book nook from encroachment by your, ah, customers." She pushed her straw-colored hair out of the way and cupped a hand over her ear. "Just listen to the clatter and chatter. A discussion of the work of a literary figure of Anna Quindlen's stature deserves a quieter, shall we say, ambiance."

I said a silent prayer that I would be able to tolerate an hour of Jocelyn's company and offered her a cup of coffee.

"Oh heavens no. I find caffeine makes me edgy lately, so I'm cutting back. I will take some herbal tea." And she marched past me, off to settle herself in the book nook.

I was pouring hot water over a tea bag that provided a nice blend of cinnamon, orange and raspberry when Lisette Ortiz stepped up to the counter and said, "Excuse me, Sassy . . ."

She'd come in so quietly I hadn't noticed her. That's the way I like my book club members, quiet and polite.

I put the kettle down and gave her my full attention.

"I was wondering how Bridgy is doing. I am amazed to see her here working. That must have been such an unspeakable experience yesterday . . . Well, I just want to say how sorry I am that you had to go through such a tragedy. To think a simple trip to the Edison and Ford estates could end like that." She wrinkled her brow. "If there is any way I can help make the burden lighter, just let me know."

I couldn't help but smile. For every Jocelyn, there were two people like Lisette, or so it seemed. People who made my life easier, happier.

As I walked to the book nook with Lisette, I scanned the dining room. Bridgy and Ophie had things well in hand. I served Jocelyn her tea and got my copy of *Still Life with Bread Crumbs* along with some pencils and paper for the clubbies. Augusta Maddox and Blondie Quinlin came in together, and as always, Augusta's voice filled the room. "I'm just saying there are better books we could be spending our time on."

I could barely hear Blondie's laughing reply, but I thought she said, "You have no romance in your soul."

Irene Lester, our newest book club member, was right behind them. I offered tea and coffee and set out a plate of Harper Lee Hush Puppies and honey butter. When everyone had a chance to take a bite or a sip, I opened with my usual question. "So, what did everyone think?"

Nothing. *Nada.*

It often took a while to get the conversation started. I tried again. "How did *Still Life with Bread Crumbs* compare to other books by Anna Quindlen you may have read?"

I was patient and counted in my head . . . one Mississippi, two Mississippi. In a very few seconds, Lisette raised her hand and said, "Until now I've only read her nonfiction. I had no idea that she wrote such beautiful fiction."

I asked what nonfiction she'd read, and Lisette gave us a wide smile that displayed her dimples. "When I graduated from college, my grandma, Josefina, gave me a slim volume titled *A Short Guide to a Happy Life* by Anna Quindlen. Grandma said that I should remember to live every moment, both the good and the bad. She insisted the book would help me do so."

Irene Lester leaned so far forward I thought she would tumble off her chair. "And did it help? The book, I mean. Do you live life to the fullest?"

Lisette laughed. "I certainly try to, but I think the definition of 'to the fullest' is different for each of us. And yes, I definitely think the book helped. I still browse through it from time to time."

I made a mental note to order a couple of copies of *A Short Guide* for the bookshelves and an extra copy for myself. On days like today I could use some direction. I brought the conversation back to *Still Life with Bread Crumbs*. "And what about Rebecca Winter? Did she live life to the fullest?"

Jocelyn sniffed. "Well, if you count playing footsie with a younger man, I suppose you could say she did."

Irene pushed back, a first for her. "Forget about the romance for a minute. Let's talk about her professional life. That certainly moved forward."

And then conversation around me took off with a lot of back-and-forth among the clubbies. I could finally relax. I let my mind wander to the events of yesterday, wondering how much trouble would rain down on Bridgy before the murderer was caught.

"Isn't that right, Sassy?" I heard Jocelyn demand. I looked at her, and she was nodding her head for me to agree. Of course I had no idea what she was asking me, which turned out to be fine, because she went right on talking. "I mean, if Anna Quindlen was a journalist, isn't it likely she stole other people's lives and turned them into a story?"

"I doubt . . ."

I was cut off by Miss Augusta, who had far less patience with Jocelyn than any of us. "Stealing lives? Writers can't do that. It's like perjury, plagiarism, one of those things. Anyway, it's wrong, plain and simple. I

102

think she is a respectable writer who makes up good stories."

Blondie Quinlin added: "And I sure do like her last name. We are only a couple of letters apart from being sisters."

While everyone but Jocelyn laughed at Blondie's joke, I made a few suggestions for next month's book from a list of books that had recently arrived on our shelves. As soon as I mentioned *Murder, She Wrote: Killer in the Kitchen* by Jessica Fletcher and Donald Bain, one of the newer books in the ongoing series, I got a quick response.

"That's it." Augusta slapped her knee. "I love Jessica Fletcher. Is it a Cabot Cove mystery? I watch the reruns on television all the time. The stories that take place in Cabot Cove are my favorite."

Irene chimed in. "That Doc Hazlitt. He's an eccentric one, he is. Oh my yes. Let's read it."

Heads nodded all around. I told them I had a few copies for sale and I would call Sally Caldera at the library and ask her to reserve any copies she might have.

Jocelyn looked at her wristwatch. "Oh, it's late. I must fly. Pastor John is hosting an ecumenical prayer service. How would it look if I didn't attend?" And she hurried out the door without so much as a wave good-bye.

Lisette and Irene opted to buy the *Murder, She Wrote* book before leaving. I got two copies down from the shelves and took a quick peek at the dining room. The crowd had thinned out. We even had one empty table. I prayed the "scene of the crime" nosy parkers were finished coming around. Their business wasn't worth the stress. Hopefully the lunch rush would be normal customers trying to decide whether they wanted a *Swiss Family Robinson* Cheeseburger, an *Old Man and the Sea* Chowder or a *My Secret Garden* Salad.

Miss Augusta and Blondie Quinlin often stayed for breakfast. I suggested they move over to the Barbara Cartland table since it was the only one available. Augusta was partial to the Emily Dickinson table, so I wondered if she was going to opt to wait for her favorite. But I guess the theme of the Anna Quindlen book caught her spirit, and she followed Blondie to Barbara Cartland. I heard her say, "This ain't so bad."

I was straightening the book nook when Bridgy tapped me on the shoulder. "I need you in the kitchen." I followed along, ready for the usual "We're running low on this and are already out of that" conversation that we often had several times a day. But as soon as I got a good look at her face, I knew it was something more.

Miguel was busy moving between the stove and the counter, plating a couple of orders of *Green Eggs and Ham.* We stayed by the door to be completely out of his way as he ran back and forth.

"Listen, Ophie went back to the Treasure Trove to cancel her appointments for the day. She'll be back soon and can help out until closing."

"I don't think it's really necessary. The endless trail of lookie-loos seems to have tapered off. We can handle it."

"That's just it. It wasn't necessary when she left but now there is no 'we' for the rest of the day. Owen called about ten minutes ago. Frank Anthony wants to speak to me again. This time he wants me to come to the sheriff's office. Owen will be here in a few minutes."

And Bridgy burst into tears.

CHAPTER TEN

"Come on, sweetie." I grabbed a napkin to wipe her face. "It won't be that bad. I promise. You'll have Owen by your side every minute. He'll save you from the evil lieutenant."

That coaxed a tiny smile. I decided to go for broke. "Hey, you're going to be surrounded by good-looking men: Owen Reston, Frank Anthony, Ryan Mantoni and who knows how many other handsome young deputies will be circling. Think what Ophie would do with that opportunity."

Bridgy actually laughed. I had done my job.

I gave her shoulder a squeeze. "Now go clean yourself up. I left a gray silk blouse on a hanger behind the door of the office. I brought it in to wear to the Rotary meeting a few days ago, but something came up and I didn't go. And I'm glad you have your black capris on. Better than denim shorts."

Bridgy protested. "Sassy, this isn't a social occasion."

"You're right. It isn't. But it is a *solemn* occasion, and that green tank top with 'SUNSET CELEBRATION AT TIMES SQUARE' sprawled across the front isn't going to cut it. Now go spiff up while I cover the dining room."

It was a good thing my hands weren't filled with dishes when Owen Reston walked into the café. I might have dropped them. I nearly didn't recognize the handsome businessman-type dressed in a light blue houndstooth suit with those tuxedo styled lapels, peaked, I think they're called. And the jacket pockets had no flaps, which gave him a very sleek line. By the time my eyes reached his face, he was taking off his aviator sunglasses. His green eyes were always attractive, even more so when he winked at me.

"I know. It's a long way from surfer dude shorts and muscle man tees, but this is my lawyer look. What do you think?" And he pirouetted as coolly as a prima ballerina. Instead of its usual wild and wavy self, I saw his hair was slicked back, probably gelled in place.

I planted my hands on my hips and rolled my shoulders in full Brooklyn swagger.

"Ain't you sumthin'? Back in Brooklyn we'd call you a 'Park Avenue lawyer.' Got that right."

Then I switched to serious. "Is she in deep and definite trouble?"

Owen shook his head. "Not if I can help it. Don't worry. Frank Anthony is doing what he has to do, working every angle to solve his case. There's a killer out there. I figure Frank knows it isn't Bridgy. But we have to remember that she is a key witness."

Right on cue, the kitchen door opened and Bridgy walked out with a far more sophisticated presence than she'd had a few minutes before. Owen's look of appreciation was completely wasted on Bridgy, because she barely noticed him. I couldn't fathom why she wasn't blown away by how handsome he looked. Her nerves must be clouding her vision.

Bridgy had clipped her hair up in a high ponytail. A few blond tendrils escaped and framed her face. My gray silk blouse was perfectly tucked into the waist of her dark pants. I was surprised she was wearing a red leather belt with a silver seashell buckle, which gave the outfit a finished look. I suspect it came from somewhere in the bottom desk drawer where we kept lots of doodads that we brought in to work and never remembered to bring home. She'd ditched her work sneakers for a pair of black sandals. Good as Bridgy looked, my first thought was that we really were going to have to clean out the office.

The ladies sitting at Robert Frost signaled for their check. I dropped it on their table, and Bridgy automatically stepped behind the register. I glanced at the two other occupied tables. No one needed my attention. I needed to push Bridgy out of here. Otherwise she'd stall for the rest of the day. Miguel, Ophie and I could handle the café.

As soon as Bridgy finished at the register, I tried to move her along. "You may as well get it over with."

She hesitated, then realized I was right and came around from behind the counter. Owen took her by the elbow and looked at me. "I promise I'll bring her back none the worse for wear."

I prayed he was right.

I began refilling the salt and pepper shakers, getting ready for the lunch rush, when Ophie opened the door and spun into the room, her magenta skirt twirling around her knees.

"I canceled any and all appointments, so I can help out here 'til closing. What is the matter? Y'all should be smiling, 'cause I'm here to help. Instead you look like death."

"Bridgy had to go to the sheriff's office for more questions."

Ophie was stricken. Her face contorted with anxiety and more than a little anger. "And you let her go alone? What were you thinking?"

"Shush." I bobbed my head toward the occupied tables. "Owen Reston went with her. He promised to take care of her."

Ophie relaxed. "I feel better already. Handsome devil that Owen is, and Mark tells me he is a top-notch lawyer."

Our conversation was cut short when customers began piling in. Within minutes the lunch rush was in full force.

For the next two hours I hustled back and forth between the kitchen and the dining room. I was still bouncy in my white quilted leather slip-on sneakers, but as usual, toward the end of the rush, my feet started to ache a bit. I began fantasizing about a barefoot walk along the water's edge around sunset. I watched Ophie spin around on her impossibly high sandals and wondered why her arches weren't screaming for relief.

I glanced at the clock. Bridgy had been gone for a long time. When the crowd slowed down, I checked my phone, hoping she'd sent me a text, but there was nothing.

Ophie walked past with a platter of *Swiss Family Robinson* Cheeseburgers and two side salads. She whispered, "Any news?"

I shook my head.

Another half hour passed, the café emptied out and still no word. I was getting antsy. I was scrubbing the countertop when it dawned on me that there was something I could do to help. Mugsy Danaher, Blondie Quinlin's nephew. I could visit him at the cab company and discover what he knew about Oscar, anything at all that might help us find a suspect other than Bridgy. I was pretty sure that all the old New Jersey stuff Oscar had talked about was useless information. Mugsy would have current information. But, would he share?

I ran into the kitchen and grabbed a large to-go box.

"Miguel, what kind of pastries do we have left? Can I get a dozen of your best?"

"*Sí,* of course. Did the customer ask for anything particular, or do you want an assortment?"

"No customer. I'm going to make a condolence call, and I don't want to show up empty-handed."

"Oscar's family is here in town?"

"Oh. I don't know." I thought quickly and decided on a half-truth. "I'm going to bring

111

the pastries to his coworkers at the cab company. Perhaps they can tell me where to send a sympathy card or if the family has a charity that will accept donations in Oscar's name. I think we should do something."

Miguel nodded in agreement, but his brain had already moved on to packaging. Both he and Bridgy had a terrific sense of visual design when it came to food presentation. I was nowhere near their league. He put the to-go box next to a platter of Robert Frost Apple and Blueberry Tartlets. I watched him roll a dozen small doilies until they were nearly pouch shaped and carefully place a tartlet in each one. He layered them in the box, snapped it shut and pulled a small white bow from the bottom drawer of the work counter. He taped it to the top while pushing the box across the counter to me. Miguel was all about economy of motion.

"Tell Oscar's work friends we are all sorry for their loss. And don't worry, Ophie and I will take care of any customers who straggle in just before closing."

Ophie was straightening tables and chairs when I waved, told her I had an errand to run and flew out the door before she could barrage me with questions.

I'd parked my trusty Heap-a-Jeep as far

away from where Oscar had parked the van yesterday as I could. Still, I stopped for a moment and looked at the spot. I said a silent prayer, then I got into the jeep and drove down island. A couple of miles later I made a left turn toward Estero Bay, and within a few yards I was inside the parking lot of the Gulf Coast Cab and Van Company.

A half dozen or so vehicles ranging from tiny four-seat sedans to oversized vans were parked neatly along the fence lined up in size places. Every one of them was sky blue with the company name and phone number prominently displayed.

A sign near the entrance said "Visitor Parking." I parked the Heap-a-Jeep right next to the sign and headed self-assuredly to the door. It was only when I got inside that my confidence began to wane. What would I say?

A woman with carrot red 1970s bouffant hair was sitting at the front desk. She greeted me with a thousand-watt smile and a deep southern drawl. "I'm Darla. How y'all doing today? Hope you're gonna let us give y'all a ride."

"Actually, I, er, I need to speak to Mr. Danaher. I'm a friend of his aunt." I was hoping making the visit sound personal would stump her curiosity.

Darla waved me in the direction of a worn leatherette bench, the same sky blue as the cars and vans. She beamed all thousand watts at me again. "Why, sure, y'all just have a seat. I'll find him soon enough."

It wasn't long before a wiry man with a shaved head and one gold hoop stuck in the lobe of a misshapen ear came down the hall. His sky blue golf shirt had a monogram I couldn't read at this distance, but it stretched across biceps and shoulders that seemed much too large for his body.

"You must be Aunt Blondie's friend." He gave me a hearty handshake and a view of the crossed anchor tattoo on his forearm. There were words in a circle, but I couldn't decipher them and didn't want to stare.

Mugsy noticed my glance. "Coast Guard back in the nineties. Great times. Went hand to hand with Hurricane Opal in '95. She nearly destroyed the Panhandle and did a job on Alabama, too. End of September, beginning of October. I can't quite recall. Anyway, Blondie says if I don't help you out, there will be no more Sunday dinners at her house for me, so what can I do you for?"

I was delighted Blondie had eased the way. I handed Mugsy the to-go box. "A book

114

club I coordinate from the Read 'Em and Eat was Oscar's last trip. I want to express our condolences."

Mugsy sniffed at the edges of the carton. "Smells sweet. I'll put these in the break room. The team will enjoy having a bite in Oscar's honor. You know, he's been a driver here a long time. Longer than the four years I've been dispatching. Oscar was friendly enough, gregarious even, but he could become feisty if he thought he was being hassled."

"The ladies on the tour loved him. All those stories he told about his life before he came to Florida. He traveled around, but he seemed to love it here."

"As an old Coast Guard guy, I appreciated how much Oscar loved the water. Did you know he worked on and off as a hand on a fishing charter?"

"Really? I had no idea. Which charter?" I was afraid Mugsy would think I was nosy, but he shook his head.

"I got no idea, but I can tell you Oscar got thrown off the boat for getting into a fight with another deckhand. I asked him once, friendly like, about the fight, but Oscar told me to mind my own business."

Mugsy shrugged off the whole idea. "Oscar was really touchy when it came to his personal life. He wouldn't say how it started or how it ended. But really, could an old guy like Oscar get into much of a fight? Anyway, I got to go back to work. Thanks for these." He shook the box of pastries toward me. "Darla can give you Oscar's family contacts if you want to send a card."

Darla handed me a photocopied paper with all Oscar's information and cheerfully reminded me to come back any time I needed a ride. As soon as I was in the parking lot, I called Bridgy. I was dying to tell her that Oscar had a fight with a deckhand, who could definitely be a potential suspect, but her phone went directly to voice mail. Not a good sign. If she was still being interviewed . . . with or without Owen, I didn't want to think about what a bad sign that would be. I hopped in my jeep and headed back to the Read 'Em and Eat. Perhaps Ophie had news.

CHAPTER ELEVEN

I was surprised that Ophie hadn't locked the door at closing. I walked into the café, where she was sitting at Robert Frost with her elbows resting on the tabletop. Her chin was pressed so deeply into her palms that her ashen face crumpled, showing wrinkles I never knew existed. I'd never seen her so distressed.

"Ophie, what is it? Is it Bridgy?"

"It's not Bridgy. I can't talk about it. I'm glad you're back. I have to go home."

As she headed out the door, I could hear Ophie's shoes scrape along the tile floor so differently from the usual peppy *click-click-click* of her spiked heels.

She left without another word.

I locked the door behind her and pushed into the kitchen to see if Miguel knew what was going on. I was shocked to see Bridgy at the sink, humming tunelessly and sway-ing left to right, right to left, while she rinsed dishes and loaded the dishwasher. She looked so happy that I didn't even mind that she was washing dishes while still wearing my gray silk blouse.

Miguel was nowhere to be seen. What was going on here? Had I imagined everything that happened yesterday and today?

"Hey, songbird. I've been calling and calling, but you aren't answering your phone. For goodness' sake, what happened today?"

As soon as she turned to me I could see that the brooding, dismal Bridgy who went off with Owen a few hours earlier had completely disappeared. Her smile was wider than a four-lane highway, and her eyes sparkled the way they used to when we went into Manhattan to stare at the Christmas tree in Rockefeller Center. I had a fleeting memory of how we'd laugh because we could see the reflection of those thousands of lightbulbs in each other's eyes. Then we'd get frustrated when we looked in a little pocket mirror but couldn't see the tree lights reflected in our own eyes.

I blurted out the first thing that came into my mind. "The killer. They caught the killer."

Bridgy did a double heel-to-toe rock and clapped her hands. "That's great news. Who was it? And why?"

118

I realized too late that whatever made Bridgy so upbeat, it wasn't the end of the investigation into Oscar's murder. I dreaded having to utter my next sentence. "I thought you were humming and swaying because the killer was caught and you were off the hook. What did happen at the sheriff's office?"

And that shot the sparkle right out of her eyes. Bridgy walked to the freezer, stuck her head inside and came out with a tub of butter pecan ice cream. She set it on the counter and grabbed some chocolate sauce from the refrigerator.

She looked at me. "Well, get some spoons." And she marched into the dining room.

We sat with the half-empty ice cream container between us. Bridgy dribbled chocolate sauce on top of the ice cream, and we dug in. After four or five minutes Bridgy set her spoon on the table. "Okay, do you want the good news or the bad news first?"

"Bad news."

Bridgy sighed. "You *always* pick bad."

"Naturally. I like to get it out of the way. So tell me. The bad news happened when you went to meet with Lieutenant Anthony, right?"

Bridgy's shoulders dropped. "It was awful. He hammered away with the same questions, over and over again. I felt like . . . like he was trying to trip me up. I will say Owen was wonderful. He kept jumping in by saying, 'Asked and answered,' but the lieutenant had a dozen different ways to ask why I went out to the van, what I did when I found Oscar, and why I said, 'He's dead. I'm sorry,' rather than 'I'm sorry he's dead.' Really? Who pays attention to sentence structure at a time like that?"

I could see the tears welling up in her eyes. I focused on praising Owen rather than dissecting Frank's questions. "It's a good thing Owen was with you. Afterward did he say anything about another lawyer?"

"You mean a criminal lawyer? Owen told me straight out it might come to that, but so far, he hasn't said it's necessary." She dipped into the ice cream and came up with a drippy spoonful of butter pecan with chocolate syrup puddled in the middle. "Oh, this is melting fast. Do you want more or should I put it away?"

"You stay right there. I'll take care of it." I cleared the table, put the ice cream away and rinsed our spoons at the sink. When I came back with a spray bottle and cloth to wipe down the table, Bridgy was gazing out

120

the window in the general direction of Oscar's last parking space. "Ophie was still here when I came in. She was really down in the dumps. I guess she's worried about you."

"Not at all. She's upset about the good news. Don't look so puzzled. There is only one thing that could make me happy and Ophie crazy all at the same time." Bridgy jumped out of her chair and started waltzing around the room singing something I didn't quite recognize. Then I realized it was one of the songs from the movie *Frozen*.

"What? Ophie is mad about *Frozen*? Is the community center putting on a show and she didn't get the part of Elsa?"

Bridgy giggled. "Don't be silly. Even she knows she's too old to play Elsa. Or Anna, for that matter."

I was starting to wish I'd paid more attention to the movie. I knew there was a clue buried in Bridgy's rambling.

She gave me an exaggerated wink. "Get it? Elsa and Anna? Sisters. Ophelia and Emelia. Sisters!"

"Your mother? She's coming here? When?" I grabbed Bridgy's hands and swung her in a circle. "No wonder you're so happy." Then I came to a dead stop. "Wait a minute. Why is Ophie so miserable?"

"For the same reason I am so happy. My mother will be here the day after tomorrow."

I stopped spinning. "But they're sisters. What did I miss? Did they have a falling-out? When?"

"Only for the last thirty or so years."

I was totally baffled. "We've spent holidays together, even long weekends. I never noticed any . . . problems. Are you sure?"

"Oh, they manage well enough for brief get-togethers like holidays and birthdays, but my mother is coming here tomorrow with an open-ended plane ticket. It's the potential time frame that has Ophie frazzled. Mom will tell her to act her age once too often, and then the bickering will begin. Think your average six-year-olds fighting over the last available swing on the play set." Bridgy chuckled. "At least they're not boring. And they do love each other. It is just that Emelia thinks she knows what's best for Ophelia, while Ophelia thinks of Emelia as her little sister who should keep her two cents to herself. And you do have to wonder what Grandma was thinking with these Ophelia, Emelia names. Like rhyming was going to make them closer. My father once mused that he thought the name game might be part of the problem. I mean, they're not clones. They're not even twins."

"Oh please. Remember Laura and Lauren Moderno? The twins who battled each other all through elementary school? The smartest thing their parents ever did was to send them to different high schools." I patted Bridgy's hand. "I'm so glad that I have you for my bestie. Closest I'll ever have to a sister." I grabbed my keys off the counter. "And in the name of sisters everywhere, let's take a ride up to visit Tony the Boatman. I'll drive."

Bridgy tucked a blond curl behind her ear and lowered her eyelids. "I hate to be a spoilsport, but I am so wiped. I'm not sure I could handle a kayak paddle, even if we took out a two-seater and I only had to do half the work."

"Well, if you are too tired to paddle around the bay, I guess we'll just have to limit ourselves to following up a lead on a genuine suspect in Oscar's murder."

Bridgy's eyes flew wide open. "A suspect? You mean someone besides me is a suspect? Let me get my purse."

Traffic on Estero Boulevard was lighter than usual, and within a few minutes I was sliding the Heap-a-Jeep into a prime spot in the parking lot at Bowditch Point Park.

When we got to Tony's boat dock, I was

delighted that he was busy cleaning out bait buckets. I wanted to talk to him without customers milling around and listening in. Over time we'd become friends. Tony liked us because when we rented canoes or kayaks we returned them on time. We liked him because he knew everything that happened for miles around and wasn't above sharing information.

"Hey, ladies." Tony took off his straw panama hat, waved it in our direction and plunked it back on his head. "Haven't seen you for a while. Want to spend an hour or so on the water? I just got a couple of new Wilderness kayaks with really comfy seats — great stability and excellent ventilation. Heat won't get you, that's for sure." The red kerchief tied around his neck was soaked with perspiration, and his Hercule Poirot–style mustache was a bit grayer and more straggly than when we'd last visited.

"I wish we could, but, well, we had a little trouble in the café parking lot, and I was wondering if you could help us out."

He looked from me to Bridgy and back again. "Is this about Oscar? Heard about that. What's this island coming to?"

We commiserated for a couple of minutes, and then Tony asked what help we needed.

Bridgy raised her hand like a third grader

who wasn't quite sure of the answer but decided to take a stab at it. "I found Oscar. After he was killed, I'm the one who found him."

Tony took off his hat again, wiped his brow with his forearm and stared at the sky. "That's a heavy burden for a young'un such as yourself." He flexed his muscles and expanded his massive chest. "Big guy like me, no problem, but you . . . I am sorry for your trouble. How can I help?"

"Sheriff's deputies have interviewed Bridgy twice already. We think they should start looking someplace else."

"Where did you have in mind? You think someone hated his driving that much?" Tony chuckled, but when we didn't respond to his joke, he moved right back to serious. "Well, if you're here, then you think Oscar might have had a problem concerning boats. Is it the *Fisherman's Dream* you're looking for?"

"We're not sure. We heard around town that Oscar crewed part-time on a fishing boat."

"Yep. That'd be the *Dream,* all right. Oscar used to fill in when guys were out sick, on vacation, like that."

I felt like we were finally on the right track. " 'Used to' is the key phrase. Rumor has it Oscar got into a fight with another deckhand. A real fight, with fists flying. We heard that fight cost Oscar his job."

Tony cupped his chin with his thumb and forefinger, then ran his fingers across his stubble. "That could be. Oscar wasn't a fighter, but he didn't like to be pushed around. Antoine Jackson is the man you need to speak to. He's the ship's captain. I hear he's a fair-minded boss, but, working for myself, I've come to the place where I don't think much of any boss, if you get my drift."

Bridgy and I'd often talked about how the freedom to make our own decisions overrode the difficulties of running our own business. It was a comfort to hear that Tony felt the same way. I steered him back to the matter at hand.

"Where can we find Mr. Jackson?"

"Call him Mister and there will be a ruckus sure as I'm standing here. Call him Captain Jackson, you might twist him around your pretty little finger and find out what you want to know. He docks the *Fisherman's Dream* over on San Carlos Island, just south of the bridge. So I guess I really can't talk you into trying my new kayaks. You got somewhere else to be."

I stretched up on my tiptoes and planted

126

a kiss on his grizzled cheek. "We'll be back for that kayak ride soon enough. Right now it's time for us to cross the bridge and see what we can learn on the *Fisherman's Dream.*"

CHAPTER TWELVE

The bridge was jam-packed with cars heading on and off the island. Traffic was at a crawl. I was glad we were going to San Carlos Island rather than continuing on to the mainland. I was nearing the turnoff when Bridgy distracted me.

"What are we going to ask him?"

"Ask who? Oh, you mean Captain Jackson?" I maneuvered the Heap-a-Jeep smartly to the right, and in a few seconds we were out of the traffic jam and on San Carlos Island.

"Well, I guess we'll ask him why he fired Oscar, and when he mentions the fight, we'll ask about the other person in the fight."

"Sassy, you make it sound so easy. Two complete strangers walk up to a man and ask why he fired someone who was found murdered yesterday. Why would he talk to us? I mean, seriously, would you?"

I was searching for a parking spot near

the marina, so I was half ignoring Bridgy's chatter until I heard her screech. "Stop. There it is."

She was pointing to a huge boat with "FISH_____AN'S DREAM" stenciled across the stern in letters about three feet high. The "E," the "R," and the "M" in "FISHERMAN'S" were missing because the gangplank was lowered. Good news for us. The ship was in dock, and there was someone aboard.

I parked rather crookedly in the first available space and jumped out of the jeep. Bridgy hesitated.

"What?"

"I told you. I don't think this is a good idea. If you insist, I'll go along, but this is *your* plan, so if it comes to naught . . ."

I got it. My plan. Any problem would be my fault.

"Look, we're here now . . ."

Bridgy got out of the jeep and led the way to the gangplank, but I knew once we got there the next move would be on me. And that is exactly where I was stymied. I had no next move planned.

We stood on the dock looking up at the enormous white ship. It was several stories high, wider than our entire apartment and longer than most mini malls.

"Well?" Bridgy was losing patience.

"I'm short on decorum. It's not like there's a doorbell. Should we just barge in? We could stand here shouting 'Permission to come aboard' from now until doomsday, but unless someone is standing right at the edge of the stern, I can't believe anyone up there" — I waved toward the upper decks — "will hear us."

We heard some banging and clanging just above our heads, and a man whose face was largely obscured by a pair of oversized round sunglasses and a faded denim bucket hat started down the gangplank. His tank top screamed "FISHERMAN'S DREAM" in big letters. He was carrying at least a dozen fishing rods along with a few tackle boxes, which knocked against the stern as he cleared the boat and headed down the gangplank.

Standing where we were, we definitely blocked his way. Bridgy took a few steps, but I figured this might be the best way to start a conversation.

"Ladies, you wanna move, please?" And he swung the fishing rods to his right since we were on his left.

"Oh, sorry, I didn't realize we were in your way. We're looking for Captain Jackson. Is he on board?"

He heaved an exaggerated sigh. Once he hit dockside, he dropped the tackle boxes and spread the rods on the gangplank. He pulled a radio out of his pocket.

"Lorgan to bridge. Lorgan to bridge. Over."

"Bridge here. Over."

"Hey, Scotty, is the captain around? He has some visitors." Lorgan glanced up at the wide glass windows of the uppermost deck, and I did the same. I thought I saw a face take a brief glance and then disappear. The radio crackled.

"Captain's busy. Tell them if they want to book a trip to go to the website or give the office a call."

Lorgan started to put the radio back in his pocket. "You heard the man."

We sure did. I decided to give it one last try. "Actually, we need to speak to the captain on a personal matter of grave importance."

"Captain doesn't do 'personal matters' on the boat." And Lorgan moved to the middle of the gangplank, crossed his arms and stood stock-still.

Mission failure.

I mustered what dignity I could, thanked him for his time and started to walk back to the car. I give Bridgy credit; she waited until we were out of Lorgan's earshot before she said, "Well, that certainly went well."

I chose not to answer.

We got in the jeep, and I turned on the engine and the radio simultaneously. I gave a quick twist to the knob so the radio was louder than normal. Unfortunately, instead of a nice, happy song, the radio was broadcasting an unending commercial about the wonders of knee-replacement surgery.

Bridgy leaned in and pushed another button on the console. I was afraid she'd turn the radio off and as soon as the silence became deafening she would fill it with a lot of chatter beginning with "I told you so," but instead she found Miranda Lambert singing "Crazy Ex-Girlfriend."

We listened until Miranda morphed into a commercial for a shoe sale at Bealls.

Bridgy always loved that song. "She wrote it, she sang it, got married and then was gracious throughout her divorce. I guess Miranda channels her negative energy through her music. When my bonehead ex-husband blew up our marriage, only you and my mother kept me from beating him with a bat."

I was happy Bridgy had dismissed the fiasco of my trying to speak to Captain Jackson, but I didn't think focusing on a cheating ex was a healthy place for her to be right now.

She went on. "With Oscar being . . . dead, I have to hope that you and my mother can keep me out of jail."

That topic was even worse. I needed to switch gears fast. Fortunately, the radio moved from commercials to Lady Antebellum singing "American Honey." We sang along.

"Childhood summers were the best, weren't they?"

I wasn't quite sure if Bridgy was asking me or musing aloud, but I answered with an agreeable "uh-hm" in case she wanted to talk.

"I'm glad my mother is coming. Sometimes a girl needs her mom. I think being a murder suspect is one of those times."

"Stop it now. You are not a suspect. You're a very special witness."

"Oh sure. Just like on *NCIS* when Tony introduces himself as 'Very Special Agent Anthony DiNozzo.'" Bridgy snorted at me.

I ignored the snort. "Listen, anytime is a great time to have your mom around. It will be like a mini vacation."

"I can see it now. Mom, me and Frank Anthony. We'll have loads of fun. At least with Mom around I don't need a lawyer. If she decides the lieutenant is being mean to me, she'll harangue him into complete silence. Remember the time those boys took our schoolbags and threw them up on Old Lady Kramden's fire escape and we were afraid to knock on her door and ask for them back? The moms not only got back our schoolbags, they went to see the fathers of each and every one of those boys. Say, why isn't your mom coming?"

I bit my tongue, deciding not to mention that I wasn't the one in trouble with the sheriff's office. "Dunno. How did you find out your mom was coming?"

"You know Ophie made me call home yesterday. I didn't want to worry Mom, so I made light of the whole situation."

I wondered how she was able to diminish the severity of discovering the dead body of a murdered man, but I didn't ask.

"This morning when I came out of the sheriff's office and turned on my phone, I found an email she sent me with her flight confirmation. I never expected her to come down here, but I'm so happy she decided she would."

I was nearing the turnoff from the bridge onto Estero Boulevard and realized I didn't know if we were going back to the café or heading home. "Right or left?"

"Huh? Oh, I don't need anything from the café. I finished the cleanup and shut down before you came back, and we definitely locked the doors, so take the right. Home it is."

We half listened to the radio asking everyone in earshot to attend a fund-raiser for one of the local nature sanctuaries.

Bridgy snapped to attention. "That sounds like fun. I am going to need a lot of activities to keep Mom occupied."

"Can't Ophie . . . ?"

"Didn't you hear a word I said? They can't be left alone. They need a mediator at all times. Do you have any book clubs coming up that Mom might enjoy?"

"I might. Remember when the moms took that French cooking class at Brooklyn Community College? The Potluck Book Club is reading Julia Child."

Bridgy clapped her hands. "That sounds perfect. Which book?"

"Well, we had a bit of a problem deciding that. Maggie Latimer suggested *Julie and Julia: My Year of Cooking Dangerously.* You know the one. It was written by Julie Powell who decided to cook her way through Julia Child's *Mastering the Art of French Cooking.*"

"I remember the movie, although we never

135

did see it. I bet we could find it on Netflix. Meryl Streep and Amy Adams, wasn't it? Anyway, I know Mom would love to read it for the book club. She'd love the chance to talk about French cooking with the ladies."

I turned the radio volume to barely there and said, "Well, it is a bit complicated. You see, Jocelyn . . ."

Bridgy laughed and flapped her hands like a toddler. "Say no more. If Jocelyn is involved, it's complicated."

I turned the car into the parking lot of the Beausoleil Apartments and remained silent.

Bridgy nudged my arm.

"Hey, don't poke. I'm parking the car."

"Tell me about the complications at the book club."

"You said, 'Say no more.' "

"A figure of speech."

I turned off the engine and said, "Okay, let's get up to the Turret, and for a cold glass of just about anything, I'll tell you the whole dreary story."

A few minutes later we were relaxing on the patio stretched out on side-by-side chaise lounges. Glasses of lemonade and a plate of sugar cookies sat on the round table at our elbows.

"Look at that view." Bridgy sighed contentedly. "It never gets old."

She was right. By a stroke of good fortune we rented an apartment on the fifth floor of the Beausoleil. Our patio and most of our windows overlooked the Gulf of Mexico, the beach and the barrier islands stretching up the coast of Florida. Sanibel, home to the Ding Darling National Wildlife Refuge, is a haven for birders and folks who collect shells. Pine Island is a fishing mecca. North Captiva, Cabbage Key, Cayo Costa and other lush islands continued northward. We were forever enthralled by the view.

Bridgy snatched a cookie and took a bite before she asked me about the Potluck Book Club.

"It was no big deal. Just the usual fuss. After Maggie suggested *Julie and Julia,* everyone agreed except Jocelyn."

"No surprise there."

"True. She said that if we were going to read *about* Julia Child, we should read something written *by* Julia Child. Jocelyn suggested *My Life in France.*"

"So which book did the club pick?"

"The argument got heated, and Jocelyn dug in her heels wide and deep. Finally, I recommended that the club members could read whichever book appealed to them, and we would talk about Julia Child, her cooking and her influence on Julie Powell. That satisfied most of the clubbies."

"Satisfied all but Jocelyn. She isn't happy unless she's triumphant."

"Well, she may still wind up triumphant. There is some really strong language in *Julie and Julia*. Who knew? I don't censor the books. I read along with the clubs. I think the vocabulary will be a major topic of discussion."

"Have you heard complaints?"

"Not yet, but I expect the meeting will be a raucous one."

Bridgy chuckled. "Won't be the first time."

A fishing boat pulled into a dock on Pine Island. We watched a flock of seagulls flying in ever-narrowing circles waiting for the crew to toss the leftover bait into the Gulf. Two deckhands emptied a half dozen or so buckets over the side of the boat, and the seagulls dived and lunged, squawking at one another to get out of the way.

"That's it. We have to get someone on that boat."

"That boat?" Bridgy pointed at Pine Island.

"No, silly. The *Fisherman's Dream*." I pulled my cell phone from my pocket. "I'll call Cady. I'm sure I can get him to go on tomorrow's fishing trip. He loves to fish."

CHAPTER THIRTEEN

Cady answered on the second ring. He instantly reminded me why I liked him so much when he opened with, "How's Bridgy?"

"She's right here beside me on our patio. We're watching a flock of seagulls devour the leavings of a fishing boat docked on Pine Island. For the moment, all is serene."

"Let's hope it stays that way. Any news about Oscar?"

Just the opening I needed. "Actually, I have a lead that could give you the scoop of the century."

His normally sweet tone of voice turned stern. "Sassy, what have you been up to? Please stay out of trouble."

I put on my brightest smile, hoping he would hear innocence in my voice. "I haven't been up to anything. Unless you consider making a condolence call with a box of pastries being 'up to something.' "

"Condolence call? Where? The paper hasn't been able to find any local relatives."

Good. His nose for news was on the scent.

"I hired the van, you know, and Oscar along with it. I don't want his friends and colleagues to be afraid to work with us in the future, so I brought some treats for their break room. Let them know we share their sorrow."

Cady's voice relaxed. "I'm sure everyone appreciated your thoughtfulness."

He was hooked, so I continued on the thread of helpfulness. "I had no idea such lovely people worked at Gulf Coast Cab and Van. Darla, the receptionist, couldn't be sweeter. And did you know Blondie Quinlin's nephew works there? His name is Mugsy. He's a dispatcher."

I may have laid it on a little too thick. Still, I could feel Cady's curiosity right through the phone. "Really? And you managed to meet him? I suppose with an introduction from his aunt. What did Mugsy have to say?"

That last question was tinged with sarcasm, but I stayed nonchalant. "He was shocked that Oscar was murdered and upset that his aunt —"

"Sassy," Cady interrupted. "Cut to the chase."

Hopefully I roused his interest enough to

get him to do what I wanted. "Mugsy happened to mention that Oscar used to be a fill-in deckhand on a fishing boat but lost that job when he got into a fistfight with another crew member." I skipped a beat. "No telling where a fight could lead."

"And did Mugsy happen to mention which of the hundreds of fishing boats on this part of the Gulf —"

My turn to interrupt. "No, but Tony said it was the *Fisherman's Dream* out of San Carlos Island."

"Tony? Boat basin Tony? Was he making a condolence call, too?" More sarcasm.

"No, but Bridgy and I ran into him after the condolence call."

"Sassy, even through the phone I can see your nose growing like Pinocchio's. You've been snooping."

"Okay. Just listen for a minute." I needed his cooperation, so I was willing to plead guilty to assorted crimes. I kept it simple. "When Mugsy told me about the fight that Oscar may have had, he didn't know the name of the boat, so Bridgy and I went to ask Tony, because he knows everything about boats. He sent us to the *Fisherman's Dream.*"

"He sent you? You mean he put you in a cab and paid the driver twenty dollars to

141

take you to San Carlos Island so you could snoop around a fishing boat?"

In need of his help or not, I was losing patience. "Skepticism doesn't become you. You know exactly what I mean. Tony told us where Oscar crewed part-time. He, too, had heard about the fight but didn't have details. He said Captain Jackson could tell us, so off we went." Then I played my trump card. "Bridgy's future could be at stake."

Cady was silent for a minute. "I'm sorry. I know you're concerned. It's just that I worry when you wander off on these investigations of yours. No telling what could happen."

Time to snap the trap. "I know I'm impulsive, and I hate that everyone worries about me, which is why I called you. How would you like to go fishing on a charter with me tomorrow? My treat."

He was silent for so long that I was afraid my smartphone had turned stupid and lost the connection. Then I heard a long, exaggerated sigh. "Well, I suppose I'd better go along. Keep you out of trouble. And I'd feel better if we went dutch. What time should I pick you up? And where?"

"Time?" I had no idea. "Let me think, but we can definitely meet at the café."

I'd noticed that Bridgy was fiddling with

her iPhone while I was talking to Cady. I thought she was texting, probably with her mom. Then she held her phone screen in front of my face to show me that she'd searched and found the advertising page for the *Fisherman's Dream.* I finger scrolled until I found tomorrow's date. All the information I needed was right in front of me. I blew Bridgy a kiss and turned my attention back to Cady.

"The *Fisherman's Dream* departs at nine sharp tomorrow morning for a half-day run. Seems kind of late to start a fishing trip. I remember having to wake up when it was still dark the day you took Bridgy, Ophie and me out on your boat."

Cady set me straight immediately. "When it comes to the charter boats, those going out for a full day leave early. Half days leave later. That prevents traffic jams in the harbor, since those boats have to follow a schedule. Small fry like me can come and go pretty much as we please."

"So it *pleased* you to make us get up early. You *could have* let us sleep in and started fishing later in the day."

"Really, Sassy? That was months ago. Did it ever occur to you I might have had a reason, like the weather or a report that the grunts or groupers were running early? As I recall, all three of you caught fish."

Bridgy could see a fight was brewing, so she started giving me the "wrap it up" signal, rolling both her hands frantically, first forward, then backward.

I held up a hand, palm out, in the universal sign for "just a minute."

"You're right. I'm sorry." I hoped I sounded contrite. "What time did you want me to be ready tomorrow?" I added a sweetener. "And what would you like for breakfast?"

I was elated by the time we hung up. Captain Antoine Jackson would be trapped in his boat with me for hours. No way I wouldn't get the information I wanted.

Then Bridgy burst my bubble. "So, what happens when Cady shows up tomorrow morning and you don't have tickets?"

I grabbed her phone and headed for my laptop. In less than five minutes Cady and I were fully registered for the next day's excursion on the *Fisherman's Dream*.

Bridgy parked her snappy red Escort ZX2 on the opposite side of the parking lot from the café. I didn't question her motives. I suspected we'd both be hard pressed to park anywhere near the scene of the crime for some time to come.

I picked up the pile of today's *Fort Myers Beach News* that was always waiting at our front door. I put the papers on the counter by the register and slipped off the string that held them together. Our current bill was right on top. I headed through the kitchen to the office to put it in our bill folder before I lost it entirely.

Miguel had things humming in his usual orderly fashion. Something smelled fabulous. I reached for the oven door to investigate.

"Don't open the oven. You'll ruin my pies."

I gave him a big grin. "Are we going to have something for the specials board today?"

"You remember my friend Benny? He's the sous chef at one of those elegant restaurants on Sanibel, and he got a bunch of us together for a great deal on pecans from a farmer up around Gainesville." He pointed to a rumpled paper tacked to the bulletin board. "There's the bill for our order. Great price for pecans fresh from the farm."

I inhaled deeply. "Pecan pie? Delish! Miguel, you are a marvel." I continued on through to our tiny office. Behind me Miguel said, "You forgot the bill."

I circled back to the bulletin board and

pulled the pecan bill off without removing the pushpin. Naturally, the rumpled paper ripped in the process. I taped the torn piece and put it and the newspaper bill into the folder that held a few other things I knew I had to pay soon.

I could hear Bridgy telling Miguel that Cady was coming by to take me fishing.

"Ay, a date so early in the morning. What will they do for the rest of the day, I wonder?"

I could almost see him raise an eyebrow in expectation. I stepped back in the room.

"Not exactly a date. We're going out on a charter boat hoping to find the deckhand that got into a tussle with Oscar. We'll be back as soon as the boat docks."

I didn't have to look at Miguel to see him roll his eyes.

"You better be back. The Teen Book Club is scheduled for this afternoon. I can't stay for even a minute. I have to shop. My mother will be here tomorrow." Bridgy practically sang the last part.

I knew to grovel. "Don't worry. I so appreciate you holding the fort down by yourself this morning, I wouldn't dare be late."

"No problem. You're doing this for me. Anyway, I sent Ophie a text, and she'll pop

146

in to help between her Treasure Trove appointments. We'll manage, won't we, Miguel?"

"Sí." He gave me the same stern look that I usually got from Cady. "But don't think I approve of your antics. I am only free from worry because I know Cady will take care of you."

I was saved from replying by the ship's bell attached to the side of our door frame. It clanged. Twice. The morning rush was about to begin.

I did as much as I could, all the while keeping an eye out for Cady. As soon as he pulled into the parking lot, I took off my apron and spent a moment telling Bridgy what the folks at my tables would need. By the time Cady came through the door, I had two large coffees and two Miss Marple Orange Iced Scones ready to go. I turned him right around, and we headed for San Carlos Island.

We were in the marina parking lot well before eight thirty, so I was surprised to see dozens of men, women and children wearing the latest fishing gear and carrying rods and tackle boxes milling around the main deck of the *Fisherman's Dream* looking for their perfect spot to cast off as soon as we were out in the Gulf.

Cady popped his trunk, reached in and tossed me a fisherman's vest festooned with hooks and lures. "Here. Put this on. You may as well look the part."

Chagrined, I put on the vest. I suppose I wouldn't do well as a spy. I thought to bring sunscreen and a visor, but fishing gear never entered my head. Cady put on his own vest and a khaki bucket hat to match. He carried three fishing rods and a beat-up metal tackle box. He slammed the trunk shut and took a few steps toward the charter boat before he asked if I had our admission tickets.

I harrumphed. I may not have thought a fig about fishing gear, but I wouldn't forget the tickets that would provide my best chance at access to information that could help point Frank Anthony far away from Bridgy. I took the tickets out of my cross-body bag and fanned his face with them.

The line was short. Two crew members wearing tanks with "FISHERMAN'S DREAM" plastered across their chests and backs were collecting tickets, so we moved quickly up the gangplank. Someone behind us yelled, "Hey, wait a minute." For a second I had the wild thought that Lorgan spotted me and was going to drag me off the boat. But the call was for the family directly ahead of us. They'd handed in their rod and tackle rental slips with their admission tickets.

Cady and I leaned against the safety rope on the side of the gangplank to let the father run down to retrieve the rental slips, and then we followed his family onto the boat deck. The fisher-folk were in high spirits. A man in the group to my left was recounting the rules to win the wager they'd all agreed upon, when another man shouted him down. "C'mon, Kirk. It's the same rules every time we go out. Do you really need to spout 'em over and over?"

Someone shouted from the crowd, "Problem is, he thinks he's Captain Kirk. Well, this ain't the good ship *Enterprise.*"

Several of the men started da-da-da-ing the theme for the original *Star Trek* television show.

With all the raucous laughter and good-natured commotion around us, I began to feel happy and confident. Once I found the person Oscar fought with, Bridgy would be in the clear. I looped my arm through Cady's. "Let's take a stroll around the deck before we choose our fishing spot."

Chapter Fourteen

As we headed from stern to bow, Cady pointed to the right side of the ship. "I always think starboard is lucky for fishing. I caught my first prizewinning snapper from starboard of a boat smaller than this one. Never fished from port side again."

I praised his prowess and wisdom but gave up because he was busy marveling out loud at the splendor of the morning. There was a slight breeze coming in from the Gulf, and the sky was cloudy, the sun not over-bright. He pronounced it perfect fishing weather. He started to explain about wind from the west and how the clouds reduced sunlight on the water and made our hooks and lures more attractive to the fish. Blah, blah, blah.

I tried to say, "Oh, really?" or, "I had no idea," at the appropriate pauses in his spiel. In the meantime, I was busy eyeing every deckhand, looking for The One. In my mind I eliminated all the females and any of the men under forty. I mean, if Oscar got into a fight, it should have been with a man close to his own age.

All of a sudden I realized I was strolling by myself. I turned to see Cady setting up our rods a few feet behind me.

"I think this'll do it. Plenty of room and no one crowding us. I hate when my line gets snagged with another fisherman's. Bad enough if it gets snagged on the boat bottom." He reddened. "It's happened more times than I can count."

Oh Lord. I'm here on a mission while he actually intends to fish.

I walked back to where he was standing and halfheartedly listened to his directions about how to use the rod he brought for me. I mean, it's a fishing rod. How hard could it be? Then I remembered last year when my father and uncle came to visit and I took them on a charter fishing trip. They babbled instructions. I paid no attention and I caused no end of trouble. I clearly remember my father using the phrase, "This is a fiasco," over and over again.

So I forced myself to pay attention even though I had no intention of fishing. I even — good-naturedly, I thought — practiced casting off. It was Cady's good fortune that I let him stand behind me and reach around

151

to hold my hands on the rod exactly as he wanted them.

Garbled instructions came over the loudspeaker, and a frisson of excitement moved through the passengers. The *Fisherman's Dream* was about to begin its journey out of Matanzas Harbor, through San Carlos Bay and into the Gulf of Mexico. Most passengers had plans to catch a shark or some delicious snapper for dinner. I couldn't wait for everyone to settle into fishing mode so I could start looking for any information about Oscar.

Cady suggested that we go to the highest deck and watch the world go by from there. Nearly everyone on the boat had the same idea. People were taking every possible picture with cameras and phones. I leaned against the rails so Cady could take my picture with the mainland in the background and then again with Bowditch Point Park and the beach stretching down Estero Island. I was getting anxious to be off on my own, so I was pleased when Cady suggested that we get back to our spot at the rail of the lower deck, ready to fish when the *Fisherman's Dream* dropped anchor.

The barrier islands were soon behind us, and a foghorn blew, signaling the first stop of the day. Everyone scrambled for their rods and reels. Crew members wove through the crowd, offering to help folks cast off or bait a hook.

Cady opened his tackle box and brought out an aerated bait carrier. "I have live cigar minnows and some frozen ballyhoo. Would you prefer to bait your hook with something that doesn't wiggle?"

I was tempted to say, "Whatever," but I remembered that Cady was doing me a huge favor by coming along on this trip. He made it so much easier for me to blend in with the other passengers, so instead I opted for the ballyhoo, because I remembered it was what my father used when he was here.

The boat rocked gently, and I had no trouble keeping my line in the water. Someone on the port side of the deck caught a nice-sized grouper, which spurred everyone to expect a good catch any minute.

The foghorn blew once more, and we pulled up our lines. I told Cady I was having a great time. Then I excused myself and started off for the cabin area. Cady grabbed my arm. "Don't go looking for trouble."

I gave him a wide but insincere smile. "You caught me. I was going below for a candy bar, but perhaps I'll get a protein bar instead. Do you want anything?"

"No, thanks. I'm going to work on your

line knot. It seems loose."

"Be right back." I took a few steps, and as soon as I saw he was bent over my line, tugging and pulling, I ran up the steps from our deck to the next and then to the next, which was tiny, vacant and had a "Do Not Enter" sign on the side rail. I saw what looked like the door to the bridge and wondered if Captain Jackson would be willing to answer a few questions to get me off his bridge and out of his hair.

I nearly made it to the door when a voice behind me boomed, "Hey, lady, this section is off-limits. Didn't you see the sign?"

Curses, foiled again. I knew just how Dick Dastardly felt in the old *Wacky Races* cartoons. Once again, I smiled, although I was getting tired of smiling at men who were determined to prevent me from doing as I pleased. Still, I threw in my best imitation of Bridgy's wide-eyed, innocent stare for good measure and turned toward the voice, and my only blessing was that the deckhand standing there wasn't Lorgan. In that case the game would be up for sure.

"I'm so sorry. I was looking for the ladies' room. A gentleman down there" — I lifted my arm and swept it around vaguely to include the entire ship — "told me it was upstairs and indoors."

"Come on, I'll show you." He started down the staircase. I had no choice but to follow. Still, he was a member of the crew.

"Thanks so much, Mr., er —"

"No thanks necessary. No "Mister," either. Name's Wyatt, Bert Wyatt. And what brings you to the *Fisherman's Dream* this fine day?"

I knew he was only making small talk, but he gave me a great opening. I was so busy formulating my answer, I didn't notice that two fishermen were waiting at the bottom of the staircase. Before I could open my mouth, the one who looked like the Skipper on *Gilligan's Island* right down to the jaunty cap asked, "Say, sailor, my friend and I have a wager."

"Save your money." Bert's answer was terse. "You won't be catching any sharks this trip."

"We ain't betting on fish. We're betting on the murder victim."

I inhaled so sharply that Bert turned and offered me his arm. "You all right there, miss?"

"I'm fine. My foot slipped." I took his arm. I had an idea what was coming, and I didn't want to miss a word.

The Skipper look-alike ignored the interruption. "I read about the murder in the paper. There was a picture of the victim,

155

large as life, pardon the expression, right there on page one. I said to the wife, 'I know that guy. Seen him around.' When we boarded today, it clicked. He was on the crew here. Even helped me with a snagged line once."

Bert nodded but took a long time to answer. "You mean Oscar. Yeah. Terrible thing. Truth is he was a troublemaker and the captain fired him months ago. So if you bet that he worked here, you win. If you bet that he worked here 'til the day he died, you lose. Excuse us."

He pushed the fishermen aside and led me across the deck to a door. "Facilities and a lounge area are in here. Down another level if you want to buy some snacks."

As he started to turn away, I grabbed his arm. "Thanks so much. I have another question. Did Oscar get fired because he got into a fight with another deckhand?"

Bert brushed my hand away like it was on fire. "What is this? A setup? You with those guys? And you're trying to pump me?"

I put my hands up in supplication. "No. Of course not. Nothing like that. It's just that my friend discovered the body, so naturally, we're curious about Oscar."

He put his hands on his hips and looked at me with that smoke coming out of the ears look that Bridgy gives me when I've gone too far. "Listen, lady, I don't know nothing, but if I did, I'm like those monkeys, 'See no evil, hear no evil, speak no evil.' I follow the monkey rule."

He rushed around the corner and out of sight.

By the time I got back to Cady and offered him one of the two granola bars I remembered to buy, the ship was stopped and he'd dropped both our lines in the water.

"Any nibbles?" I nudged my head toward the fishing lines while I unwrapped my granola bar.

"Nothing yet." He shrugged. "But it's early, only the second stop."

He waited until I took a big bite of my bar and got what felt like a sunflower seed wedged between two molars to ask if I had any nibbles. When I reached for my rod, he said, "I'm talking about your snooping. Did you find out anything?"

I made loud, crunchy noises while chewing granola and pointing to my mouth. My mind raced at warp speed. Was I gone too long? Did Cady see me with Bert Wyatt? Worse, did he follow me and hear me ask about Oscar? I swallowed and decided to come clean.

"No nibbles at all. I only confirmed that Oscar worked on this ship and was fired months ago. I couldn't even confirm why."

Cady handed me my rod. "Let's focus on fishing."

From that moment on, the trip was actually pleasant. Cady caught a grouper that would make a delicious dinner, and I caught a snook so small that he had to be thrown back. I wished the little guy well and hoped a barracuda didn't eat him before he was fully grown.

Miguel greeted us at the door. That was never a good sign. The first time he'd ever done so, the refrigerator was broken. The second time it was because Ophie had invaded his kitchen and he was not taking that well at all. Somehow I didn't think the third time would be a charm. "Owen Reston was here a little while ago. He doesn't like that the sheriff persists in talking to Bridgy, so he took her to meet with a criminal lawyer on the mainland. The lawyer is a friend. Owen said Bridgy could trust her."

I was in a hurry to prepare for the Teen Book Club, but I invited Cady to have something to eat. He'd been such a pal all day, it was the least I could do. When Miguel offered to make *Green Eggs and Ham,* a *salsa verde* omelet that was one of Cady's favorites, Cady practically salivated.

"I have to go to the car and get my grouper out of the cooler and put it in your fridge temporarily, okay?"

"*Sí.* We have plenty of room. That way you can enjoy your eggs without hurrying."

When Cady brought in his fish wrapped in paper and stored in a plastic bag, I brought it into the kitchen. As soon as I opened the door, I sniffed.

"I smell the deep fryer."

Miguel nodded. "You have the best nose for cooking. Better than Bridgy, even."

Well, that may have been true, but we both knew she was the better cook. Still, I took the compliment.

"I made fresh potato chips for the Teen Book Club. It is time for them to learn that the best food often does not come in a bag." He slid Cady's *Green Eggs and Ham* on a plate, then added some green grapes and a few of the still-warm potato chips.

When I placed the dish in front of Cady, he nearly swooned. I left him to enjoy his feast while I set up for the meeting. Pencils, paper and extra copies of *I Am the Messenger.* I was anxious to see what the kids thought of it.

Cady leaned back in his chair and patted

159

his stomach. "Too delicious. Miguel is a wiz in the kitchen." He saw that I was circling chairs and remembered that the Teen Book Club was coming in momentarily. "Say, what did the kids read this month?"

Before I could answer, the front door burst open and Holly Latimer and her posse marched in waving pieces of brightly colored knitted material over their heads while chanting, "Yarn bomb. Yarn bomb."

What? I thought.

CHAPTER FIFTEEN

Holly slid her backpack to the floor. "Sassy, we decided we want to liven up the book nook for our meetings. Even Jenna agrees." She pointed to the youngest member of the group, a shy thirteen-year-old. "So, we took knitting and crocheting classes at the community center and made these. This one is yours." She held up a mint green and butterscotch striped rectangle about three feet by two feet.

Mystified, I took it and thanked her.

Angela reached behind her head, pulled her long, dark ponytail over her shoulder and started to twist it, something she does whenever she's uneasy. She elbowed Daphne. "Look, she doesn't even know what it is."

Cady to the rescue. He took the knitted fabric out of my hand. "You said it was a yarn bomb, didn't you? Totes fabu. You will rock the book corner."

The girls began fist bumping each other, and Cady joined in. I understood "totally fabulous" but couldn't fathom what made him think the girls would rock the book nook. And what is a yarn bomb?

Cady held the rectangle in front of me. "Wow, the pale green and deep yellow really makes the red in your hair pop."

I was still at a loss for words.

He thrust a hand toward Jenna. "I see straps and buttons. I bet these are going to cover the chair backs. You did a great job on Sassy's. Now let me see yours."

Instinctively she put her rectangle behind her back, but when Cady stood and waited patiently with his hand extended, Jenna's good manners overcame her shyness, and she gave him her rectangle. It looked like the woolen throws my grandmother used to make for the sofa in her "parlor," as she liked to call it. Jenna's rectangle was filled with smaller rectangles of at least six or eight different shades of brown.

"Wow." Cady held it up to the light. "It looks like the bark of a dozen gorgeous trees."

Jenna flushed with pleasure and thanked him. The other three girls were anxious to get their praise and were busy showing Cady their colorful stitch work when the door opened. The final two clubbies came in. Julio greeted everyone with a smile. Macho and muscular Larry gave Cady the once-over, instantly deciding that he was much too ancient to be of any serious interest to the girls. When Holly introduced the boys to Cady, Larry stuck out his right hand and proceeded to lead Cady in an intricate handshake. I was astonished to watch Cady respond to it with very little difficulty.

As Cady handed her yarn chair cover back to Jenna, Julio asked what it was. Jenna shrugged and said, "It was Holly's idea."

Holly circle-waved her own vibrant burnt sienna and bright orange cloth over her head and then held it up high. "We are yarn bombing the book nook. You know, personalizing. Making it our own while we are here. And when we leave, we can take it with us."

"That makes no sense. You made those things? All that work for what? To decorate for an hour? Is that even a thing?" Larry was unimpressed.

"Dude, don't be a hater. Yarn bombing is killin' it. Think graffiti that's not permanent. You still make your mark, but you can take it away again — no problem — and set it up anywhere you go. Mad awesome." Holly won the verbal smackdown.

Ah, now I got it. I was about to corral everyone and get the meeting started when Julio asked if the girls could teach him to knit a motorcycle do-rag. "Maybe black with orange flames on the side."

Larry was all over it. "Or like a Flydanna, you know, with tails. A couple of guys riding Harleys, really big hogs, on Estero Boulevard told me it keeps their shaved heads from getting sunburned while they are cruising."

Angela smirked. "Surfer dude, football hero and now a biker wannabe. You definitely get an A for dangerous behavior."

Having watched Angela and Larry scuffle at previous meetings, I knew they could escalate in seconds, so I decided to wade in. "Let's get started everyone. *I Am the Messenger* is waiting, and Miguel has a mega delicious treat for you today. Big surprise."

I grabbed everyone's attention at "delicious treat."

They headed for the book nook, scrambling for a favorite seat. The girls began to fasten their needlework to the back of their chairs. Daphne grabbed mine and said, "Sassy, we'll put this where you usually sit," and she draped it over the chair next to Julio.

Unimpressed, he mocked, "We're going to

have to look at those colors all day? Barking mad is all I'm saying."

Holly smacked back, "Do I hear the voice of envy?"

The girls laughed while the boys squirmed uncomfortably.

Angela dropped her backpack and pulled out two more woolen rectangles, each one very blue. "You think we'd leave you out? No way. We're a tight club." And she threw a sky blue and white striped chair cover at Julio.

He held it out and looked at it. "The colors. *Azul y blanco.* The colors of the Guatemalan flag. *Perfecto.* I was born in Guatemala, you know."

He stood and began trying to figure out how to fasten it to his chair. Holly was quick to help.

The dark blue and green went to Larry, who shouted, "Seattle Seahawks. Way past fabu. Who do we thank?"

Holly said, "Aw, no biggie. We all worked on yours and Julio's." Then her eyes sparkled as she continued. "Angie is the ace. She developed the patterns and guided us all. You really need to thank her."

Larry turned a shade of scarlet that was a becoming contrast to his chair cover. He bobbed his head and mumbled a thank-you in Angela's general direction.

Angie preened as if she had been awarded the top spot on *America's Got Talent.*

If she and Larry ever started dating, I hoped that they would still be clubbies. I wouldn't want to miss an episode of that relationship. It would never be boring.

"Okay." I held up a copy of *I Am the Messenger.* "So what did everybody think?"

Cady waved good-bye from the doorway and signaled me to call him later. I nodded and sat silently, waiting for one of the kids to start the conversation about the book.

Holly, always energetic, began, "When I heard that Markus Zusak, who wrote *The Book Thief,* wrote this book, I was all for reading it. And I should have known better than to assume I'd like a book because the author wrote a book I did like. The two books are so different."

Daphne nodded her head, blond curls bouncing. "I know what you mean. I expected more, I don't know, *similarities,* I guess is the right word."

I let the silence wrap around us for a few moments, and eventually Larry said, "Well, I liked it. I think Ed is a really cool guy. I'd hang with him. Wouldn't you, Julio?"

Julio was quick to agree with Larry, but there was an unmistakable hesitancy in his voice. I tried to draw him out. "Julio, why do you think it would be fun to hang out with Ed Kennedy?"

"Well, for one thing, Ed needs to have some cooler friends. Except for Audrey, his friends are losers."

The whole group laughed as Julio and Larry high-fived and fist bumped each other.

Jenna, usually quiet but filled with good ideas when she can break through her shyness to share them, said, "I think that is the whole point. In the beginning, didn't you expect Ed to turn out to be a big loser?"

Holly bobbled in her chair. "Exactly. When the book opened with Ed foiling the bank robber and becoming a hero, I thought he had no place to go but downhill. I kept waiting for him to fail. I think he kept waiting for himself to fail."

I felt my phone vibrate. I slid it out of my pocket just enough to see that it was Bridgy. I excused myself, answered and said, "Hold on, please."

As I practically ran out the front door, I heard Daphne say, "Must be an important call." She lowered her voice to a stage whisper. "Do you think it's her boyfriend?"

Larry asked, "When we came in, the fella who was here, isn't he her boyfriend?"

I reached the door, opened it and stepped outside before I could hear the answer and any further speculation the clubbies might have about my personal life. I looked around and, satisfied there was no one around to overhear, said, "Okay, I can talk. You've been gone forever. What's going on? Why are you talking to a criminal attorney?"

"No big deal. Owen thought it was time I met with Clarence Darrow and put her on retainer in case the sheriff's deputies persist in bothering me."

"Clarence Darrow?"

Bridgy laughed. "Not really, but close. Her name is Georgette Darrow. Believe me when I tell you, she has one office wall covered with pictures and ancient newspaper clippings. It looks like every snap ever taken and every word ever written about Clarence Darrow."

"Are they related?"

"I was afraid to ask for fear she would bring out some genealogy charts and we'd be there a few more hours while she explained something about third cousins twice removed. Better not to know."

"So what did she say about . . . Oscar?"

"Not much. She mostly listened. I told her that I found Oscar and how Lieutenant Anthony has been questioning me ever since. Georgette seems to think that the questions are coming hot and heavy because they think I may have seen or heard something that I don't realize I saw or heard. It's like I'm the sheriff's department's personal game of *Clue*."

"If she's right, and all they think you have is information, that's a huge relief. Listen, I have to go. I have the Teen Book Club here. See you in a few?"

"Actually, I am really wiped. Owen said he would take me for a bite to eat and then drive me home. Do you have your key for the Escort? If not, I think there is a spare —"

"I'm sure I have mine. It's always on my key ring." I pulled my keys from my pocket. "Yep. Got it. I'll bring your car home safe and sound. See you later."

I stood up, and as I shoved both my phone and my keys in my pocket, I knew I'd heard something in Bridgy's voice that hadn't been there for a long time, and I wondered if she was starting to like Owen enough to go on a date or if a bite to eat was just a bite to eat.

I opened the door, and the clubbies were happily munching on freshly made potato chips and telling Miguel he was the best cook on planet Earth.

Angela dug in the bowl for another hand-ful. "Or maybe in the universe. I'm not convinced there are extraterrestrials out there, but one thing I do know: If they are there, you can out-cook 'em."

"Ow, little green men. Sure. And what would you do if you met one?" Larry practi-cally growled.

I couldn't take another round of Larry and Angela, so I went over to wrap up the meeting. No one had any suggestions for our next book, so I said I would email three names to them tomorrow, and they could vote. We'd read the book with the most votes. Everyone "yessed" me. The yarn bombs were far more interesting at the mo-ment.

I offered to find a spot where I could store the chair covers between meetings, but to my surprise, even the boys wanted to take the yarn bombs with them. I had a feeling the chair covers would visit lots of places before the Teen Book Club met again.

Laughing and teasing, the group headed for the door. I was sliding the cover off my chair when Holly came running back. "Oh, my mom really needs to talk to you. Could you give her a call? She told me to tell you it's about Oscar. She treats me like such a baby. She probably didn't want to say it's about the murder. Honestly, mothers."

And she ran out the door behind her friends. I pulled my phone from my pocket and began scrolling for Maggie Latimer's number.

CHAPTER SIXTEEN

I consider Holly's mother a friend. Not only is Maggie a talented instructor of yoga and meditation who has taught me wonderful approaches to both, she's also an enthusiastic member of several of our book clubs. I found Maggie in my cell and was just about to press the picture of the little green phone under her name when Miguel came out of the kitchen and asked if I needed a ride home.

I told him I was driving Bridgy's car home.

"Then you heard from her?"

"I did. She's fine. I think this meeting was Owen's way of preparing her so that if she needs a criminal lawyer down the road, it won't be such a shock, since she now has the lawyer on retainer. Not like bringing in a stranger."

"*Ay!* May she never need this lawyer. Still, for the peace of mind, it will be money well spent. Can I get you anything before I leave?"

"No, thanks. You were a huge help today, and the potato chips were a stroke of genius. Calmed those kids right down. They are such fun, but they can be a handful, especially when I have other things on my mind."

Miguel laughed. "Think how their poor mothers feel. *Mañana, chica.*"

I locked the door behind him, sat down and called Maggie. She answered the phone immediately. "Sassy, good. Holly swore she would deliver my message, but, well, you know kids. She might actually think she delivered the message, but . . ."

"Miguel and I were just talking about the difficulties of raising kids, which is pretty funny considering neither of us have any. So what's up? Holly made it sound serious."

I could picture Maggie leaning her head toward her left shoulder with her shiny blond ponytail dangling. I'd observed it dozens of times. The deeper the lean, the more serious her thoughts.

"Well, it could be nothing, but Tammy Rushing has, how can I say this? She's disappeared."

"Disappeared, as in vanished?"

"Without a trace. The cottage she rented

173

for the season is empty. She's gone and so are her belongings and her lease isn't up for another two weeks. I heard it directly from Jake Gilman, who owns the cottages. He takes my "Yoga for Arthritis" class. You know Jake's cottages, the ones near the bay, past the library? Anyway, Tammy's been complaining about a dripping faucet. It was interrupting her sleep. Not the speediest of landlords, Jake finally got around to sending the plumber this morning, but Tammy didn't answer the door. Plumber called Jake, who went over to let the plumber in with a passkey. Tammy was gone. Not a good-bye to anyone, and she didn't leave so much as a hairpin behind."

I was stunned. "She didn't tell Jake she was leaving?"

"No. He said that was the weird part. When people have to leave early, they always try to get some money back. Tammy didn't even ask for the return of her security deposit. Left the key on the kitchen table and a quart of milk turning sour in the fridge."

I thought for a second or two. "Maybe she had a family emergency and was too distracted to think about money. She just needed to get home ASAP."

"Noooo. There's something more. I was

at the community center a little while ago, dropping off some old jigsaw puzzles for the rec room. The sewing class was letting out, and I bumped into some of Tammy's pals. You know that Margo and her friend Sonja. There was another woman . . ."

"Could it be Angeline Drefke? She takes the sewing class with them. I know because they are all in the Cool Reads/Warm Climate Book Club. They once did a little show-and-tell with some aprons they made. And every one of them was with us at the Edison and Ford estates."

"Exactly. They were all on the trip when Oscar was killed, and now Tammy has bolted for no reason anyone can think of. Well, I can tell you the ladies thought it was highly suspicious. They didn't think she was scheduled to leave so soon and were more than willing to point a finger straight at her. Seems to me, she didn't have a true friend among them. Snowbirds."

I couldn't help but notice that Maggie used the same tone of exasperation when she talked about snowbirds that Holly did when she talked about mothers. It was totally comical. Although Tammy Rushing's disappearance was not.

"Maggie, do you think, er, is it possible that Tammy had a falling-out with Jake? We all know he can be a tad gruff. Maybe she just found another rental for the last few days of her stay. Under those circumstances she wouldn't be looking for a refund. She'd just go."

Maggie's "Well . . ." was drawn out into several syllables. Then the rest of the sentence tumbled out. "Why isn't she answering calls, texts or emails from her snowbird buddies in the sewing club?"

She had me there.

Then she dropped the bomb, and it wasn't made of yarn. "Could her leaving so hurriedly have anything to do with Oscar's murder? Do you think we should tell Ryan?"

I didn't hesitate. "Great idea. I'll let Ryan know. He and Frank Anthony can worry about Tammy Rushing. I have enough on my mind with Bridgy being questioned all the time."

Maggie said she would be coming to the Potluck Book Club and asked if Miguel was going to make any special Julia Child dish. I think she was disappointed that I had no idea.

Every time I turn my key in the lock and open the door to the Turret I get a warm feeling in my heart. Not only are Bridgy and I lucky enough to live in paradise, we also have an expansive view from five stories above. I opened the verticals that kept the afternoon sun from fighting with the air-conditioning for control of the apartment temperature, and I sighed. Yep. It was all still there. Sea, sand and greenery.

I headed for the shower, still thinking how lucky we were. I found myself humming the theme from *Star Trek*. For a moment, I wondered how the music came to be rattling around in my brain. Usually, I was more of a country music singer in the shower, a little Carrie Underwood, or some Martina McBride. Then I remembered the men on the *Fisherman's Dream* teasing their friend Kirk. I quoted, "To boldly go where no man has gone before," and turned the water full blast, ready to scrub away the stress of the day.

Of course, the thought of the *Star Trek* groupies reminded me that I hadn't had any success in finding out anything about the fight Oscar had with his shipmate. I still didn't know if there truly was a fight. If so, who was the other deckhand? It was like the entire trip had been a waste of my time.

I was massaging conditioner into the ends of my hair when I heard my smartphone. I loved my new ringtone, Cookie Monster singing his theme song. It rang again while

I was tidying the bathroom, and I sang along, but not before yelling, "I'll call back," as if Cookie could relay the message.

Much as I wanted to slide into my footie pajamas, there was always the chance Bridgy might bring Owen home with her, so I opted for clean shorts and a bright pink tee, while I decided how to spend my evening.

I remembered that Bridgy's mom's idea of crisis resolution had always been to fill the days with busywork until the crisis went away. While we were waiting for our college applications to come back yea or nay, she found dozens of chores to keep us occupied. First, Bridgy's grandma needed her closets cleaned, then a neighbor needed babysitters for her five-year-old twins, and of course Sister Cornelius was running a bake sale for the elementary school summer camp and needed dozens and dozens of cupcakes, along with a pineapple upside-down cake or two.

Once Bridgy's mom got to town, I wouldn't have the time or the peace and quiet to keep up with my book club reading. I decided to get through a few chapters of *My Life in France* while I waited for Bridgy to come home.

I barely had the book in my hand when Cookie Monster started singing again.

Cady. I told him that Bridgy was on her way home. Then I complimented him on his terrific handling of the kids earlier in the day.

"You really connect easily. That is quite a gift."

I could almost see him blushing right through the phone. Then he said, "Ah, listen, Sassy . . ." and I knew he switched from blushing to running his palm across his head, smoothing his hair front to back as if he'd managed to survive a windstorm.

I gave him a noncommittal "Uh-hm."

"I thought it was a bad idea for us to go on the *Fisherman's Dream,* because I knew you would start nosing around, and I was afraid you would get into trouble. That's why I went with you."

He paused, and when I didn't respond, he continued, the relief in his voice palpable. "As it turns out, I'm glad we went, because you didn't get into trouble, and now you have no reason to go near the boat again."

When he stopped talking, I knew I'd have to say something. "Cady, thanks for indulging me today. I promise to give you no further cause for worry."

We chatted for a few more minutes, and when we hung up, I was satisfied that he bought my shtick. Whatever I chose to do, it wouldn't be his concern.

I found *My Life in France* to be a fascinating book. Julia Child may have written it with her grand-nephew, but her voice shines through every page. The history buff in me was captivated by the descriptions of life in post–World War Two France and the role of her husband, Paul, in what was essentially the American diplomatic corps. Nothing could prepare me for the fact that there was a time when Julia Child was a terrible cook. So I enjoyed her journey through the schools and kitchens of France.

Along with Julia, I was happily accompanying Paul on a business trip to Cannes when I heard Bridgy's key turn in the lock. I jumped from my corner of the couch and met her in the foyer. I looked over her shoulder. No Owen. And when I took a good look at her face, I was glad that she was alone. I took her arm and guided her into the kitchen.

"Sit." I poured a glass of orange juice and placed it on the table in front of her. "Here."

I noticed her hand was shaking as she picked up the glass. I sat opposite her.

"Bridgy, what is it? You look like you've been shot out of a cannon."

She drained the glass and slammed it on the table so forcefully I thought it might crack.

"Everything was going so well. I actually like Georgette, and crazy as she is when it comes to Clarence Darrow, I think she is a competent attorney. But I never thought I'd actually need her to represent me."

She held out her glass for more juice. I filled it from the container on the counter and placed it in front of her. This time she only sipped.

"Anyway, after our meeting, Owen and I went to Bahama Breeze for something to eat. We were hardly in our seats when his phone rang."

She took a long sip of orange juice. "It was Frank Anthony. He said . . . he said that he wanted to give us a heads-up. Someone from the state attorney's office would be calling to 'invite' me to their office to 'discuss' Oscar's murder. Frank ended the call by warning Owen that it was time for the criminal lawyer."

She put her head on the table and began to cry.

Not knowing what to say, I petted her head and crooned, "Don't worry, your mother will be here tomorrow. Everything will be all right."

CHAPTER SEVENTEEN

The next morning when I told Bridgy that she looked great and asked how she pulled herself together, she winked. "It's all a façade. Mom will be here in a few hours, and that is my first priority. I'll let Owen and Georgette worry about the state attorney for now."

We got to the café extra early, probably because we were both so tense that we were moving at lightning speed. Bridgy threw the Escort's gear into park. Then she tapped my arm.

"Before we go in, I want you to come to the airport with me to pick up Mom. Okay?"

Instead of answering, I looked across the parking lot to the café. Bridgy followed my gaze.

"Oh, it'll be fine. Ophie is willing to work at the café. I asked if she wanted to ride over to the airport with me, but she said I should take you and offered to move her appointments around again to help us at the café."

When I didn't reply, Bridgy read the big question mark on my face correctly and answered as if I had asked.

"I told you Ophie would be edgy with Mom around. She probably doesn't want to feel trapped in the car with only me to run interference between the two of them. They usually do really well if they are surrounded by lots of people in a large space."

"And you need someone to come with you to pick up your mother because . . . ?"

"Because I might not be able to drive safely while she bombards me with questions about . . . about Oscar. Suppose I start to cry, right in the middle of all the traffic on Daniels Parkway? You know how crowded Daniels can get." Bridgy gave me a look that was half pleading, half direct order.

I knew I had no choice. "Of course I'll go. And I'll drive. Now let's get ready for the breakfast crowd."

The café was mobbed for most of the morning. Judge Harcroft, always set in his ways, came in at his usual time dressed in a dark blue suit complete with white shirt and a patriotic red, white and blue tie. No matter that he had retired from traffic court ages ago, he generally dressed as if he might

183

be summoned to handle an emergency hearing at any moment. I came out of the kitchen with a tray stacked with breakfasts, and he stepped in my path, nearly causing a calamity. I stopped dead.

"Can I help you, Judge?" Although I knew exactly what his complaint would be.

He harrumphed not once but twice and pointed to the area of the café right next to the book nook. "You can see the problem for yourself. Someone is sitting at Dashiell Hammett. We have an agreement. That table is reserved for me." He looked at his wristwatch. "Especially at this time of the morning."

I set my tray on the counter and looked him steadily in the eye. "Our agreement is that we will *try* not to seat guests at the table you prefer to use, but when we have an overflow crowd such as we do this morning, it is not always possible. Now, would you like to take a complimentary copy of the *News* and sit on the bench outside to read it until the table is vacant?"

He harrumphed once more, probably for emphasis, turned on his heel, took a newspaper from the pile by the cash register and walked out the door. I hustled to serve the food before it got cold.

Things eventually began to slow down.

Soon enough, Judge Harcroft was able to spread his copy of the *Fort Myers Beach News* across the top of the Dashiell Hammett table while he waited to be served his standing order of Hammett Ham 'n Eggs over hard. He lingered longer than usual, and when I collected his payment at the register, he didn't forget to say good-bye with his standard, "Enjoy your day. I must *Dash.*" He took a step toward the door and then stopped. "Er. I hope we won't have this confusion about my table ever again."

I looked to heaven for patience. Bridgy was a few feet down the counter packing a to-go order. She rolled her eyes and shrugged flamboyantly. If she could shrug off the judge's nonsense with all the turmoil she faced, I mentally dismissed him as one of life's minor irritants.

During the lull between late breakfast and early lunch, I refilled the salt and pepper shakers and lined the ketchup and mustard bottles where they would be easily accessible. Bridgy was making the rounds of the few remaining occupied tables with the coffeepots, brown topped for regular in one hand, orange for decaf in the other. I heard her say, "More tea? Sure, no problem." I poured hot water from the electric kettle into a carafe and pushed it across the counter to her.

She served the tea and walked slowly back to the counter, fiddling with her iPhone. I hoped she wasn't getting a troubling message from Owen or that criminal lawyer, what was her name? Georgette. I didn't want the state attorney's office spoiling Bridgy's first day with her mom.

When she got to me, she slipped the phone back in her pocket and beamed a smile wider than the countertop. "According to the airline app, Mom's plane is in the air. I'd better call Ophie and give her a deadline. Otherwise she'll come waltzing in whenever she chooses. I don't want Mom hanging out by the information desk waiting for me."

The café filled up once again. Running from table to table, I didn't notice the time until the door opened and Hurricane Ophie blew in. My brain instantly paraphrased Bogie in *Casablanca*. Of all the outfits in all the world, she had to show up in black. Black lace yet. On a day we were all trying to cheer Bridgy up, Ophie was dressed as though she was about to attend Abraham Lincoln's funeral. Her black wrap dress was trimmed with black lace, and her waist was cinched with a black patent leather belt at least as wide as the three-inch heels on her

186

matching spiked sandals. Black lace finger-less gloves reached her elbows, and her shoulder-length oat-colored hair was gathered up in some kind of black hairnet.

"Ophie's here to save the day. And don't y'all worry about my finery. I brought a full-length apron to protect my dress against spills and whatnot."

Of course every head in the room turned toward her. Ophie did a couple of "look at my pretty dress" pirouettes into the center of the room and then stood still and gave a royal side-to-side wave to her adoring audience. I was surprised no one clapped. She pulled a gauzy white frou-frou apron from her enormous black patent leather tote. Then she tossed the tote at me from five feet away. I lunged and caught it, remembering that Ophie's well-mannered ladies' rules included "No well-mannered lady should carry a purse indoors."

Bridgy came out of the kitchen and affected the southern drawl that sometimes overrode the cultured voice she developed in college when she was working at diminishing her Brooklyn accent. "Why, Aunt Ophie, look at you. Stunning, darlin', absolutely stunning." And they did the big ole bear hug that they'd perfected long ago.

I heard Ophie whisper, "It will all be fine."

I hoped she was talking about Bridgy's predicament and not her own anxiety because Emelia would be landing shortly in Fort Myers.

Ophie pulled away from Bridgy and turned around, shaking her head back and forth. The lacy pouch resting on her neck captured her hair as it wiggled from side to side. "So, y'all tell me. What do you think of my snood?"

"Your . . . what?" I couldn't help myself, even though I really knew better.

"My snood. Don't you pay attention to fashion? A snood is the latest thing in head-wear."

Maybe in the 1940s. I wisely kept my thoughts to myself.

A few minutes later, Bridgy pulled the Escort onto Estero Boulevard. "Unless the bridge is jam-packed, we should get to the airport in plenty of time. Maybe we can relax. Have a cuppa before the plane lands."

"Sounds terrific. So tell me, what is it with Ophie and her super outlandish getup? This mournful outfit is way over the top, even for her."

"Don't even think about it. She just wants to shock Mom. If she didn't have to work today, she might have shown up in a bikini. We are only at the very beginning of the

188

battle of the Brice babes."

"Brice babes?"

"Their maiden name is Brice. The Brice babes is what Grandpa called them."

I wondered how tough the fighting would get but was distracted by the miniature golf course as we approached Summerlin Road. I pointed off to the left. "Isn't that the 'golf with the gators' place? That would make a nice outing for you and your mom. I bet she's never fed live gators before."

"Come now. You've been at my mother's table for Thanksgiving. Feeding gators would be easy compared to trying to get my cousin George's twins to settle down and eat their dinner."

We both laughed long and loud. It was wonderful to see Bridgy carefree if only for a while.

"Of course, the newly constructed connection from I-75 to the Terminal Access Road at Southwest Florida International Airport got us a bit confused, and it took us a little longer than we expected, but when Bridgy parked the car in the airport parking lot, she looked at the dashboard clock and whistled. "We have plenty of time to spare. We'll check the arrivals board, but I think Mom will be coming in on Concourse B."

"Great. Isn't there a bagel place somewhere along there? We can get a coffee and maybe a nosh."

"A nosh? Toto, we're not in Brooklyn anymore." Bridgy gave a high-spirited laugh, stepped out of the car and rushed to the elevators. Energized by the thought of seeing her mother in a short while, she never even looked back to see if I was behind her. Although she did yell over her shoulder, "The bagel place is behind the TSA station. You're going to have to settle for a donut."

I caught up with her just as the elevator door opened, and we rode down to the terminal walkway and entered the building. Bridgy headed right for the arrivals and departures boards, but a large white sign caught my eye. It said the Port Authority was in the midst of celebrating the tenth year of its partnership with Lee County Alliance for the Arts. They were sponsoring a decorative project called *Art in Flight,* and visitors would find paintings of talented local artists hanging on the walls along Terminal B and Terminal D.

"Mom should land in about twenty minutes." The exhilaration in Bridgy's voice was palpable.

"Great. Let's take a look at the paintings." I pointed to the sign. "Local talent. It's always so exciting to discover homegrown artists."

"I thought you wanted coffee." Bridgy grabbed my arm and tugged me toward the coffee bar nearest the spot where her mother would be deplaning.

I resisted. "We can always get coffee. These paintings aren't going to be here forever." I tried to spend a few moments enjoying each painting, but Bridgy made it clear she was humoring me and hurried along as if her mother would magically appear next to the final canvas. She came to a sudden stop in front of a cherubic blonde with lilac wings standing in a lush flower field. The fairy was waving to others who were flying far into the sky. I could feel her turn was coming, and coming soon.

Bridgy nudged me. "Look at the title." *Let the Fairy in You Fly.* "When we left Brooklyn, everyone said we were looking for a fairy-tale life. And we found it here in Fort Myers Beach." Her tone hardened. "And I'm not going to let Oscar's murder ruin it."

Mentally, I saluted the artist. As a painter, Paula Eckerty has the ability to touch the soul.

Bridgy's phone pinged. She read her mother's text out loud. "On the ground.

191

Hugs in a minute xoxo."

We scanned the trickle of travelers coming around the TSA barrier. As the crowd swelled, we stretched on our tippy toes, as if our being an inch taller would make Emelia easier to see. Abruptly, Bridgy ran into the crowd waving wildly and shouting, "MOM. MOM."

The second I saw her, I realized what Bridgy had been trying to explain about the difference between the sisters. I don't know why I never noticed it all these years. Emelia was dressed in a tan Chanel styled suit with broad-heeled sensible shoes. Barely there pearl button earrings set off her short pixie cut with longish side bangs that kept her gray hair neat and tidy. I doubt there were ever any "she took my best sweater" fights between these sisters.

Then I saw the woman striding confidently alongside Emelia. She had wild red hair, many shades brighter than my own, and was wearing a flowing caftan highly reminiscent of Van Gogh's *Starry Night.* Suddenly, I was the one waving wildly and shouting, "MOM. MOM."

CHAPTER EIGHTEEN

Bridgy and I managed to block the entire exit ramp as we each grabbed a mom and squeezed. A TSA employee wearing a navy blue Sikh turban tapped us on the shoulders. "Ladies, there is plenty of room for greetings. Please take a few more steps," he said and encouraged us to move toward the main terminal.

I grabbed Mom's carry-on and dragged it behind me. One wheel rolled quite smoothly, while the other thumped along. Normally, my practical side would be planning on picking up a replacement suitcase at Bealls Outlet, but my brain was dizzy. As we walked through the terminal, arms around each other's waists, I realized how happy I was to have my mom here.

Bridgy and I took turns supporting each other in times of crisis, but we'd never had to face anything as serious as Bridgy finding Oscar dead in his van. We needed all the help we could get. Nothing was better than having the moms.

"I'm so glad you're here."

"I know you are, my little petunia. When I first saw you, your aura was very cloudy, even murky, but as soon as you saw *me,* the clouds started to dissipate." She stopped, turned to look at me directly and stared for a long minute. "See? Better already. Cloudy is gone and your pink is getting brighter. That's because I'm here. Pink aura equals loving, giving, family, friends. And matters of the heart. Oh, do you have a BAE? Is that why we're here?"

"A bay? You mean a horse? Or water, like Estero Bay?"

She patted my cheek. "Living on this island you are so far behind the times. I learn more on one subway ride to Lincoln Center than you can learn here all year. I listen to the young people. A BAE is someone who comes Before All Else. I'm asking if you are newly in love."

The last thing I needed was for Mom to get off on one of her "why aren't you married?" tangents. It was time to be firm and stop her gibberish. "Luna, stop. Emelia is here to support Bridgy, and you're here to support me while I help Bridgy."

"Oh, Sunflower, haven't I told you to call

me Sage? Really, it's not that hard to remember."

"Sage? What happened to Luna?"

Only my mom could give the evil eye
while speaking in a cooing tone. "That was
when I was in my moon phase." She stopped
for a beat. "I am in my earth phase now."

*In your earth phase? I guess I'm lucky you
aren't calling yourself Mud.* I hoped my
thoughts weren't dimming my aura.

It didn't take long to get the moms settled
in the Turret. As planned, Emelia took the
guest room. I turned my room over to
Mom, er, Sage. I was glad that we had a
very comfy sofa bed in the living room.
Looked like I'd be sleeping there for a while.

Bridgy's mom changed into an Alfred
Dunner–ish pale denim skort topped by a
white man-tailored tie-front shirt. Her pearl
button earrings were replaced by tiny beige
seashells, and she had white and navy deck
shoes on her feet. I was beginning to understand why she arrived with so many pieces
of luggage.

When I asked Sage if she wanted to
freshen up, she sighed. "I am refreshed by
the very sight of you, my little girl. And the
sea. How glorious is the sea."

I wondered if she would move into her
water phase while she was here. What name

195

from the sea would she pick? Octopus? Crab? Not likely. She'd want a romantic name like Coral or something regal like Queen Conch. I could hardly wait.

I snapped back to attention. Mom was asking if I had any poetry books handy. She said watching the water move to and fro always made her think of poetic meter and rhyme schemes.

"I don't have one here, but when we get to the café, I have at least one copy of *The Road Not Taken* by Robert Frost. It includes dozens of poems, not just 'Road'. I also have some volumes by Emily Dickinson that I'm sure you'll like."

We piled into the Escort. Bridgy waved me away from the driver's side door and drove us to the Read 'Em and Eat, where Miguel had promised he would have *Cubano* sandwiches and *batidos* for Emelia. With both ham and pork in the sandwiches, I hoped Sage wasn't on one of her vegetarian cleanse cycles. I remember she once did a vegan prayer fest that lasted for two weeks. If that was where she was in her life cycle, she couldn't have a *batido,* either. Well, there was no point fretting. We had lots of food in the kitchen.

Bridgy rang the ship's bell and then opened the door. Miguel had dressed for the occasion in a dazzling white chef's jacket with round gold buttons. His chef's *toque blanche* sat on his head at a rakish angle as he came from the kitchen with a bounce in his step and a welcoming smile. When he saw Sage, he began to clap his hands. *"¡Qué estupendo!* How wonderful! We have both moms. Brooklyn's loss is our gain. Come, *señoras."*

He had pushed the Robert Frost and Emily Dickinson tables together and covered them with a lovely turquoise and white tablecloth and matching napkins. Several small bud vases sat in the center of each with a different colored rose. So thoughtful. I started to thank him, and then I remembered Ophie. The bud vases looked like her touch. *Where was Ophie?*

Saying he would get another place setting, Miguel went back into the kitchen, and within seconds, Ophie came out. By the look on her face, Miguel had practically pushed her into the dining room.

Bridgy's mom froze. She stared at every inch of black from the much-too-young-for-her footwear to the outlandish lacy gloves that her sister was wearing. Finally, she drew out the name, "O-phel-ia."

Ophie answered in the exact same tone. "E-mel-ia."

Right then I knew there wouldn't be a big ole bear hug for these two. They stood about a foot apart, grabbed each other by the elbow and air kissed both cheeks like Parisian matrons of a certain class.

Miguel froze in the kitchen doorway, his mouth open and napkins and silverware in his hand. We were all a little afraid to breathe, until the sisters' greeting ended. Then we all talked at once and began scraping chairs along the floor, clanging tableware and trying to pretend there was no tension whatsoever in the air.

Ophie gave my mother a warm kiss on the cheek. "Sage, this is a welcome surprise. I didn't expect y'all to come."

I was taken back that Ophie knew my mother had moved into her earth phase and changed her name. Then I remembered Ophie keeps track of the entire universe through Facebook. I guess Sage made the name change on her page and I missed it. Too bad I didn't miss Emelia's response to Ophie.

"Ophelia, Sage is one person, not the 82nd Airborne. The word 'all' isn't necessary."

Like a flock of magpies, everyone started to speak at once. I asked Sage and Emilia how the flight was. Bridgy asked what flavor

198

batidos everyone wanted to drink. Miguel offered to bring in the salad and fled to the safety of the kitchen. Sage told me that Miguel's lovely green aura indicated that he was extremely creative and a hard worker. The sisters ignored us all. Emelia sat with her hands folded primly on the edge of the table, while Ophie adjusted and readjusted her snood.

Bridgy cleared her throat, raised her voice an octave or two and tried again. "Miguel makes the most delicious Cuban milkshakes called *batidos.* We have three flavors: orange cream, papaya and mango."

"Sage, try the papaya. It's awesome," I recommended.

She agreed. One down.

Bridgy prodded. "Mom? Aunt Ophie?"

I caught Ophie glancing sideways at Emelia. I got it. Neither would order until she heard what the other one was having. This was going to be a long visit.

I raised my hand as though I was the brightest kid in the classroom. "Why don't we fill juice glasses with samples of each *batido*? I'll help you."

The silence in the dining room was looming larger by the minute. I pushed Bridgy ahead of me into the kitchen. As soon as the door closed behind me I whispered, "Is it going to be like this for the entire visit?"

Bridgy got defensive. "I did warn you, this isn't twenty people for Thanksgiving where everyone mills around. They can each get lost in the crowd. By ourselves, we're too small a group."

Sarcasm roiled. "What's our option? Should we throw a party?"

"*Chicas,* you are squabbling like Ophie and Emelia. Stop it. Serve the food, and pretty soon they will be busy eating and the hostility will — poof! — be gone."

I hoped Miguel was right.

Putting on their best "Sunday company" manners, Sage and Emelia raved over each bite of their *Cubanos* and alternated so many sips from each of their sampler *batidos* that you would think they were drinking tequila shots at two-for-one night in the local pub. Ophie was quieter than usual but still managed to throw in a rave review now and again.

Of course when the eating stopped, so did the conversation. Miguel came to the rescue with a tray of individual fluted flans plated with a dollop of whipped cream and sliced almonds.

Bridgy and I cleared the table to make room for the dessert. I offered tea and coffee. Sage asked for herbal tea. Everyone else waved me away and dug into the flan, which brought glowing reviews all around.

Ophie pushed her chair from the table. "So nice to see y'all, but I have an appointment at the Treasure Trove."

Emelia let the "y'all" slide right past her, but her tone was frosty. "You take care, Ophelia. We'll see you tomorrow."

My first thought was, *Oh no, we're going to have to go through this again.*

Always willing to be a distraction, Sage stood. "Is it walking distance? I need to stretch my legs. Do you mind if I walk with you?"

"Come along. The Treasure Trove is at the other end of the parking lot. You won't get lost if I send you back on your own."

As soon as they left, Bridgy and I began the cleanup. I was at the kitchen side of the pass-through pulling a tray of glasses when I heard Emelia say, "Bridget, while we have the chance . . . while we're alone, please tell me what is going on with this murder. Do the police seriously suspect you? Oh, and your father sent a check for the lawyer."

I tiptoed over to Miguel, who was cleaning his work counter. "We really need a back door to this place. We're trapped in here while Emelia grills Bridgy. And she brought a check for lawyer fees. It's like that song from years ago. 'Lawyers, Guns and Money'?"

"*Sí*, Warren Zevon. Very popular during beach week when I was in school. Of course we were silly, not dangerous, but at nineteen, it sounded *muy macho.*"

I went back to the pass-through and listened to Bridgy explain to her mother that Oscar was killed with a pair of scissors.

"I was looking for sunglasses, not scissors. I never carry scissors. As soon as the sheriff's department figures out who owns the murder weapon, I doubt they'll bother me anymore. I have a terrific lawyer. His name is Owen, and you will adore him. And wait until you meet Georgette."

"Georgette? Is that his wife?"

"Oh no. Georgette Darrow is my other lawyer. She's the one I'll be using Dad's check for. Thank you so much." I heard Bridgy slide her chair, and then there was some sweet mother-daughter kissy face time.

I was deciding if it was okay for me to go back into the dining room when I heard a knock on the front door. I flew out of the kitchen, but Bridgy was ahead of me. She turned the lock, and Ryan Mantoni stood there, dressed in civilian clothes, dark chino shorts and a light blue tee shirt. It's pos-

202

sible that he owns the largest collection of law enforcement tee shirts in the world. This one had a fake collar, gold buttons, a big sheriff's star and a brown belt all painted on a blue shirt. He looked exactly like a Keystone Cop.

I'm not sure if he noticed Emelia, but he definitely ignored me and looked squarely at Bridgy. "I'm here unofficially. You got a minute?"

CHAPTER NINETEEN

Bridgy stepped aside to let him in, but Ryan gestured for her to come outside. For one insane moment I thought he was going to arrest her. Then I remembered how long we'd been friends. There was no trickery about Ryan.

Emelia was twitching with curiosity. "Who is that young man? I think I met him when I was here last year, but I can't place him."

I told her that we'd known Ryan since shortly after Bridgy and I arrived in Fort Myers Beach. I didn't think it was prudent to mention that he was a sheriff's deputy, so I used the safe catchall word "friend." "Between the café and the bookstore there are always customers around, so our friends are used to inviting us outside for conversations."

"I am getting tired. Perhaps when Bridgy comes back, we could go home and I could take a brief nap. It's been a stressful day."

Emelia opened her purse, took out a gold compact and examined her face as if searching for bags spouting under tired eyes or a new wrinkle or two. She closed the compact and twisted her head so she could see the door. I could almost hear her thinking, "Where is that child?"

"Of course you are tired. Sage must be, too. I'm sure we'll be ready to leave in a few minutes. I just need to get the kitchen straightened." A great excuse to ask Miguel if he'd heard any gossip while we were at the airport.

Always the king of neat and tidy, Miguel was hanging tomorrow's clean apron and *toque blanche* on his clothing hook when I walked into the spic-and-span kitchen. "I think your mothers had a nice treat, *sí?* Although I hope the strain between Ophie and Emelia does not ruin the visit."

Miguel had a knack for saying exactly what I was thinking. We didn't want the pressure on Bridgy to worsen. I hoped having Emelia here would help, but if she and Ophie were determined to go at it constantly . . .

"I hope so, too, but right now I'm wondering why Ryan took Bridgy outside for a chat. Did he happen to stop in earlier looking for her?"

"Ryan? No. Do you think . . . ?"

"I don't know. He wasn't in uniform, so let's assume the best." I pulled out my phone. "I better get Sage back here. Emelia wants to go home for a nap. Can't say I blame her."

I was in the midst of telling Emelia that Sage was on her way and we'd be going home shortly when the door opened and Bridgy came in looking dejected. Ryan was nowhere in sight.

Bridgy slumped into the chair she'd vacated a few minutes ago. Emelia and I exchanged looks, and then she wrapped Bridgy in a mom hug that was part smother, part comfort. It took a while, but finally, Bridgy pushed her away and said, "It's okay. Honestly, it is. Ryan told me that the scissors aren't going to save me. It turns out that the weapon is an extremely common pair of five-inch straight scissors that can be bought pretty much anywhere from Jo-Ann Fabric to the local ninety-nine-cent store." She heaved an exaggerated sigh. "We're going to have to work hard and find a way to prove that it wasn't me who stuck that ordinary pair of scissors into Oscar's neck."

We met Sage in the parking lot and piled into the Escort for the quick ride home. I was feeling like Scarlett O'Hara.

"Tomorrow is another day."

The next morning the delightful fragrance of coffee woke me. I padded into the kitchen to find Sage with her head stuck in the pantry, rummaging through the shelves. "I already checked the refrigerator. I don't find any chicory. I'm sure I can get some in the local health food store. Coffee's not the same without it."

Well, this was new, but not surprising. If Sage was in her earth phase, I supposed she was paying a lot more attention to plants.

"Last night Bridgy and I decided that we would take the Heap-a-Jeep to work today and leave the Escort for you and Emelia. It's easier for you to drive than the jeep."

Emelia stood in the doorway, looking extremely unrumpled in her tan man-tailored pajamas. It was as though she slept standing up. "Drive? Where are we going? I thought I'd spend a restful day on the beach until Bridgy comes home from work."

Bridgy crept up behind her. "That sounds perfect, Mom, and we'll take you to Times Square for ice cream tonight."

"Times Square? Oh, the plaza by the pier. The one with the clock."

"And the shops." No matter what phase

she was in, Sage never lost her yen for shopping.

Emelia looked at me. "I was wondering if you have some books I could borrow. Beach reads. That sort of thing."

I had two books sitting on the table in the entryway. I brought them in and handed them to her. "*Julie and Julia* is the book for tomorrow's Potluck Book Club meeting, although some of the members may have read *My Life in France,* so I read them both."

Emelia clapped her hands. "*Julie and Julia.* Fabulous movie. Did anyone see it? No? Meryl Streep was extraordinary. Then again, she always is. Thanks, Sassy. I'll enjoy these. Perhaps I'll come to your book club tomorrow. What time is it?"

Before I could answer, Bridgy was pushing me out the kitchen door. "Hurry. Shower and change. Miguel will be wondering where we are." And she gave me a look that said, "Don't question, just go with it."

When we were in the elevator and safely out of earshot, I asked Bridgy why she got jumpy when I gave her mom the Julia Child books. "You're the one who told me she'd love them."

"That was before I got a text from Ophie checking the time for the meeting. It seems Blondie Quinlin was talking about the book at their ecology club meeting, and Ophie is a big Julia Child fan. She read the book and said she'd come to the meeting."

As if having Jocelyn to contend with wasn't enough, I'd probably have to referee the Brice babes. "Well, your mother and your aunt may both love the same book, and that would solve the problem."

Bridgy shook her head. "Don't count on it."

We had a nice-sized crowd for breakfast and did a brisk business at lunchtime. When things slowed down, I called Sage.

"My little rose petal, I hope your day is as glorious as mine. Emelia and I spent hours lounging on the beach. Then we took a walk along the shoreline and collected some of the most whimsical shells. I can only imagine the superb creatures that called them home. Do you know anything about the identity of seashells?"

"Actually, Bridgy is more the expert. I'm sure she can answer whatever questions you have." I could see that Sage was quickly becoming enamored of all things sea related.

"That would be wonderful. In the meantime, Emelia is taking a nap." Then in a faux whisper she added, "I had no idea she was so low energy."

I thought it best not to respond. "And

besides collecting shells, how are you amusing yourself this afternoon?"

"Oh, I have so much to do. I saw a lovely group of palm trees just past the edge of the building patio out by the pool. I think it is the perfect spot for me to practice my tai chi. I really need to relieve the physical stress of being cramped up in that airplane yesterday. My inner circulation is extremely restricted. I can feel it."

I wasn't sure what inner circulation Sage was referring to, but I was glad she had something to do that would keep her busy while Emelia napped. That left me free to entice Bridgy to come to visit the *Fisherman's Dream* with me. It should be docking just after we closed.

Miguel left for the day with his usual cheery *"Mañana, chicas."* And he clanged the ship's bell attached to the wall outside the front door as a final good-bye.

Bridgy and I were nearly done with the café cleanup when I asked if she felt like taking a ride to San Carlos Island.

"I don't know. Home is sounding really great right now. We could rest up a little and then take the moms to Times Square. Peaceful and pleasant. I could use some of both." She gave me a pleading look with big puppy dog eyes, but I wasn't buying it.

"Listen, we have two possible suspects who aren't you. One is Tammy Rushing, who disappeared right after the murder, and the other is some sailor who had a fistfight with Oscar a while before the murder. Either one has better potential as a murder suspect than you do."

"Oh, you're right. We need to tell Frank Anthony."

"Definitely, but first . . ." I double-checked to make sure the teakettle and other small appliances behind the counter were unplugged. "First we should find out the name of the guy who played Manny Pacquiao to Oscar's Floyd Mayweather."

Bridgy's facial expression was totally puzzled, so I answered the question she hadn't asked.

"Boxers. Professional boxers." I looked at the big clock over the front door. "We'd better hustle. The *Fisherman's Dream* is going to dock any minute. Today we're going to find out who fought with Oscar. Then we can feed the information to Lieutenant Anthony."

When we pulled into the marina parking lot, a half dozen sunburned fishermen were straggling down the gangplank of the *Fisherman's Dream.* Good. That meant the crew was still on board.

211

There are not a lot of places to hide on a dock. Bridgy and I looked around and took up our post next to one of the decorative streetlights that I was sure would make the marina look very romantic after sunset. We couldn't hide behind its graceful, slender pole, but at least we could pretend to be interested in its material and structure. I wish I'd brought an art pad and some chalk. Of course then I'd have to know how to draw. *Sigh.*

We watched a few more fishermen and women come ashore, then folks wearing tank tops with the FISHERMAN'S DREAM logo began to meander down the gangplank. Bridgy asked me what we'd do if we ran into Lorgan again.

"Easy peasy. We just tell him we're waiting for a friend."

"What friend? The passengers are all gone."

"My new best friend Bert Wyatt. He's a member of the crew."

I took offense when Bridgy laughed at me. "Oh right, and he is dying to be buds with you. Me, too, probably."

"Exactly right." I'd show her.

Of course Bert Wyatt chose that precise moment to march down the gangplank with a scruffy gray and black duffel bag slung

212

over his shoulder.

"There he is. And he's alone."

I waved with all the enthusiasm best friends have for one another, but Bert wasn't up for it.

Instead of waving back, he shooed us away with the back of his hand as if we were horseflies about to light on his burger.

But I'd learned a thing or two from Lorgan, and I grabbed Bridgy and planted both of us squarely at the bottom of the gangplank.

Bert stopped in front of us and looked directly at me. "Hey, I've already had a long day. I'd like to say it's great to see you again, but we both know it isn't. And who's this?" He hooked his thumb at Bridgy. "You brought along a friend to double-team me? I already told you, I don't know nothing about nothing."

Before I could say a word, Bridgy gave him the most soulful look and with a tear flowing gently along her cheek said, "We're sorry to bother you. We really are. But I'm desperate. The Lee County Sheriff's Department has me listed as the only suspect in Oscar's murder. And I have two lawyers pushing me back and forth. And . . . and my mother is here for a visit. What do I tell her?" And she opened her big blue eyes extra wide.

Even before he set the banged-up duffel on the deck, I knew Bert was a goner.

CHAPTER TWENTY

Bridgy and I moved away from the foot of the gangplank, and the three of us began ambling toward the parking lot.

"Okay, young ladies, how can I help?"

Bridgy got us this far, so I stayed mum until she asked the first question. "Is there anything you can think of that might help the sheriff's deputies find any other suspect? Then maybe they'd leave me alone."

"You really know how to tug at the heartstrings, don'tcha? Let's just say that Oscar had a bad habit of always thinking he'd met you someplace else, years ago. He never realized some folks don't want to be remembered."

We mulled that over for a bit. Then I asked, "Can you think of anyone in particular? Someone who was really annoyed by Oscar?"

Bert snorted a hardy guffaw. "If you knew Oscar, and you say you did, he annoyed everybody. Never knew when to quit."

Well, that was certainly true. I'd seen his teasing move from playful to irritating many times. I decided to go for the million-dollar question. "What about the fight that got Oscar fired? Who was involved? How did that come about?"

Bert pursed his lips and looked out to sea. I figured he was trying to decide what needed to be said and what could be left alone.

"Think about what I said. There was Oscar always believing he knew a person from some other time and place. The deck-hand Oscar scuffled with, a guy called Lolly, it was that kind of thing. Oscar kept insisting he remembered Lolly from the old days when he worked in Vegas. Lolly kept saying he'd never been to Vegas. Finally, the snippy-snappy words came to pushing and shoving. That's when the captain sacked 'em both. I wouldn't give you much for either of them as workers anyway. Still, it caused a rift in the crew for a while. Some taking one side, some taking the other."

Bert stopped in front of a red truck with a rusty dent on the left fender. "This is my 'Lucky Lola.' Got more than a few miles on her but, she kept me safe more than once. See that dent? If I was driving some little nothing, a sports car kind of thing, I'd be in the morgue when that SUV ran the stop sign. Lola, here, took the hit for me. I keep the fender just like it is so I don't forget I owe her big-time."

We spent a minute or two lavishing praise on the old truck, and then I pushed the envelope maybe a little too hard. "Bert, one last thing. Do you have any idea where we might find this Lolly?"

He frowned so hard that his eyebrows met. "What do you want to be going off stirring up trouble for?"

Bridgy saved the day again. "No. No trouble. I promise. It's just that if Lolly knew Oscar well enough to get into a scuffle with him, then maybe he knows who else might've done the same. Someone meaner, vicious, even."

Bert crumpled again. "Okay, I know a place he might be. Ever been to the Dirty Pirate?"

Bridgy and I exchanged looks. As restaurant owners, we'd at least heard of every food or drink establishment for miles around, but this was a new one for us. "Hm. Didn't think so. It's a rough-and-tumble joint. Don't have many of those around here. Not that I care for it much myself. Only been there a couple or three times, but Lolly spends a fair amount of time there. I know Oscar'd been seen bending his elbow there now and again."

"Where . . . ?"

"Oh no. It's not a fitting place for ladies such as yourselves."

Bridgy said, "No prob. We can always run a Google search for it. How many Dirty Pirates can there be?"

Bert looked to heaven. "Okay. I suppose even a place as skanky as the Pirate has a presence on the Web. Instead of you looking for it, why don't we stop in for a quick drink?"

Before he had a chance to change his mind, I pointed to the Heap-a-Jeep sitting alone in the next row. "That's my car. We'll follow you."

He gave the jeep a glance of approval. "Sounds good. We'll take Main Street a few blocks and then turn back toward the water. Follow along. No way I'll lose you."

Bert pulled into the driveway of a vacant boat shed and signaled me to pull in next to him. As we got out of the car, he said, "Like the jeep. Fits right in. Glad you don't drive one of those bright-colored girlie cars."

Bridgy whispered to me. "I'm glad we left my shiny red Escort for the moms."

We followed Bert to a wooden building

just across the way. Peeling white paint made the words "DIRTY PIRATE" barely legible above the door. The wide glass picture window was covered with grime. As we walked by I tried to peer in but couldn't see anything but darkness.

Bert opened the door. As he ushered us in, he said, "Now, don't let the wharf rats give you the heebie-jeebies."

Bridgy let out an "eek" and jumped away from the door frame looking cautiously at the ground.

I couldn't help but laugh. "Not the four-legged kind. Bert means folks who hang out around the harbor."

Bridgy tried to recover her dignity, but when she crossed the threshold, she immediately slipped and nearly lost a sandal. "What the . . . ? Oh . . . sawdust."

As our eyes adjusted to the gloom, I saw there were three or four empty tables with mismatched chairs scattered about the room. Bert walked directly to the center of the long bar. He stopped behind a bar stool that had stuffing hanging out of a ripped cushion and pushed it out of his way. He propped one foot on the wooden ledge that ran along the bottom of the bar. Then he plunked his elbow down on the scarred and scratched wooden bar top.

"There we go lassies, foot up, elbow down. I'm ready for a cold one. How about you?"

What kind of cold one? I was pretty sure he wasn't ordering a cosmo. I raised my hand. "Designated driver here. I'll have water, please."

The bartender, a burly man wearing a gray tank top and black diver shorts, stepped in front of us. "Hey, been a while, Bert. These the two pretty daughters you're always bragging about?"

"Nah, my girls are still away at school. These are my nieces, here for a visit. Say, I'll have a pint. Give this lass a half pint, and the driver here" — he pointed to me — "will have water, in a bottle if you got it."

Bridgy and I exchanged looks and said not a word.

I scanned the bar. To our left, an ancient man with a ZZ Top kind of beard was reading a newspaper painstakingly. His eyeglasses were perched on his nose, but every now and then he'd pick a second pair off the bar and hold it against the paper to magnify the print.

To our right, two middle-aged men dressed in fishing gear were arguing about something to do with football. At first I thought they were premature. The football

220

season wouldn't start for months. Then I heard the name Joe Montana and realized that they were arguing about a game that probably took place before I was born. I was beginning to think that Lolly wasn't among the small group of regulars.

The bartender set our drinks in front of us and took Bert's twenty off the bar. He came back and laid the change on the bar ledge. Bert took a long sip of golden beer. "Ah, perfect, Ernie. Just perfect. No one handles the spigot like you. Just enough head to make a perfect glass of beer."

Bridgy and I are hanging out with Bert and Ernie. How wild is that? When Oscar's murderer is caught and we can laugh again, this will make for some great jokes.

Bert raised his glass for a toast. We clinked glasses as he said, "To the Gulf of Mexico. Isn't it grand?"

We echoed, "Grand."

And Bert replied, "Drink up, ladies."

Ernie went to refill the ZZ Top man's glass with some kind of whiskey served neat. When he was done, he began to absently rub a linen towel along the top of the bar. Bert watched him for a while and then asked, oh so casually, "Lolly been around?"

Ernie shook his head. "Not for a few days. He heard there was work up north a little ways. He went off-island to see about it. Ain't been back."

Bert took a long sip and praised the beer again. "Ah, that is good." He waited a beat. "Shame about Oscar. Here's to Oscar."

That got everyone's attention. All glasses were promptly raised, followed by a loud amen from one of the football fans.

Ernie came back and stood in front of Bert. He leaned across the bar. "Funny thing. He was in here night before it happened. Lolly, too. You knew how Oscar could get, kept talking loud as could be about the boxing lessons he was taking, just in case some youngster started up with him again. Next time he'd be ready. Lolly ignored him for as long as he could. Oscar being Oscar finally walked over to the corner where Lolly was sitting, right there" — Ernie pointed — "and he stood right behind Lolly and asked, 'You got that, kid?' Then, while the whole place fell out laughing, Oscar waved a big good night and told me he'd see me again soon. 'Course he didn't know he wouldn't."

One of the football fans called Ernie and held up his empty glass.

Bert drained his beer and stood up straight. "Okay, ladies, time to go."

He left a nice tip for Ernie. In my line of

work, we notice things like that.

When we stepped outside, the sunlight was dazzling. I searched my purse and found my sunglasses.

Bert shaded his eyes with a beefy hand. "We've done all we can do here. Sorry it was a wash."

Bridgy reached up on her tippy toes and kissed him on the cheek. "You've done no end of good here today."

Bert blushed. "I'm sorry you didn't get to talk to Lolly."

Bridgy started. "About Lolly —"

I cut her off. "It's too bad we didn't get a chance to talk with him, but I'm sure he'll be back after his job hunt, at least to say good-bye to friends. Maybe we'll have a chance to meet him then."

Bert looked uncertain but nodded in agreement. "Anyway, it's been a pleasure, ladies." He shook my hand. "I sure hope you come fishing with us again real soon. I haven't had this much fun at work since, well, since the fight between Oscar and Lolly. That was a day, I can tell you."

"Who started the physical fighting, do you recall?"

Bert grinned. "I can still see it. There's Lolly, young enough to be Oscar's son, and after one too many 'I know I've seen you in

223

Las Vegas' rags from Oscar, Lolly throws a roundhouse that couldn't have hit the port side of a forty-foot cabin cruiser, if you get my meaning. Then old Oscar gives Lolly a two-handed push that lands him plumb on his butt. Right there on the main deck in front of half the crew and a few early-bird customers. No choice at all for the captain. Had to toss 'em both."

Bert was delighted when we invited him to bring his family to the Read 'Em and Eat. He promised that as soon as college let out for the summer, he'd bring his wife and daughters.

Always the kitchen maven, Bridgy handed him her card and said, "Give us a call before you come and tell us your favorite pie. I promise we'll have it ready."

Bert's eyes lit up. "Both my girls love lemon meringue. I, myself, am partial to good old American apple pie, with a touch of ice cream."

Bridgy said, "Done."

As soon as I pulled out of the boathouse driveway, Bridgy sighed. "Well, that was a waste of time. We'll never find Lolly if he left Fort Myers Beach for a job elsewhere."

"You did get the main point of Ernie's story, didn't you?"

"There was a point?"

I looped the Heap-a-Jeep onto the San Carlos Bridge. "Lolly was in the Dirty Pirate the night before Oscar was killed, and he hasn't been around since. I think it's time to send Lieutenant Anthony looking for both Tammy Rushing and Lolly the Sailor.

CHAPTER TWENTY-ONE

I'd scarcely pressed the elevator button when I heard Sage call my name. Bridgy spotted her first and started to chuckle. I knew what the sound of that particular chuckle meant and immediately groaned. Sage was up to something.

"Take a deep breath, maybe a deep yoga breath, and then look," Bridgy advised.

Sage called again. Louder this time.

I inhaled and turned to see my mother walking across the Beausoleil lobby, both arms hugging dozens of palm fronds.

What the heck?

"My sweet daffodil, give me a hand, please. I don't want to drop any of these divine gifts from Mother Nature."

I thought the long and tangled leaves looked more like plunder stolen from the compost heap, but I held my tongue and clumsily accepted the fronds she thrust at me.

"Be careful. Don't hurt them. They are still alive, barely off the tree."

Bridgy, still struggling to hide her laughter, stretched out her arms, and Sage obliged by filling them with greenery.

A young couple, who, I think, lived on the third floor, declined to get into the elevator with us. I didn't blame them. My arms were already itching.

Sage cautioned all the way to the fifth floor, "Watch it. Be careful. Don't squish."

It was the longest elevator ride of my life, which is saying something, considering I've ridden to the top of the Empire State Building a half dozen times.

With all three of us trying to get out our door keys without "squishing" the palm fronds, the conversation went something like this: "I can't quite reach . . ." "I know mine is in my side pocket." "Be careful of the greens." "If I could just see the inside of my purse . . ."

Fortunately, Emelia heard the commotion and swung the front door wide open. She stepped back instantly, a look of dismay clouding her face. I'm sure she thought we'd visited the Little Shop of Horrors and were being devoured by palm trees.

Emelia retreated out of the way, and Sage bounded into the kitchen. Bridgy looked at me. I would have shrugged if I could, but with my arms full it was easier to speak. "Let's find out what she plans to do."

Sage motioned for us to put the fronds on the counter. I vetoed that instantly. She dismissed me with a look and said, "I suppose the table will do." And dropped her pile as if to end the discussion.

"Sage, not in the kitchen. Aren't the greens better off on the patio? Fresh air. Sunshine."

"My darling lily, palm fronds weave without difficulty when they are green. If we put them outside and they dry, well, they could snap and break while we are working with them."

Clearly, Sage had a group project in mind. I tried another tack. "What spurred your sudden interest in palm fronds and, ah, weaving?"

"It's not sudden. Some time ago I saw a special on the public television station about natives on some Pacific island building huts out of palm leaves. So when the gardeners outside began to prune the trees, I went through the piles and pulled out all the green or mostly green leaves. Quite a job, I can tell you."

I escalated to firm. "Pick those up." I head-butted toward the fronds on the table.

"And bring them to the patio."

When I turned to walk across the foyer to the patio door, Emelia scuttled ahead and pulled it open. I dropped my bundle on the floor near the railing and took a good look at my arms, both covered in scratches. Bridgy followed my lead, and Sage came along behind her. Rarely one to acknowledge defeat, Sage said, "Buttercup, I'm so sorry. I didn't plan ahead. I saw the opportunity to rescue these fronds. The gardeners were feeding the cuttings to a big machine that was slicing and dicing the leaves to death." She shuddered.

Oh pul-eeze.

"If you want to leave the palm fronds on the patio, be my guest, but you cannot keep them in the apartment."

She opened her mouth to protest.

I turned up the unyielding tone in my voice. "Sage. I mean it."

Sometimes I wondered who was the mother and who was the child.

Reluctantly, Sage bent to put her leaves on the patio floor, and as she straightened up, she noticed the scratches and welts on my arms. "My dear goldenrod, what happened to you? Look at your arms."

"I got beat up by your palm fronds. Those pointy edges are *hard*. Look at Bridgy. She's banged up, too."

Sage looked at her own arms, which were covered by the long, fitted sleeves of her hot pink yoga shirt. Other than a broken leaf tip stuck to her left sleeve, she appeared to have escaped unscathed. "Oh, my poor babies. I am so sorry. Why don't you both hit the showers, and I'll make us a light dinner."

Emelia, who'd been dead silent, said, "I thought we were going to Times Square."

Sage agreed. "Of course we are. Times Square for ice cream, but first a light supper. Our girls need a minute's rest."

After a refreshing shower, I changed into denim shorts and a white peasant blouse. The welts on my arms had disappeared, and the scratches were tiny and painless. I found Bridgy on the patio towel-drying her hair.

She glanced over my shoulder, and when she was satisfied that the moms were busy in the kitchen and couldn't overhear us, she said, "We can't stall any longer, Sassy. When are we going to tell the deputies about Lolly, oh, and Tammy? Are we sure she left town?"

"Maggie is sure, and Tammy's landlord, Jake Gilman, is sure, so yes, we are sure."

"Do you want me to call Ryan or . . . ?"

I sighed. "I'll call. I'm tired of getting accused of holding back information. Maybe if I dump this whole pile of 'maybes' in the deputies' laps they'll realize I don't try to thwart them on purpose. Sometimes . . ."

Bridgy laughed. "Sometimes it just happens, I know."

I was relieved when Ryan didn't answer. I left a message and hung up fantasizing that perhaps we could have a peaceful night with the moms and not worry about murder and murderers until tomorrow.

Emelia stuck her head through the patio door, and a delicious scent wafted over her shoulder and enveloped us. "Dinner's ready."

Sage made rigatoni and spinach with a pungent garlic and olive oil sauce. She was happy to share the glory with Emelia. "You know those garlic cloves didn't chop themselves."

Emelia sniffed her hands. "I love the smell of garlic but not on my fingers. Fortunately, I found a lemon in the produce drawer. A few minutes scrubbing with the lemon and I smell like a citrus garden." She waved one hand across the table like Tinkerbell sprinkling fairy dust.

By the time we pushed away from the table, I was sure I couldn't eat another bite, and I wanted nothing more than to lounge on the patio with a magazine. So I was slightly taken aback when Bridgy said,

"Okay, I'll get the kitchen cleaned up, and then who's ready for ice cream?"

I groaned internally but somehow prevented myself from groaning out loud. I pitched in by loading the dishwasher. I almost choked when Emelia said, "I'll just go to my room to buff up a bit before we leave."

"Buff" was Ophie's favorite word, which, loosely translated, meant "make myself presentable to go out in polite society," or some such. The thought crossed my mind that the sisters might have more in common than they suspected.

We decided to walk along the water's edge to Times Square. The sun was still an hour or so away from setting. It hung over the horizon and blazed sparkling pathways across the Gulf right to our feet. Emelia had a bulky black camera hanging from a thick strap around her neck. She swiveled this way and that, looking for the perfect picture. She snapped three in quick succession of a group of royal terns poking their bright orange bills in the wet sand, looking for dinner.

"Don't startle them," Sage whispered. "If you startle them, they'll fly away."

"We'd rather look at them than make them leave," I agreed.

But, as always, Sage had a nature point to make. "Forcing birds to fly when it isn't warranted by their own wants or needs makes them waste energy. They need that energy for survival. Suppose a predator came along and the birds couldn't get proper liftoff because we scattered them with our boisterousness?"

It was easier to say I got her point than to sing "Circle of Life" from *The Lion King,* a movie she'd taken me to see a half dozen times before it was released in video and she could buy her own personal copy.

We were still a football field length away from the pier when Emelia made us stop so she could take a picture from every angle. Bridgy and Sage took the opportunity to examine the shoreline for seashells. Sage was delighted to find a perfect tulip shell in shades of brownish mauve. She opened her oversized tote decorated with small gray kittens tumbling around and took out a plastic bag and shook it open. She placed the shell inside gently and was about to put it in the bag when Bridgy asked to see it.

"Oh, that is a flawless gastropod. You should hold on to that shell. Even the edges are impeccable, not the slightest chip or crack."

Sage and Emelia were fascinated.

233

"What did you call it?" Emelia asked.

"Gastropod. You know how clamshells are bivalves — two half shells and a hinge? Well gastropods are univalves. No hinge. The snail pushes part of its body through that opening in the shell to push itself around the Gulf floor. And when the snail is done, it leaves a lovely, well-shaped shell."

I'd heard Bridgy gush about shells so often, I was afraid once she got started, we'd spend the rest of the night on the beach looking for a few dozen more gastropods. "The pier is just ahead. Would you like to walk out over the Gulf or go directly for ice cream?"

The moms agreed a short walk on the pier to watch the sun hit the horizon was a great idea. The gastropod was forgotten for the moment.

We were leaning on the rail watching some Jet Skiers loop-de-loop when my phone rang. I mouthed to Bridgy, *It's Ryan,* leaving her to entertain the moms while I edged a few feet away.

When I said hello, Ryan was bubbly. "Hey, Sassy, thanks for calling. Great game tonight. Lee County brought Charlotte County to their knees. Score was nine to four. I hit a double, and Frank, er, the lieutenant hit two singles. You had to see

Tina Wei. She hit a home run and trotted those bases like Derek Jeter. Oh man, I wish you guys had come."

"That's fantastic. Good for you." What else could I say? "Listen, I didn't realize you were off duty. Enjoy the after game celebration. We can talk tomorrow."

Ryan's demeanor changed instantly. "Hold on." He covered the phone, but I could hear a mumbled conversation, then he was back. "Where are you?"

"Bridgy and I are on the pier. We're taking the moms to Times Square for ice cream."

"I'm with the lieutenant. We're on the mainland, almost at the bridge. Stay in the square. We'll find you," he said, and he clicked off.

Bridgy sidled over to me. "Well?"

"They'll meet us over there." I pointed toward the four-faced clock that gave Time Square its name. "I'm not sure what we're supposed to do with the moms. Of course, Ryan and Frank are coming from a ball game, so I suppose they're not in uniform. That might help, but the moms are going to find the conversation creepy. I can see Emelia beating Ryan with her camera while Sage starts singing incantations and maybe even lighting incense. Who knows what she

235

carries in that tote?"

The sun was sinking into the horizon and taking my spirits with it. We moved the moms off the pier and toward the ice cream shop. I was certain that disaster would strike in the next half hour.

CHAPTER TWENTY-TWO

The disaster that struck immediately wasn't the disaster I was expecting, but in some ways it was much, much worse. We settled the moms at a glass-topped table surrounded by pretty wrought-iron chairs. It took them a few minutes to decide how far from healthy eating they wanted to stray, but finally, we had the order straight. When Bridgy and I came back with two scoops of pistachio with granola in a cup for Sage, a double scoop of chocolate chip mint in an extra-large sugar cone for Emelia and our own ice cream, the moms had their heads bent together and were giggling like two schoolgirls.

"We had a really grand idea, and we have put it in motion. Are you ready for a surprise? We . . ." Emelia started then hesitated. "Sage, do you want to tell them?"

Sage reached out and grabbed Emelia's hand. "Don't be silly, we'll tell them together. One. Two. Three."

"Surprise! You're going to Key West." In perfect unison, they were loud enough to turn heads. A couple at the next table started clapping and then stopped abruptly when no one else joined in.

Emelia said, "We did some investigating and booked you a round trip on that Key West boat that leaves from somewhere here in Fort Myers Beach." She circled her hand loosely above her head. "And you don't have to come back the same day you go, which is a very good thing because . . . Sage."

"We also booked you a three-night stay at a charming hotel on Duval Street, a few blocks from Mallory Square," Sage added cooperatively.

Bridgy looked as if she'd been struck by lightning. She was in the midst of raising her butter pecan ice cream cone with the hard chocolate shell to her mouth, aiming, I thought, for a quick bite of chocolate so she could nibble her way to the butter pecan. The moms spoke, and Bridgy's hand froze at shoulder height. Her eyes opened wider than I'd ever seen, and a deep red sheen crept up her neck and covered her face.

I had no choice but to recover first. "What are you talking about? We can't go any-where. We have the bookstore and the café

238

to run." I thought it best not to remind them we were involved in a murder investigation, and while Lieutenant Anthony had not yet said the immortal words "don't leave town," we probably shouldn't leave town.

"Oh, the café," Emelia sniffed. "We can do that. Ophie claims that she helps out all the time. If she can do it, how hard can it be? After all, Miguel does the cooking. All we'll have to do is to wake up early and be polite to customers. Difficult? I don't think so."

The chocolate coating on Bridgy's cone cracked, and one thin ribbon of ice cream dribbled across her fingers. I passed her a fistful of napkins, and in that instant I was happy that I sacrificed the calories of a cone for a small scoop in a cup. This conversation might cause my ice cream to melt, but it would melt neatly and not ruin my new white tank top with dolphins leaping across the hem.

I was struggling to think of an appropriate response to Emelia's observation about how easy running the Read 'Em and Eat must be. Finding none, I would have settled for any response at all, but I was startled by a hand clamping down on my shoulder.

"Sorry we took so long." Ryan Mantoni was looking down at me apologetically.

"The bridge." He said those last two words as if that explained everything, and to islanders, it certainly did.

Frank Anthony was standing behind Ryan. They both wore white pin-striped softball shirts with green letters declaring: LEE COUNTY SHERIFF. The shirts were dusty enough to show that they'd played hard. I jumped up, determined to do a quick introduction in the hope that I could grab on to the conversation and then remain in charge.

"I don't know if you've ever met our mothers. This is Emelia Mayfield and Sage Cabot." I indicated who was which. "These are our *friends,* Ryan Mantoni and Frank Anthony." I emphasized the word "friends" in the hope that Ryan and Frank would catch on.

I didn't count on Sage deciding to impress them with her psychic impressions. "Look at those auras. Nearly identical. So much blue. Calming. And peace. Such peace. Are you peace officers, by any chance?"

Sure, like she hadn't read their shirts and figured that out.

Ryan responded with a snappy, "Yes, ma'am."

By this point Bridgy had tossed her ice cream in the trash. I'm sure she was as antsy as I was. We wanted to give our information

240

to the deputies and be relieved of the burden. Then we wanted them to go away. The moms complicated everything. If they heard us talk about Bert, Lolly and the Dirty Pirate, there would be no end of questions. Not to mention the fact that Tammy Rushing disappearing would be a great excuse for them to hire private security guards to protect their little girls.

I was trying to find a way out of this potential calamity when Bridgy stood. "I am so stuffed after that delicious meal you fixed." She beamed at the moms. "I need more exercise. Maybe a longer walk on the pier would do me good."

I caught on immediately. "Why don't you sit here and relax while we stroll along the pier for a bit with Ryan and Frank." I gave Sage a sly wink, and her thoughts immediately turned to romance. I'm sure she was trying to figure out which man was the match for me and which one was for Bridgy.

Emelia started to get out of her seat, but Sage patted her arm. "I couldn't move a muscle. Let's just sit here." She shooed us toward the pier. "You run along now. We'll be right here when you get back."

Before the moms changed their minds, Bridgy and I led Ryan and Frank away as fast as we could.

As soon as we were out of earshot, Frank turned all lieutenant on us. "Okay, you sent for us. Now what is going on?"

Much as I resented his tone, I gave up my news immediately. "We have some new suspects."

"*You* have some new suspects? I don't remember deputizing you. I do remember telling you to stay out of this case, which, no matter how often I say it, no matter how much I emphasize it, you seem loath to do."

He had a point, but when he heard what we had to say, I was sure he'd be glad we'd nosed around. "One of the ladies who traveled to the Edison and Ford Winter Estates with us has disappeared."

That got his attention. He looked at Ryan, who indicated a discreet "I know nothing" with a slight shake of his head.

Frank put his hands on his hips and stretched an inch or two above his full height. "Who disappeared and how do you know this to be true?"

Bridgy took a step back. This one was all mine, and I relished the job. I started with the Teen Book Club. "You know Holly Latimer, don't you?"

"The yoga teacher's daughter. What has she got to do with the disappearance?"

I babbled about *I Am the Messenger,* the

242

yarn bomb and Miguel's homemade potato chips. The longer I talked, the more irritated Frank got, which pleased me no end. Finally, I told him Holly asked me to call her mom, and I summed up Maggie's conversation with Jake Gilman as confirmation that Tammy Rushing had left town suddenly.

Frank looked at Ryan, who nodded and said, "I know right where Jake Gilman is."

I watched Frank relax, pleased that he'd gotten information from me with a minimum of fuss. It was time to slam him with the other news we'd dredged up.

"And then, of course, there was the fight." I smiled perhaps a bit too triumphantly.

"This Tammy Rushing had a fight? Who'd she fight with?"

"Not Tammy. All she did was up and disappear. It was Oscar who had the fight. He got into a brawl with a deckhand on the *Fisherman's Dream.* Sailor called Lolly."

Ryan was using a stub pencil to take notes along the margins of his softball scorecard. He spelled aloud. "L-o-l-l-i, as in lollipop?"

"I don't know. In my head it's L-o-l-l-y. But I'm sure Ernie, the bartender at the Dirty Pirate, would be able to give you his full name. Lolly hung out there all the time."

Frank leaned in so far and so fast that I felt slightly menaced. He jabbed the air in front of my face with his index finger. "How do you know the bartender in the Dirty Pirate? For that matter, how is it you know about the Dirty Pirate at all? That den of wharf rats is a world apart from the Read 'Em and Eat. Completely different universe."

I kept my eye on Bridgy and was glad she didn't flinch at the word "rats." In fact, she wore a tiny smile. She was never happier than when Frank Anthony and I were waging war. Never mind that this time I was doing battle to save her. She liked watching us get on each other's nerves. On the other hand, Ryan was getting more fidgety by the minute. For a deputy, he really couldn't take confrontation. Or maybe he just didn't like witnessing conflict between his lieutenant and a good friend like me.

I adopted as prim a stance as I could manage. "You needn't worry. Bridgy and I had an escort. An impeccable gentleman."

Frank turned away, looked out over the Gulf for a while and then waggled his hand back and forth between me and Bridgy. "I don't know what you two think you are doing wandering around the docks. And Cady had no right to tag along as if he was protection enough."

I'd always suspected Frank Anthony didn't

care for Cady any more than Cady cared for him. Now I could tuck it away as a fact. I'd probably be able to use it to my advantage someday in the future. Not today. Today I was going for mystery. "Cady? Cady had nothing to do with this. He's not the only man we know." I tossed my head, hoping my auburn hair fell attractively back in place. "Are we done here?"

Frank crossed his arms, assumed his "I'm in charge of the world" stance and pressed me for a name. "We're not done here until you tell me who took you to the Dirty Pirate and why."

Bridgy gave me a sharp poke in the back that, roughly translated, meant "just tell him."

"Bert Wyatt."

"Who is Bert Wyatt?"

Well, if he didn't connect Bert to Oscar, then our information was valuable. Keeping that in mind, I doled it out in crumbs.

"He's a deckhand on the *Fisherman's Dream.*"

"So you were snooping around and got caught by a deckhand."

"Don't be silly. It's a charter boat. I went fishing and happened to meet Bert. We got to talking about Oscar. The next day, he invited Bridgy and me for a drink. If that's all you need to know, we'd better go back. Our moms are going to be worried."

"Okay. It's not like we don't know where to find you. Tell your mothers we're sorry for the interruption."

There was no way for the four of us to walk from mid-pier back to Times Square without walking together. Always more socially adept than I was, Bridgy immediately asked Frank and Ryan about their softball game.

Ryan was gleeful. "We trounced Charlotte County, and your friend Tina Wei was a star." He proceeded to recount the game hit by hit until we were back in the plaza and approaching the moms. Frank and I walked along silently. I think we were both glad the grilling was finished, at least for today. The deputies said a quick good night and headed back to Estero Boulevard.

Sage raised an eyebrow. "Well?"

"Well what?"

Sage stood and linked arms with me. "Did you invite your friends? Are they going to Key West with you? Tell me about it while we walk. There are a bunch of shops right around the corner that I want to explore."

Life wasn't complicated enough. Oscar had been murdered. Bridgy was a suspect. Both Tammy and the boisterous Lolly had

246

disappeared. Yet I was positive that Sage playing Cupid was going to be the thing that pushed me right over the edge.

CHAPTER TWENTY-THREE

I woke up the next morning to the smell of coffee and a hum of whispered conversation from the patio. When I opened the sliding glass doors, Sage said, "Good morning, daffodil. Isn't it a glorious day?"

I looked out over the Gulf of Mexico and our neighboring islands to the north. And, as most days are, this one was superb.

Bridgy popped out of her chaise lounge. "I'm off to the shower. Here, take my seat and I'll bring your coffee. We have to leave for work in twenty-five minutes." She tapped the imaginary watch on her wrist.

I've often thought she would have made an exemplary drill sergeant.

"Your aura looks tired. Kind of fuzzy. Did you sleep well? I feel terrible pushing you out of your bed and onto the couch. Perhaps I should sleep in the living room. Or we could alternate."

I patted Sage's hand. "Don't worry. I am

fine. It's just . . ."

Bridgy slid the door open, handed me a steaming mug of coffee, and warned, "Twenty-three minutes."

Sage laughed. "Bridgy inherited Emelia's efficiency gene. I wish she had more of Ophie's amusing gene."

"Bridgy is lots of fun. You know that. It is a really stressful time for her. For all of us." I gulped down my coffee while Sage murmured the momisms that always made me feel better.

Bridgy stood holding the apartment door open with one foot while she stage-whispered, "Hurry up." Apparently, by showering and jumping into shorts and a tee shirt I'd missed her deadline by four minutes. She wasn't happy that I had to run back into the living room to get my copies of *Julie and Julia* and *My Life in France* for the Potluck Book Club.

In the elevator, she watched me stuff the books in my tote, befittingly stenciled with a long, fat, curly worm sprawled below the word "BOOK."

"I'm glad you got those books out of the house. If Mom doesn't see them she may forget about the book club and we can avoid a clash between her and Ophie."

Once we got to the café, there was no time

to think about Emelia, Ophie, the Potluck Book Club or anything else. Within five minutes of opening the door, every table was full, and the dining room stayed busy for several hours.

The breakfast crowd was thinning out and I was at the counter pouring a cup of tea when the landline phone next to the register rang. It startled me and I splashed hot water on my fingers. I grabbed an ice cube with my burnt fingers and answered the phone with my other hand.

Pastor John Kendall was one of my favorite people. Caring and generous to a fault, he considered everyone he met to be part of his flock and was always ready to help no matter what the problem. His one flaw as far as I could tell was that in what must have been a moment of insanity he married the cranky and demanding Jocelyn, often the bane of my book club meetings.

"Sassy, I am in such trouble. I've invited several of the local clergy to lunch today, and it seems . . . it seems I forgot to tell Jocelyn. Well, clearly, she had a right to be upset and she . . . well, she went off to the community center . . ."

"And you need lunch in a box for how many?"

The relief in his voice was palpable. "Oh,

could you? Really? I can pick it up if that's convenient."

I looked around. More than half the tables were now empty, and according to the big clock above the door, we had a while until the lunch crowd descended on us. I'd rather run a basket over to Pastor than prepare for a book club meeting that might well prove disastrous.

"Don't be silly, Pastor. We deliver." Since when? Well, we do now.

He was having three guests, all from the mainland. I suggested *Old Man and the Sea* Chowder with Drunken Raisin Scones, *My Secret Garden* Salad and one of Miguel's fabulous pecan pies. "Do you need a jug of sweet tea or coffee?"

"Sweet tea would be splendid." Then his voice tremored slightly. "Let me ask you about the drunken scones . . ."

I had to laugh. "Don't worry, Pastor, only the raisins are drunk. I mean, Miguel soaks the raisins in a tiny bit of whiskey to plump them up and then mixes them in the scones. No one will be the slightest bit impaired."

"In that case, I can only say you are a lifesaver."

I went into the kitchen to prepare the order. When I told Miguel that it was for Pastor John and his friends, he said, "I made

251

fresh whipped cream this morning. Let me put some in a bowl for the pecan pie. Shall I sprinkle cinnamon? No. Let me . . . Ah, shaved chocolate. That will make the dessert festive." And he put an ounce or so of shaved chocolate in a small container.

I always got a kick out of Miguel. Not only was he extraordinarily particular about how the food he prepared tasted, he was totally fussy about the way it looked when served.

"*Chica,* write down these instructions. On paper, not in your phone. You have to leave them with Pastor John. Oh, and I included two different salad dressings. Make sure they are labeled." He dictated precise heating and serving directions that would make the pastor's luncheon that much easier.

A few minutes later I pulled into the church parking lot. I parked as close to the pastor's house as I could and was struggling to get everything out of the car in one trip.

"Can I help you there, Little Miss?"

I knew that voice. Tom Smallwood, my favorite handyman.

We didn't often cross paths, so I was happy to see him. He'd bestowed the title "Little Miss" on me after an adventure we once shared, and I wore it with pride.

"Sorry to hear about Oscar. Must have been a shock for you and Bridgy."

It never occurred to me that he knew
Oscar, but the island was a small community, and everyone knew about the murder within minutes of Bridgy finding the
body.

I was handing him the cardboard box that
Miguel had packed so carefully, and I nearly
dropped it when he asked if anyone knew
what happened to Oscar's boat.

"Oscar had a boat?" I recovered the box
and pressed it securely into Tom's hands.

"Old tub. He was refitting it, mostly by
himself. Called it the *Jersey Girl.*"

"I had no idea. Where does he . . . did he
moor it?"

"He used to keep it at Tony's, but Oscar
made so much noise and mess with his
repairs, not to mention that he was using
the boat to store odds and ends, so Tony
made him leave. You know how particular
Tony is. Oscar had the boat towed to a
repair dock on Pine Island."

Pastor John met us at the front door. He
took the box from Skully, who pastor always
called Tom, and thanked me profusely when
I gave him Miguel's notes.

"Come inside and visit for a minute.
Company's not due for a while. Join us,
Tom?"

Skully shook his head and pointed to a

253

small building toward the back of the churchyard. "No thank ye. I want to get that crossbeam seen to before the end of the day. That will give me all of tomorrow to work on the others." He turned to me. "Fine to see you, Little Miss."

"You, too. Stop by the café before you leave the island. Miguel is in the mood to bake lots of pies, and I'm sure there'll be a piece that suits you." Then I turned to Pastor John. "Sorry, I can't stay even for a second. Any minute the café will be bursting with the lunch crowd and then there's the Potluck Book Club."

"Busy, busy. I do know that feeling. Thanks for your help. Oh, and the bill?"

"It's in the box. Got to run."

I made it back to the café just as the lunch rush was moving into full swing. I knew I'd be caught short at the book club meeting if I didn't find time to squeeze in a final review of topics I wanted to cover, but helping Pastor John was a special pleasure, mostly because he spent so much time helping everyone else. I wrapped an apron around my waist and got to work.

A young family came in. I sat them at Dr. Seuss, and the mom asked me if I would heat a jar of baby carrots. When I went into the kitchen, Bridgy was huddled over the sink on her iPhone. Miguel signaled me to be quiet.

I popped the lid on the baby food jar and put it in a pan of water. I turned the burner to simmer, moved next to Miguel and head-butted toward Bridgy.

He mouthed, *Owen.*

More lawyer stuff. This needed to end. I stirred the carrots carefully until the contents of the jar were warm but not hot, and when I left the kitchen, Bridgy was still on the phone.

When the café quieted down, I began to set up for the Potluck Book Club. I set out extra copies of *Julie and Julia* and *My Life in France* along with notepads and paper. I started to write the questions I would use to move the conversation along if it stalled. That rarely happened, but I liked to be prepared.

I wrote my first question: "What do you think would move you to spend a year of your life cooking every recipe from a specific cookbook?" and was brainstorming for a second when the moms burst through the door.

"Ah, my sweet begonia." Sage planted a loud kiss on my forehead. She was wearing a flowing white chiffon caftan that looked more like a nightgown than day wear. Luckily, we are a beach community, so nearly any outfit is doable. I know people who, nine months a year, wear bathing suits and tee shirts every place they go except church. In January, they change into shorts and a sweatshirt.

Emelia, elegant in dove gray capri pants and a matching pullover, took one look at Bridgy's face, grabbed her for a hug of smotherly love and asked what was wrong.

"Nothing, really." Bridgy was fighting back tears. "Same old, same old. This time I have to go to the state attorney's office for still another interview. It's just — I can't understand what they could possibly want. I've already given a voluntary DNA sample, been fingerprinted and answered every question under the sun."

Emelia began wailing at "DNA" and showed no signs of stopping. Thank goodness there were only three tables that were still occupied. Of course, the diners were very busy pretending not to notice the drama, but I could tell Bridgy and Emelia had everyone's rapt attention. I guided them into the kitchen, went back to the dining room, picked up the coffeepots and made the rounds offering regular and decaf while asking if there was anything else they needed. I was thankful that all three, including the young couple with the baby, who had barely sat down, asked for their checks.

The book club members began to arrive. Maggie Latimer walked in raving about *Julie and Julia* and then gave me a wink. "But some of Julie's language. What will the ladies say?"

I was surprised when I saw Angeline Drefke was carrying both books. She held the door open with her hip until Augusta Maddox and Blondie Quinlin came in behind her.

"All I'm saying," Augusta boomed, "is that it ain't my concern if she talks like that, but no lady should write that kind of language."

I made a quick decision to address the language in *Julie and Julia* at the very beginning of the meeting; otherwise, it was sure to come up over and over again.

When Jocelyn Kendall, the final group member, came in, I hurried everyone to the book nook, anxious to get the meeting started.

Jocelyn wasn't even in her chair when she pushed her strawlike hair out of her eyes, looked around and scowled. "Who on earth picked this book?" She waved *Julie and Julia* in the air. "I am a pastor's wife. I cannot read this smut."

I looked at her, my eyes goggled in amazement. "Jocelyn, weren't you the one who objected to *Julie and Julia* in the first place? Didn't you say you preferred to read a book written by Julia Child herself? Isn't that why you picked *My Life in France*?"

Heads nodded all around. Clearly, I wasn't the only one dumbfounded by Jocelyn's outburst. Maggie and Angeline each swatted Jocelyn in less than dulcet tones.

"Really? I read both books because of you."

"The bad language was right in the beginning. You could have stopped reading."

The battle would have reached high gear except at that moment the front door opened. It was Owen Reston with what was a wonkish-looking woman dressed in a tan suit. Owen signaled Bridgy. It was time to go.

CHAPTER TWENTY-FOUR

Everyone stopped. It was as though we were kids playing Red Light, Green Light and Owen yelled "Red light." In fact, he hadn't uttered a sound.

Emelia rushed to Bridgy and gave her a kiss. I heard her ask Owen if she could go with them, and I was surprised she didn't argue when he shook his head. She walked them to the door, started back to us and then made a turn into the kitchen. I was grateful that Sage left the club meeting and followed her. I doubted Miguel was equipped to handle a frantic mother.

The clubbies, realizing that there were more serious things swirling around us than a disagreement about a book club selection, quieted down.

Angeline cleared her throat and said that she decided to read both books because she had the time. After reading *Julie and Julia,* she went on to read *My Life in France.* "I enjoyed it so much that I bought a copy of *Mastering the Art of French Cooking,* written by Julia Child herself along with another woman. It's the cookbook that Julie used on her blog, and later in the book."

That led to a conversation about how Julie made cooking seem so hard while Julia made it seem so easy. Blondie Quinlin opened her copy of *Julie and Julia* to a page she had bookmarked. "Right here Julie says that ' "simple" is not exactly the same as "easy." ' Once you look at it that way . . .'"

Emelia came out of the kitchen, her eyes red, and she was wringing a paper towel in her hand. She patted my shoulder and then sat quietly, half listening to the group banter. Sage was nowhere to be seen. I hoped she wasn't fiddling with Miguel's kitchen. She had a penchant for poking around in drawers and cupboards. Miguel kept everything so organized I feared Sage would get in his way.

Jocelyn, having been neutralized in the clash about proper language, was determined to be right about something. She insisted that we had no way of knowing how much of *My Life in France* was written by Julia Child since she collaborated with her great-nephew, Alex Prud'homme.

A lively discussion ensued. The tone was

civil, everyone was pleasant and I started to relax. Then the front door opened. Emelia and I turned, hopeful that Bridgy was back, only to see Ophie twirl in on her usual high-heeled sandals, this pair turquoise with rhinestone trim. The color was only a shade or two darker than her surplice dress. Emelia stiffened immediately.

"So sorry I'm late, y'all. What are we up to?"

Hoping to move the conversation to safer ground, I rolled back to Blondie quoting that simple did not mean easy when it came to recipes.

"Of course it does. All you've got to do is follow along with any of Rachael Ray's *30 Minute Meals* recipes." Ophie nodded as if that settled it.

"How can you say such a thing?" Emelia exploded. "Julia Child has presented cooks with brilliant recipes since Mama was a young bride. That Rachael Ray is a new-comer. I bet she uses slick tricks for quick fixes. I bet you never even read either of these books." And she pointed to the two books in my lap.

"You don't know what you're talking about. I read the Meryl Streep movie book, the one with the young girl trying to cook. Amy Adams played her in the movie, and

261

all I'm saying is that Rachael Ray would have made it much easier to fix those fancy meals."

Not smart enough to see that the argument between the sisters had nothing to do with cooks or cookbooks, Angeline Drefke tried to intercede. "Well now, that might be a topic for us at a future meeting. Everyone could read a cookbook written by a different chef, and then we could all bring our opinions to the club for discussion."

She waited. And waited.

When no one said a word, Angeline got the message. "Of course I'm going home to Pennsylvania soon. This is my last meeting. Still, you could think about what I said."

I was hugely grateful to see Miguel come out of the kitchen carrying a large platter that had an appetizing tower of . . . I wasn't sure. Pancakes? When he set the platter on Dashiell Hammett, I got a closer look. Crepes! I crossed my fingers in the hope that he didn't copy the spinach crepes that Julie made from Julia's recipe. I'd much rather a crepe dessert.

"Ladies, I present *Gâteau de Crêpes*. A cake made of pancakes. I read about the spinach, mushroom and Mornay sauce gâteau in the *Julie and Julia* book. I knew you would appreciate the concept, the design, but I took the liberty of adapting it to a dessert I used to make when I was pastry chef at the big resort at the south end of the island. I hope you will enjoy."

He hoped we'd enjoy? Seriously? He had our undivided attention at "dessert."

Miguel picked up a broad, flat knife from the platter and began cutting the gâteau into airy, elegant wedges. We could see about a dozen crepes were alternating with a white filling mixed with berries. He deftly set each wedge on a plate. I'm sure I would have managed to fumble the wedges until they broke into several pieces. Miguel had no such problem.

I passed the plates to the clubbies, who examined the wedges and pummeled Miguel with questions. How many crepes are in the stack? Ten. What kind of fruit is in the filling? Raspberries. What is the base of the filling? Vanilla cream.

Then Blondie Quinlin, who should have known better, set the usually unflappable Miguel off when she asked if he made each crepe by hand or ordered a set from a bakery?

"*¿Por qué preguntas?* Why do you ask? When have I ever brought in commercial desserts? Commercial anything, for that matter."

"Hold on to your britches there, Miguel. I didn't mean nothing by it. Just wondered where I could get these tasty pancakes. If they're only available here, that'll do me just fine." She took another bite of the gâteau and sighed with delight.

Somewhat mollified, Miguel bowed to the group and went back into the kitchen. Now I really wondered what Sage was up to. She wouldn't even leave the kitchen to join us for dessert.

I offered iced tea and lemonade but had no takers. We ate in silence partly because the cake was so delicious but mostly because no one wanted to set off another round between the Brice babes.

The book clubs were my responsibility, and I thought I could end this disaster on a high note as long as everyone was eating.

I dreaded the question, especially after Angeline's recommendation, but it was our customary ending to every meeting. "Does anyone have a suggestion for next month's book?"

More silence.

Finally, Maggie squirmed in her chair. She was a little hesitant. "There is a series of books I've heard about called *Best Food Writing,* well, fill in the year. A writer named Holly Hughes has been editing a book each year for more than a decade. She gathers articles from all over the world that have been written about food or food preparation, sometimes even about how food is grown. I thought one of the volumes would be interesting reading for us."

"Long as Miguel can find a recipe that goes with the book, I'm fine with it." Augusta took a meaningful bite of her gateau, effectively breaking the glacier that was rapidly enveloping the book nook.

Grateful that Ophie hadn't mentioned Rachael Ray again, I quickly answered, "That sounds like a great series. I don't have any on hand. Let me check with Sally, and if the library stocks the series, I'll put the most recent year on hold for us and order a few copies for the bookshelves."

Maggie stood. "That sounds great. Hate to eat and run, but I have a class in a few minutes." She patted her stomach. "After that delicious dessert, I'm going to have to work harder, but tell Miguel it was so worth it."

The clubbies started rounding up their books and packing their totes and fanny packs. Everyone wished Angeline a safe trip "back north." I thought it was really sweet when Blondie and Augusta said they hoped to see her next year.

Jocelyn took a parting shot. "Sassy, I really think you are going to have to read the book club choices *before* the club reads them. Decent women really can't be subjected to such language." She took a few steps toward the door and then stopped to turn and wave her index finger at me. "Someone has to be the moral guardian, and as book club moderator, that job falls on your shoulders." And she was gone.

Ophie looked at me. "Lord love a rock, what all is she yammering about now?"

With only Ophie and Emelia left in the book nook, conversation of any kind wasn't the best idea. I opened *Julie and Julia* to page eight and pointed to the offending word written repeatedly, sometimes in all capital letters.

Ophie was horrified. "Well, that doesn't match my image of Julia Child."

Emelia snapped, "That's because it isn't Julia Child talking, which you would realize if you bothered to read the book."

I slid away from them and pushed open the kitchen door, looking for reinforcements. "Sage, battle stations." One look at Miguel's face, and I knew that whatever had been going on, there was no harmony in the kitchen, either. Couldn't anybody around here act like an adult?

Sage followed me back to the Brice babes, where Emelia was shouting that Ophie was so busy taking shortcuts through life and then was always surprised when she didn't know the full story.

Sage stopped me dead with a quick yank on my arm and put a finger to my lips. We stood by the counter and let the battle rage.

Although there were no actual years attached to the accusations being hurled, the gist was something like, "You ate my Milky Way" and "It was my Patti Playpal" and "You lost my library copy of *A Tree Grows in Brooklyn.*" None of those words were actually used, but the singsong tone of a sibling argument was definitely there.

I whispered to Sage, "Shouldn't we do something?"

She shook her head. "They're running out of steam."

And she was right. Words that had been tumbling out of their mouths a few seconds ago were slowing to a normal pace and volume. Finally, Ophie took a deep breath, did that spin on her super high heels that she always manages to do without breaking a leg and walked past us with a wink and a smile. "I'll see y'all later." She opened the front door and gave herself the final word. "Too bad that's how you feel, Emelia, but done is done."

Sage poured a glass of sweet tea, handed it to Emelia and, leaving an empty chair between them, sat down. No way I was joining them. Best to leave Sage to comfort Emelia. I knew we were all on edge because Bridgy was being interrogated again. I fled for the peace and quiet of the kitchen. Miguel was scrubbing the top of his work counter. *"Chica,* is it possible to keep your mother out of my kitchen, *por favor?"*

I knew better than to tell him whose kitchen this actually was. Who paid the rent for the kitchen along with the rest of the café. I knew exactly what he meant — maybe not exactly, but I knew Sage well enough to know that she would easily find a way to interfere with how Miguel ran the kitchen, all the while thinking she was being helpful.

"I'll do my best. What is it? Your aura is too fuzzy when you stand by the stove?" I hoped that a good-humored poke would help Miguel shake off his dusty mood. No such luck.

"I took two packages of rosemary out of the refrigerator and was snipping them into small sprigs to sit decoratively along with a leaf of red lettuce on the serving plates tomorrow for any sandwiches that may be ordered. The rosemary is very fresh and adds a nice aroma to the plate without changing the flavor of the food."

I knew before he said another word. Sage is in her earth phase. "She saw the bags and said you should be growing your own herbs instead of buying them."

"*Sí*, but an herb garden is not practical with my wonderful Bow. She might chew on the herbs and make herself so sick. *Ay, no.*"

"Don't worry, Miguel. I'll distract Sage," I said with far more confidence than I felt. I heard voices in the dining room. I stuck my head in the pass-through. Bridgy was back. Emelia and Sage were fluttering around her, alternating between telling her that she was all right and begging her to tell them how she felt.

"Well, at least I'm not in jail." Bridgy sounded more surprised than happy.

Chapter Twenty-Five

"Now that's something worth celebrating." I startled all three of them. As they turned toward the sound of my voice, Sage and Emelia burst out laughing. Sage said that my talking head popping out of the pass-through looked like a cross between a bobblehead doll and a jack-in-the-box.

That started Bridgy laughing. "I guess we're so used to using the pass-through that way, I don't think of it the way you do, but it is pretty funny."

It was such a relief to see her laugh. I came out of the kitchen clapping my hands. "I have a terrific idea. Sage, do you remember when Bridgy and I moved down here you said you were a big fan of the writer Randy Wayne White? You know his hero, Doc Ford, lives on Sanibel Island right next door, don't you?"

"Of course I do. I still read every Doc Ford book. Why, in *Bone Deep* I learned so much about history and geology."

That might have been the start of Sage's earth phase. I was never sure what moved her from one immersion to another. I once asked my father what he thought was the reason, and he said, "Your mother loves life and wants to touch every part of it." I was beginning to agree.

"We're going to eat at Doc Ford's."

Sage thought I was teasing. "Sassy, Doc is a character in a book. He's not real."

"But his restaurant is."

"Restaurant? There is a restaurant?"

"Randy Wayne White owns at least three Doc Ford restaurants on the barrier islands. The closest is right on San Carlos Island overlooking Matanzas Harbor. I say we go there for dinner tonight. Who's with me for shrimp and grits?"

Miguel came out of the kitchen dressed in his civvies — bright green surfer shorts and a black tank top. "What's this I hear? Shrimp and grits? Great idea. We haven't had that on the menu for a long time. I'll have to make some calls and see what I can get from the shrimp boats." He turned and headed to the door. *"Buenas noches."*

"Miguel, wait. We're going to Doc Ford's for dinner. Why don't you join us?"

"Thank you so much for asking, but

tonight I am having company. My neighbor Liam Gerrity and his Tess are going to come for dinner. Cynthia Mays will be joining us for dessert. It is time for our annual hurricane planning meetings to begin." And as he usually did when he left before we did, Miguel gonged the ship's bell outside the door as his final farewell.

Emelia said, "What an energetic man. He cooks all day and goes home and has a dinner party!"

"Miguel loves to cook. Besides, Miguel, Mr. Gerrity and Dr. Mays are the steering committee for the part of the Hurricane Evacuation Committee that deals with pet safety."

Emelia looked puzzled, so I explained. "Back in the day, pets were not allowed in public shelters during hurricane emergencies. Most people didn't want to leave their pets behind when the families evacuated. It could be a death sentence for the animal. At the least it would be a frightening experience for a pet to be all alone during a raging storm. So Miguel and Dr. Mays, our local veterinarian, have been working on the annual preparation for pet shelters and shelters for families with pets since, well, at least since Hurricane Charley, and that was more than ten years ago."

I was returning the book nook chairs to their tables, and Emelia helped as we talked. "And they do this every year?"

"They do. After they update the mainland shelter locations where pets will be welcomed and readapt last year's plan accordingly, they revamp the list of pets living on the island. They do this scrupulously prior to hurricane season, all the while hoping it won't be needed."

Bridgy checked the supplies behind the counter while I ran a damp mop over the floor. In a few minutes we were set to go.

Since we had both cars with us, Bridgy took her car, and her mom and I took Sage in the Heap-a-Jeep. I looked on it as my opportunity to suggest that she stay out of Miguel's way in the kitchen.

"Really, my sweet delphinium, I am only trying to help. You have all this glorious weather, brilliant days full of sunshine with just enough rain. Everything is lush and green. Why wouldn't Miguel want to grow his own herbs? Besides, it was only a suggestion."

Having grown up under the command of Sage's "suggestions," I knew a sledgehammer when it hit me, and I'm sure Miguel did, too. I remembered Bridgy talking about finding things to occupy Emelia. It was definitely time to introduce some tourist attractions to the moms.

"Sage, Miguel has a life and an adorable Maine Coon cat named Bow. She runs freely around his yard . . ."

"I know where you are going, but there is no reason why he couldn't grow his herbs in pots and train the cat to stay away from them."

Sage had never met Bow. Train Bow. Ha!

It was not quite the beginning of the dinner rush, so Bridgy and I were able to park side by side. Sage was out of the car before I'd unbuckled my seat belt. "This is glorious. All blue sky and sea air. And look, there's the Doc . . ." She pointed to a wooden multistoried building topped by a green sign proclaiming "DOC FORD'S RUM BAR & GRILLE."

We were not yet at the entrance when the door opened and Margo Wellington walked out, hanging on to the arm of a nattily dressed man. Margo blanched at the sight of us and dropped the man's arm as though it was on fire. Made me wonder who the man was. She recovered quickly and introduced us to her husband. Nothing off base, then. Perhaps we startled her by turning up unexpectedly and "catching" her eating in a place that wasn't the Read 'Em and Eat. I chuckled to myself.

Bridgy introduced the moms. Sage impulsively grabbed Margo and wrapped her in a hug. "Honey, your aura is so dark. I guess the murder had a deep effect on your psyche."

I think we were all shocked when Margo's husband looked at her quizzically. "What murder? Margo, were you involved?"

Margo grabbed his arm and planted a sweet kiss on his cheek. "I didn't want to worry you. Let me out of your sight for half a day and there's a murder nearby. You wouldn't let me go as far as the supermarket by myself if you knew."

Without giving the poor man a chance to answer, Margo smiled broadly, said, "Nice to meet you," to the moms and pulled her husband toward their car.

I said, "That's so odd. The whole town is buzzing about Oscar's murder, and Margo didn't bother to tell her husband. What's up with that?"

"You heard her; she didn't want her husband to know she'd been in harm's way. Nothing unusual about that." Emelia looked at Bridgy. "You know there are lots of things I don't tell your father."

Bridgy sighed. "Mom, hiding the fact that you are a witness in a murder investigation is not the same as ripping the tags off an expensive new dress and calling it 'this old thing' when Daddy says how nice you look."

"I agree," Sage said. "There is so much more here. I was shocked by her aura. That woman is paralyzed with fear and worry. Emelia, do you think when the girls are at work tomorrow we could visit Margo, find out more about her?"

I was never so grateful to have a hostess interrupt a conversation to lead us to a table. Although it was becoming clear how I got my nosy gene.

As soon as we were seated, I knew it was well worth the few minutes we had to wait to sit outdoors on the harbor side. The terraced patio was built of heavy wood and decorated with potted palms. Every seat had a terrific view of the harbor.

Bridgy and I stuck with water, but the moms each ordered a glass of wine. Emelia led us in a toast about love, loyalty and family. As we clinked our glasses, I couldn't help but wonder if her definition of family included her sister Ophie.

We shared an appetizer of Caribbean Jerk Tostados while we waited for our entrées. I took one bite of the jerk chicken and Cuban black beans mixed with salad and covered with cheese, and I was in heaven.

"Try this." I pushed the serving plate to Sage, who was leaning back in her chair and taking in the view.

I followed her gaze. "Beautiful, isn't it?"

"Oh, it is. Magnificent, really. What are all those boats?"

"Those are fishing boats."

Emelia piped up. "You mean like the charter boats my husband's firm rents for the annual company fishing trip?"

"Mom, these boats are the real deal. Look at the size of them. They're commercial fishing boats. Maybe the crusted grouper you're waiting for came in on one of those boats this morning. Fort Myers Beach is a major hub for commercial fishing. It's probably one of the largest fleets in the Gulf of Mexico. The old-timers will tell you that around here there was a time that shrimp was called 'pink gold.' "

The server brought our meals. The food was plated artfully. I knew Miguel would approve. Except for the occasional "um-hum" or "so good," we were too focused on our food to talk.

Emelia held a forkful of grouper in front of her. "Fresh fish caught in the Gulf of Mexico. I had no idea. Tell me more."

Bridgy shook her head. "Don't have to. I can send you to the experts. There is a tour.

The Fort Myers Beach Working Waterfront Tour. It starts right around here someplace. First there is a history lesson, and then the tour includes a visit to the docks and you'll learn everything there is to know about the commercial fishing industry."

"I want to go. Sage?"

"Oh yes, of course. Sounds fascinating."

I liked the sound of that. A guarantee that I could keep her out of Miguel's kitchen at least one day.

When we got back to the Turret, Sage opted for a shower and Emelia went off to catch up on her email. Bridgy and I stretched out on the patio.

Bridgy said, "That was a great dinner."

I agreed and added, "And you are a genius telling the moms about the waterfront tour. That should keep Sage out of Miguel's hair for a while."

"Oh no. What happened?"

I told her about the herb incident and was surprised when she laughed. "Your mother is something else. I wouldn't have the nerve . . ."

"She doesn't know any better."

"Ah, but you do."

"I know. I should have told her not to bother Miguel."

"That's not what I meant. Didn't you say

Skully is fixing something at Pastor John's?"

"Crossbeam in one of the outbuildings."

"And who knows more about the outdoor life of this area?"

"No one. I get it. I get it. I bet he knows a place where he can show Sage all the natural Florida plants and herbs and whatever. And I bet Emelia would go along. If I can talk him into taking the moms around for a day . . ."

"We could pay him. Like a tour guide," Bridgy offered, but I knew that Skully would never accept money. We'd have to think of another reward.

"That's two days that we can keep the moms out of our way. Should we try for three?"

Bridgy was moving further and further away from the thing I wanted her to tell me. "Before the moms pop out here, how did it go at the state attorney's? You didn't seem too upset."

"I couldn't cry in front of the moms."

As soon as my face crumpled, she punched me in the arm. "Just joking. This was so much better than being interviewed by Lieutenant Anthony."

I could understand that. Getting a dental cavity filled was better than being interviewed by Frank Anthony. But I wanted to hear everything.

"Hurry up before one of the moms comes looking for us."

CHAPTER TWENTY-SIX

"When Frank called Owen and told him that I better bring a criminal lawyer with me to the state attorney, I thought that meant the questioning would be longer, and a whole lot meaner. But it wasn't. It wasn't like that at all."

I waited.

"The lawyer, Mr. Dodson, read a bunch of questions to me. The same questions that I'd already answered over and over again at the sheriff's office. He read a question. I gave an answer. When he reached the end of the list, he said I was free to go."

"And that was it?"

"Yep, that was it. The only thing different was that Georgette spoke into the recorder at the beginning and said that for the record I was there of my own free will and could leave at any time, and she made Mr. Dodson say that was true."

"Owen couldn't do that?"

"I'm sure he could. In the car coming home Georgette said that the process was standard and this may only be the first step. Owen said that Frank might have expected the state attorney to push harder or something. Maybe Frank Anthony was just being cautious on my behalf when he suggested that I get a criminal lawyer."

That didn't sound like Lieutenant *Law & Order* to me, but as long as Bridgy had been treated well and didn't come home crying, I was content.

The patio door slid open, and Emelia sat on the edge of Bridgy's chaise lounge. "Your father sends kisses and more money if you need it. Legal fees and all that."

I crept out to give them some quality mother-and-daughter time. I could hear my mother singing softly in my bedroom. It sounded like a Beatles tune. "All You Need Is Love" or "Here Comes the Sun," something from the era right before the group became full-fledged hippies.

I knocked on the door. Sage was dressed in either pajamas that looked like shorts and a tank top or shorts and a tank top that looked like pajamas.

"Come in, my goldenrod." She pointed to a bed pillow on the floor. "I'm just about to meditate. Join me. Please." And she dropped another pillow. "Would you like me to chant aloud?"

I gave her a quick hug. "No, thank you. I have really gotten used to mental visual meditation. I find it peaceful. I see the horizon over the Gulf."

We sat on our pillows, each finding a comfortable position. Sage squeezed my hand and whispered, "Listen to the voice within yourself." The same thing she had been saying to me since my first meditation when I was a very little girl.

I closed my eyes and was nearly focused on the horizon when the voice within me spoke. It said, *Oscar has a boat somewhere on Pine Island. Could it contain a clue to Oscar's murder?*

The next morning as soon as the breakfast rush was over, I found Skully hammering away in the outbuilding he'd been repairing on Pastor John's church property. When there was a break in the pounding, I called out from the doorway. He pulled off the hospital mask that covered his mouth and ushered me outside.

"Too much dust in the air. I been doing a bit of sawing."

Seeing how busy he was, I asked if he could find time to introduce my mother to

283

some of Florida's edible plants.

"Sure thing, Little Miss, I'm happy to help. Driving Miguel crazy, is she?" Perceptive as always, Skully understood the problem. "Happens I have a friend, Hector Clifford, lives down island and has a nice little herb garden filled with all sorts of treats. Your mom might like to visit. I could bring Bridgy's mom, too."

I thought it best to explain that the moms wouldn't be great at riding in Skully's canoe, so it would probably be best if I picked up Skully and drove all three to Mr. Clifford's house.

"Smart. When I'm done here this afternoon, I'll check in with Hector to see if tomorrow works. What's a good time?"

"Between ten and eleven I should be able to get away to drive you there."

"Sassy, Sassy Cabot. Wait right there." The voice sent shivers down my spine. Jocelyn Kendall was marching across the yard.

"Better she's looking for you than for me, Little Miss." Skully gave me a wink and a nod. Then he headed back inside the building, and the hammering recommenced. Whether slamming the hammer was necessary or it was Skully's method of warding off Jocelyn, I had no idea. I only knew I was trapped like a rat.

Jocelyn massaged her temples. "First the sawing, now the hammering. I tell you, it gives me a headache. John says it would be more of a headache if the building fell down. I suppose he's right. Still, it is only an old storage shed. Who would miss it? Of course, as John keeps reminding me, it is parish property."

As she blathered on, I moved closer and closer to the Heap-a-Jeep. But we were apparently attached at the hip by some invisible string, and she stayed by my side.

I reached for the driver's door as unobtrusively as I could, but it didn't get by Jocelyn. She switched topics instantly. "We did not finish our conversation about the language in that book." She stopped and looked at me expectantly.

"You mean the f-bomb in *Julie and Julia*?"

"I do indeed. And if you think back, we also had to tolerate a mature woman having a 'relationship' with a younger man."

Now she was talking about the Anna Quindlen book.

"I have to insist that you carefully screen the reading material for the clubs. You have an obligation —"

"Screen?" I'd had about enough of her nonsense. Rather than pull every over-bleached straw-textured hair from her head in huge fistfuls, I decided to put her in her place, maybe not on everything, maybe not forever, but definitely here and now on reading choices for the book clubs. "You mean censor, am I right? You want me to read a book *before* a club chooses it, and then you want me to *decide* if the book is wholesome enough for us to read."

She should have caught on when I said the word "censor," but she didn't. "Exactly. If you do your job effectively, it will save no amount of trouble."

"I won't even consider it." I pulled the jeep door open and counted to ten, waiting for her to tell me that she would have to quit the book clubs. Instead, she stood on the lawn with her mouth open. I closed my door and drove away.

When I got back to the café, things were quiet. Judge Harcroft was still at Dashiell Hammett, the *Fort Myers Beach News* spread out in front of him. Two other tables were occupied, but no one seemed to need attention. Bridgy was cleaning the unoccupied tables. When she saw me, she went to the kitchen and signaled me to follow.

"Ryan called. He and Lieutenant Anthony are coming in later to interview you and Miguel."

"What about?"

"Oscar, silly. What else? Oh, I hear something in the dining room." Bridgy went through the kitchen door, and I heard her ask Judge Harcroft if he enjoyed his breakfast. He answered with his usual, "I must *Dash.*"

I told Miguel that Skully had a friend with a garden that should enchant Sage, and he was willing to take the moms there tomorrow. "It's on the south end of the island. I offered to drive; I couldn't imagine the moms paddling along in Skully's canoe."

Miguel and I were laughing at that vision when Bridgy stuck her head through the kitchen door and said that we had new customers. The early lunch rush had begun.

Angeline Drefke and Sonja Ferraro came in, opted for the Robert Frost table and unloaded their totes and packages on an empty chair. When I brought their menus, I smiled in the direction of the packages. "Getting some last-minute shopping done, are we?"

Sonja said, "We're both going home soon. Can't go home without goodies."

"I want to take home your delicious buttermilk pie. I wish you'd open a mail-order business so I could eat it all year long." Angeline rubbed her stomach and laughed. "Maybe better I don't."

"Don't let Ophie hear you give me credit for the buttermilk pie. She shared her special recipe with Miguel, but even Bridgy doesn't know how to make it, and Ophie is her aunt."

"Speaking of Bridgy . . ." Sonja looked over her shoulder and lowered her voice. "How is she? I mean, even we had to go in to the sheriff's office this morning for a second interview. She must be on her fourth or fifth by now. Poor girl. As if she could harm a flea."

Angeline agreed. "Bridgy is too sweet to kill anyone. And Fort Myers Beach is too charming a place for a murder. I don't get it. If Oscar had been killed in Atlantic City, well, that I could understand. Remember I told you my first husband was a gambler? There was a rough crowd in Atlantic City back in the day. That was Oscar's day as well — you never know what comes back to haunt you."

Before they started reading their menus and asking about the day's specials, I asked how well they knew Tammy Rushing.

Angeline shrugged. "Barely. We saw her at book club, of course. And we were in the same sewing group at the community center."

"Don't forget Mexican Train Dominoes.

We joined a group, and Tammy and Margo were part of the rotation. You know, we had different opponents every week. Our group was red, teams one through six. They were a blue team. Or was it green?" Sonja was uncertain.

"Margo Wellington?"

"Oh yes. Margo and Tammy were besties. They did everything together. It was like, well, if I couldn't get to a game or a class or a meeting, Angeline would still go, wouldn't you?"

Angeline nodded.

"And if she couldn't make it, I'd go without her. But those two never went anywhere alone. You saw both of them or neither of them. When did you ever see one of them at a book club meeting without the other?" Sonja challenged me.

I realized she was right. I never had seen Margo without Tammy or vice versa.

I took their orders and brought them glasses of sweet tea.

Bridgy and I were both in the kitchen when I made the mistake of repeating the conversation I had with Sonja and Angeline. When I mentioned the sewing club, she got excited. "Sewing club. Sewing scissors. That's it. Tammy Rushing killed Oscar. Stabbed him with her sewing scissors and then fled."

"Really, Bridgy? We need hard evidence. You can't jump to conclusions like that."

At the work counter, Miguel laughed. "Sassy, aren't you like the pot who calls the kettle black?" And he went back to chopping carrots, satisfied that he had ended our argument.

We had a long, teary good-bye with Angeline and Sonja. They even insisted that Miguel come out of the kitchen for hugs. I had to beg, but he did succumb.

They were out the door less than three minutes when Sonja came back, slightly out of breath. She handed me a plastic bag, and by the heft of it, it held a hardcover book.

"Give this to Margo when you see her. She lent me her copy of *The Florida Life of Thomas Edison,* but with all the chaos and confusion I forgot to return it. Got to go. Angeline's waiting at the curb." She gave me a last quick hug.

I put the package under the counter and promptly forgot about it when Deputy Ryan Mantoni and Lieutenant Frank Anthony, both ramrod straight in their dark green uniforms, walked through the door.

CHAPTER TWENTY-SEVEN

I tried to pretend that I wasn't worried. "I understand you want to talk to me and to Miguel. Would you like a cup of coffee first? Or perhaps a piece of pie?"

When Frank shook his head and said they didn't have time, Ryan looked disappointed. I know he never met a piece of pie that didn't make him happy.

Frank looked at the kitchen door. "We won't interrupt your workday for long, but we need to go over your statement and Miguel's. Is he in the kitchen?"

Knowing how Miguel hated to have anyone in his kitchen, I hesitated. "He is, but could you use the bench outside to talk to us? The kitchen gets busy . . ."

Frank looked around at the dining room, which was more than half empty. I could see the decision milling around in his brain.

"Sure. See if Miguel has time for us now."

As if Miguel had a choice.

I went into the kitchen and told Miguel he was up at bat. He gave me strict instructions not to touch the pot of broth simmering on the back of the stove. He spread paper towels over the cutting board covered with bell peppers, some already chopped, some waiting for the knife. "Don't touch. I'll finish afterward." And he went off to speak with the deputies.

I puttered around the dining room, keeping one eye out the window. Miguel, Frank and Ryan were standing in a kind of football huddle formation, heads leaning toward one another as if they didn't want to be overheard by passersby.

I was refilling sweet tea glasses for the couple sitting at Robert Louis Stevenson when Miguel came back inside. He was whistling some catchy tune I didn't quite recognize. When I looked at him, he bobbed his head toward the door and the deputies waiting outside. I served the sweet tea and went out to meet my fate.

Frank was standing directly opposite the bench where customers sat if they had to wait for a table. This time of day it was empty. He waved toward the bench. "Have a seat."

"Why? You let Miguel stand." Even as I said it, I knew I sounded like a pouty six-year-old. Ryan looked up to heaven, but Frank took it in stride. "Stand if you like." And he folded his arms in a way that showed off his well-shaped biceps.

I wasn't about to let his muscles distract me. "How can I help you, Lieutenant? I have a business to run." Now I sounded like a cranky old lady. Could I never get my tone right when I talked to this man?

Ever polite, he told me we were merely reviewing my previous statements about the day Oscar was killed. I did beautifully with all the lead-up questions. Where had we gone? What time did we get back? Did everyone enter the café at the same time? I was patting myself on the back when he got to the tough questions.

"So when you heard Bridgy call for help, you ran out to find her, is that correct?"

"It was Ophie who heard Bridgy calling for help. Ophie called me, and I ran out to find Bridgy."

"And when you found her?"

I closed my eyes, unwilling to recall the scene. Haltingly, I told him about finding Bridgy with Oscar's body, and how upset she was.

"And what did she say?"

"That she was sorry."

"Sorry?"

"Yes. Sorry. Like she was sorry he was dead, sorry she couldn't save him. Sorry."

He glanced at the narrow black leather-bound notebook in his hand. "In your last statement you quoted Bridgy as saying, 'He's dead. I'm so sorry.' Is that still your recollection?"

Really? He's going to push me about Bridgy? I'd had enough. I turned to the front door. "Probably. Are we done?"

"No, we are not done. 'Probably' isn't an answer. Do you recall Bridgy saying, 'He's dead. I'm so sorry'?"

I sighed. "Yes. But she meant . . ."

"She told us what she meant. Thank you. That will be all." And he closed his notebook with a slap of pages hitting against each other.

He may as well have shouted, "Dismissed."

But I was not a woman to be set aside so easily. "I have a question. Have you found Tammy Rushing or Lolly the Sailor?"

His eyes shot darts at mine, but I held steady.

"You know better. I can't discuss an ongoing case. Besides . . ."

I waited.

"I'm surprised *you* haven't found them already."

Ryan, standing just over Frank's left shoulder, was frantically pulling his hand across the space in front of his neck signaling me to stop. No such luck.

"Well, what clues do you have? What did you find in Oscar's house or his locker at work?" I demanded as if I was *his* boss, afraid to be chewed out by *my* boss because we didn't gather enough information.

The lieutenant gave me a cold, hard stare, did an about-face and walked off to his green and white department car.

I was surprised that Ryan glared at me, too. "Anybody ever tell you about getting more flies with honey . . . ?" And he followed behind Frank, marching in lockstep without so much as a good-bye.

A voice off to my left asked, "What did you say to annoy those handsome young men? I was on the other side of the parking lot, and I could see the steam rising. And not the good kind of steam, the kind a well-mannered lady could instill without being too obvious."

"I just asked a question, and Frank got all huffy, which bothered Ryan no end."

"Can't y'all show one little bitty bit of sweetness to that handsome lieutenant?"

Ophie always put her duty as teacher of womanly wiles ahead of all else, but she switched right back to rebuking me. "I swear I'll be in my grave long before I see you married."

Ugh. Sometimes it was easier to talk to Lieutenant Starch-In-His-Drawers than Ophie.

Bridgy blanched when she saw Ophie walk into the café with me. That's when I remembered the moms were coming to meet us so we could take them to an art show over on Matlacha. If the moms showed up in the next few minutes, we might well have another O-phel-ia/E-mel-ia storm in the making.

Oblivious to Bridgy's reaction, Ophie headed to the kitchen. "I have some company coming over to play Bunco tonight, and I was wondering if you had a spare pie around somewhere. Dessert and tea should do them."

Bridgy's face turned to alarm. "Bunco? Isn't that like a swindling scheme? Something that could land you in jail?" Bridgy gave an involuntary shudder at the thought.

"Y'all are just being silly. Bunco is a table game. Sure, we use dice, but it's legal as sunshine. Best played with twelve people. I learned it down at the community center and thought I'd have a Bunco party. Now about that pie."

Definitely relieved that the invitation to join us at Matlacha wouldn't have to be issued, Bridgy followed Ophie into the kitchen.

I began the daily cleanup then decided to dust the bookshelves before I washed the tables and cleaned the floor. I loved the smell of brand-new books, spines never cracked. Shelf by shelf, I ran the dust cloth along the tops of the books and down the spines. Then I switched to a different cloth to do the dividers and shelves. I was only partway done when the front door opened and the moms came in laughing about some story Emelia was telling.

The kitchen door opened, and out came Ophie, pie in hand.

Still laughing, Sage said, "Ophie, Emelia was just telling me about the time you two skipped school and went to Coney Island to watch some teams practice for a major bicycle race on the boardwalk because you had a crush on a dreamy cyclist from the neighborhood."

Ophie broke out into a grin. "Emy had a hole in her pocket and lost our money and our subway tokens. We had to borrow a dime from a nice old lady and call home. Dad came to get us. He said Mom was too mad to drive. I don't remember the punishment, but I do remember we tiptoed around Mom for a good long while."

As if she was talking to anyone but Ophie, Emelia chortled. "We got one of Mom's jumbo punishment packages."

Ophie set the box holding her pie down on the counter and put her hand on her sister's shoulder. "Oh yes, she gave us the old the double H. Extra homework. Extra housework."

"And when she heard you begging me to trade hosing out the trash cans for scrubbing the work sink in the basement because you didn't want to ruin your nails, she gave you work sink duty for the next month."

Ophie was wiping happy tears from her eyes. "I guess she knew who the real troublemaker was."

Emelia shook her head. "No matter where you led, I always followed."

We were all still laughing when Emelia said, "Until you left."

The room fell silent.

Ophie looked like she'd been slapped. "We both left. You went to Albertus Magnus. I went to Belmont Abbey. It was college."

"The difference, Ophelia, is I came home again."

"So did I." Ophie placed her hands on

her hips and thrust her chin defiantly in the air.

"Barely. Graduated in June, married in October and off to Macon, Georgia, without so much as a fare-thee-well."

"Emy, Shane McLennon and I were engaged for nearly two years. You helped me plan the wedding. You were my maid of honor. What is this about?"

"Don't 'Emy' me. You know what this is about. We did everything together. Our entire lives. That's why Dad thought it would be a good idea for us to go to different colleges. 'Time for the Brice babes to shore up their independence,' he used to say. Not sure he expected you to be so independent that you'd never come home again."

Ophie's face turned pasty. Suddenly, she had jowls I'd never noticed. "All these years? That's what's been stuck in your craw all these years? And here I thought after we had those college years apart, you realized that you didn't like me very much. The only time you ever came to visit was when Shane died. Even then . . ."

"Even then you wouldn't come home." Now Emelia had assumed the family hands-on-hips pose. I feared the worst.

Just then the kitchen door swung open

299

and Miguel set a large tray covered with bowls of ice cream — some chocolate, some vanilla — along with a plate of Robert Frost Apple and Blueberry Tartlets on the counter. *"Señoras,* when the *chicas"* — he pointed to Bridgy and me — "have a tiff, a big bowl of ice cream generally makes them more, ah, reasonable. Perhaps if you nibble a bit, you will become more reasonable as well."

He smiled all around, said *"Mañana"* and headed for home. Of course he rang the ship's bell outside the front door, startling Emelia and Sage. It was just the distraction we needed to get everyone into seats at the Emily Dickinson table. Bridgy and I placed bowls of ice cream and the platter of pastries on the table and passed around spoons. No one touched them.

Bridgy and I sat and began eating our ice cream, telling each other how delicious it was. Sage caught on, picked up a spoon and asked that a little vanilla be added to her chocolate. That gave me the opening I needed.

"Emelia? Ophie? Would you like to mix flavors in your bowls?" I noticed they both had vanilla, so I grabbed an extra dish of chocolate and stood between their seats, ready to serve.

Ophie gave in first. "Emy doesn't really like vanilla. Why don't you give her all the chocolate."

Emelia nodded at her sister. "Why thank you for remembering." And she held out her bowl for me to make the switch.

Bridgy and I exchanged looks. While it was hardly an official peace accord, we both could see the sisters softening. I wasn't brave, but Bridgy took a chance.

"Ophie, we're going to the art show on Matlacha. Would you like to come?"

Emelia stiffened, and I feared we had gone too far too fast.

CHAPTER TWENTY-EIGHT

"That sounds like a fine trip." Ophie patted her sister's hand. "Such a colorful place. Y'all will love it. And the shops. I can tell y'all the shops are charming. Some of them are the closest thing to my Treasure Trove to be found anywhere in Lee County. But I can't join in. I'm having company tonight."

Emelia actually looked disappointed for a split second. "No problem. Now that we've got our little wrinkle ironed out, as Grandma would say, we'll have plenty of time to play." Then she flabbergasted us by asking, "Isn't that right, y'all?"

Ophie laughed first, and we all joined in.

Bridgy and I finished tidying the café and loaded the dishwasher. Bridgy hung a sign she'd made months ago out of a chunk of driftwood — "Dirty — please press start" — so that when Miguel came in the next morning, he would start the washer first thing.

As Bridgy stepped away from the dishwasher, she mused, "I wonder what Miguel will think when he finds out his ice cream trick instantly dissolved a battle between Mom and Ophie that has been going on for my entire life."

"Seriously? Why wouldn't it work? He uses it on us all the time."

We went to round up Sage and Emelia, who were browsing through the bookshelves.

Emelia was looking at the Mystery section. "Sassy, do you have any of those books . . . ? I've been watching the show on public television . . . *Vera*?"

"You mean the Vera Stanhope books by Ann Cleeves? I just sold our last copy of *Harbour Street* yesterday. I have more on order. I do have one of Cleeves's Shetland books, *Thin Air,* in stock. Jimmy Perez is the detective in those. That is an excellent series as well. Why don't you try it for now? I'll set a copy of *Harbour Street* aside for you when it comes in."

"Done. Now let's get to the fantastic and colorful shops Ophie told us about."

I had to smile at Emelia's sudden enthusiasm for all things Ophie. Bridgy was positively beaming. A major stress had dropped from her shoulders. Now if we could find out who killed Oscar, life would go back to normal.

Rather than take two cars, we decided to take the Heap-a-Jeep. It might be crowded, but I could open the top, and the gorgeous weather would more than make up for bent knees. We crossed the San Carlos Bridge and, soon after, the Cape Coral Bridge. Within a couple of miles we were on a long-ish ride on Pine Island Road, crossing over wetlands and water. Sage and Emelia were enchanted by the countryside. When we got to the tiny island community of Matlacha, it was jam-packed with sightseers and art aficionados. Beach shacks, long ago painted bright colors and turned into shops, art studios and restaurants, lined both sides of the street. The crowds milling back and forth across the street often stopped traffic entirely. It didn't take long to figure out there wasn't a parking spot to be had. It was one of those problems that presented an opportunity.

"What a mob scene," Sage observed. "I see lots of happy aurae, though." Only Sage would hark back to the Latin root instead of using "auras" like everyone else.

Emelia chimed in, "If it isn't conve-nient . . ."

Bridgy was almost pleading, afraid she

304

wouldn't be able to add fuel to her mother's festive mood. "Any chance of finding a spot?"

"No problem. I have an idea. Bridgy and I have been talking about checking out a new supplier on Pine Island, just down the road another mile or two." I gave Bridgy a look so she'd know not to ask what I was talking about. "Why don't we let you two out? You can shop and explore while we take care of business. We'll come back and meet you."

Sage was always up for a spontaneous moment, but Emelia was hesitant. "Where will we meet? We could get lost. It is so crowded here."

Then I spotted an excellent distraction. "We'll pick you up in front of the post office."

Heads swerved. Sage and Emelia were searching every storefront while Bridgy gave me an evil grin.

"I don't see . . ."

Bridgy jumped in. I guess she didn't think I should have all the fun. "Look across the street. See that building with the huge orange fish with the big green eye painted along the side wall? American flag? Mailbox out front? Do you see the emblem on the

305

wall above the fish's head? Voilà, post office."

Instant delight. "It has island art all over the front, too. Sage, let's go see if they sell postcards. I'd love to mail some from that quirky little building."

And the moms were pushing the seat backs out of the way so they could get out of the jeep. No one worried about crushing me or Bridgy.

"Careful crossing. We'll pick you up in an hour," I shouted after them, but they were busy locking arms and laughing while they dodged cars. Their only response was a backhanded wave from Sage. I got the feeling they were no longer concerned about getting lost. Island time and island spirit had grabbed them.

I eased the Heap-a-Jeep into the never-ending line of cars heading for Pine Island.

As soon as we were moving, Bridgy asked, "So what's really going on?"

"Oscar has a boat in a repair dock on Pine Island. I checked online, and there are only a few places it can be. Wouldn't it be cool to take a look?"

"Wouldn't it be cooler still to tell Frank or Ryan?" wasn't the reaction I expected from Bridgy, but it was the reaction I got.

"And how will we know the boat when we see it?"

"Skully said it's a cabin cruiser named *Jersey Girl.* Come on, we've got some extra time. Can't we spend it looking for the boat? Maybe there is something that could help identify the killer."

"Oh sure. So once we find the boat, you want to search the boat. Breaking and entering? Great idea. The killer probably left a selfie on Oscar's spare cell phone. Please. We already witnessed one miracle today. Mom and Ophie made peace. Let's not push our luck."

"Don't be such a drama queen. We're not breaking into the boat. We're just looking. Maybe we want to buy it from Oscar's heirs. Stop worrying."

"It's hard to stop worrying when I'm interrogated and re-interrogated every day." Bridgy tossed her blond curls and stared out the window.

I crossed onto Little Pine Island, and the lush scenery kept us both occupied for a while.

I decided to offer a compromise. "I have the names of four repair docks. How about we look at two of them, and if we don't see the *Jersey Girl,* we go back to get the moms."

Silence. Then Bridgy let out an exaggerated sigh. "Okay. But I'm not getting out of the car. You are on your own, and if you get arrested, I'm going back to Matlacha without you."

There she was — the drama queen again. There were moments that it was so obvious that Bridgy and Ophie were related. This was one of them. Still, we were so physically close to the repair docks that it would have been a shame to turn around. So, I thought, *Let her sit in the car if that's what she wants to do. Didn't she realize I was doing this to clear her name?*

I turned left on Stringfellow Road, which was the north/south spine of Pine Island, and in no time at all I saw a directional sign identifying Rudy's Repair Dock. I made a right turn and followed an endlessly winding road that suddenly opened up into a parking lot. There were only a few dozen boat slips, and more than half were empty. I'd know in a minute if Oscar's boat was here.

I squinted around a really wide dwarf palm in order to check out the front of the massive repair shed, blue paint flecked with chips of rusty metal. The doors were closed and belted with chains. If the *Jersey Girl* was inside, I was plain out of luck. But at least I could snoop without getting caught by a boat mechanic. I ran up and down each dock, checking all the occupied slips. No *Jersey Girl* to be seen.

I ran back to the parking lot, and when I opened the driver's side door, Bridgy handed me a bottle of water. I guess she'd been watching me run around. "Thanks. The next place is a little farther south."

I backtracked on the winding road and turned south on Stringfellow Road. Bridgy's phone dinged a text message, and she took a peek. I made another right, heading toward a row of boat sheds each with "BOAT REPAIRS" and a phone number stenciled in letters and numbers about four feet high on each shed.

"Mom sent a text. They're having fun and we needn't hurry back." Bridgy slipped her phone back in her purse. "That doesn't mean we can search every repair dock on Pine Island. We agreed on two. This is the second."

Honestly, sometimes she acts like I can't count. This parking lot was three times the size of the lot at Rudy's. Ten or so cars were parked near the water by the boat sheds, and I followed suit. I told Bridgy I would be right back and walked with more certainty than I felt toward the nearest dock line of slips. It was long and stretched far out into the Gulf, but it didn't take much time for me to realize that *Jersey Girl* wasn't among these boats, which ranged from several two-seater motorboats to one so big that it could easily be considered a yacht.

I made my way to the second row of slips, and a blue flat-bottom boat caught my eye. It wasn't the boat I was looking for, but I stopped for a minute, envisioning lazy days cruising Estero Bay on the flat boat instead of in a kayak. I shook the thought from my head. No time for fantasies.

Two slips down on the left-hand side. There she was. A cabin cruiser about thirty feet long with *"JERSEY GIRL"* stenciled in curlicue letters on the bow.

I looked around the boatyard. Except for Bridgy waiting in the Heap-a-Jeep, I didn't see a soul. I crept over to the *Jersey Girl* and looked around again. Still nobody. The boat was moored securely to the dock, so I grabbed on to the boat rails and hoisted myself aboard. I opened the cabin doors and bent down to peek inside. A few weathered copies of *Salt Water Sportsman* magazine were wedged to prop open the door of the galley refrigerator. Coffee mugs and some papers that looked like bills and handwritten notes littered the countertop. And there were three or four large plastic storage bins that looked to be stuffed. My foot hadn't even touched the first step when I heard a growly voice. "What do you think you're doing?"

I turned around slowly to face my accuser, who turned out to be a twentysomething security guard, clipboard in hand, who'd obviously deepened his voice to startle me.

Now that he had my attention, he fell back to his normal tone. "Who are you? What are you doing here?"

A bit of fibbing was probably my best option. "This is my uncle's boat. He passed suddenly, and my aunt can't find his Marine Corps ring. She knows he wanted to be buried wearing it."

"Uncle's name?"

"Oscar. Oscar Frieland." I looked as solemn as I could.

He tapped a ballpoint pen on his clipboard. "Yeah, I got it. Now what's this about a ring?"

"Uncle Oscar always took his ring off when he was cleaning fish or scrubbing the boat. Now it's missing. My aunt sent me here to see if I could find it and bring it over to the 'Rest in Beech.' "

"Where?" The guard scratched his cheek with the pen.

311

"Oh, that's the nickname of the Michael J. Beech Funeral Home over in Fort Myers Beach."

He relaxed. "Sorry, I didn't know you were an island girl. You'd be amazed at the tourists who show up here and begin wandering on and off the boats, taking selfies and Vine loop videos, shouting, 'Great vacation,' to friends and family. It's like theft of imagery or something."

I was relieved to know the crime he was policing. "Well, that's not me." I gestured to the cabin below. "If I can just look for the ring. I'll be out of your way in a . . ."

He tapped the clipboard again. "Sorry. You're not on the approved list for this boat. You have to get off and stay off."

Bridgy was much better at faking her way through these kinds of situations than I was, but I tried my best. I squeezed my eyes shut and stuck my lower lip out as far as I could and wiggled it as if I was going to sob.

He melted. "Stay here. I'll look."

There was nothing I could do but listen to him open and shut cabinets and drawers belowdecks. It wasn't hard for me to project disappointment when he couldn't find the ring. I was disappointed — disappointed that I hadn't had a chance to rummage

among Oscar's papers in the hope of finding a clue to his killer.

CHAPTER TWENTY-NINE

I told Bridgy about my run-in with the security guard, and it totally brightened her mood. When she wasn't snickering, "Uncle Oscar's Marine Corps ring," she was laughing out loud. Pleased as I was to see her happy, it was tedious to have her make fun of me all the way back to Matlacha.

We pulled off Pine Island Road into the parking lot next to the Matlacha Post Office. Emelia and Sage had their arms loaded with packages. Sage carried a new tote bag, which sported a colorful picture of the Earth as it looks from outer space.

Like children exhausted after a day at Disney World, they tossed their packages into the jeep and tumbled in after them, both laughing and talking at once. They weren't even settled in their seats when they began demanding that we schedule another trip to Matlacha.

"There is so much to see and do here. It

would take days to spend enough time meandering through every shop. Oh, and I'd like to come back for a lesson at the art studio. I'd love to paint a big orange fish like the one on the side of the post office."

I had no idea Emelia was interested in becoming an artist.

More laughter from the moms.

Sage chimed in, "I'd like to paint a mermaid, surrounded by seashells. Speaking of shells, could we stop in Times Square? I looked at some shells here, but I remember a few I saw for sale in the shop there. I'd like to compare while they are still fresh in my mind."

I was ready to call it a day, but Bridgy was all for heading to Times Square. "My muscles could use a stretch. While you two 'shop 'til you drop,' Sassy and I can walk on the beach. It's always so soothing."

The main plaza of Times Square was extra crowded. A group of teens with matching tee shirts that read "SAVE THE DOLPHINS" came off the pier and tried to scatter in all four directions, but their chaperones herded them into an untidy group and moved them toward the ice cream and candy store.

A busker, wearing pirate garb complete with a patch over one eye, was singing sea shanties next to the tall four-sided clock. We listened to him sing for a while. The moms were especially happy to clap along to "Blow the Man Down," and I wasn't surprised that Sage knew most of the words to "Fiddler's Green," an old Irish song describing a fisherman's view of heaven; a song I remember my grandfather singing.

The moms went off to do more shopping while Bridgy and I headed under the pier. We took off our sandals and buckled them around the belt loops on our shorts.

"Wriggling your toes in the sand never gets old, does it?" Bridgy pushed her sunglasses on top of her head and looked over the Gulf of Mexico lapping at the shore straight out to the horizon. "Look at that sky." She pointed to the horizon. "Seems to be getting ready for another dazzling sunset. I'm going to walk the water's edge."

"Enjoy. I'll meditate for a while." I sat in the sand and twisted and turned until I found a comfortable spot. I watched Bridgy walk to the shoreline. She stopped and bent down here and there to look at an interesting seashell.

I stared at the horizon. Streaks of white clouds in a light blue sky rested on the straight edge of the dark blue water of the Gulf. A few boats sped across the scene, no more than tiny images that didn't add so much as a ripple to the water lapping gracefully on the shore.

A thousand thoughts crowded around me. Oscar's murder. Bridgy as a prime suspect, no matter how much the deputies denied it. The stress between Ophie and Emelia. Then watching the tension between them evaporate over a bowl of ice cream. I swatted each and every thought away, intent on the horizon. The word "peace" rolled across my mind, and then, as happens so often, there was nothing but the horizon. I closed my eyes and focused on relaxing each body part, starting with my toes, then my ankles, my calves and so on. In a while, my body and mind felt refreshed.

Gradually, I opened my eyes. The sun was slightly lower on the horizon. I heard voices calling my name. I turned, and the moms were leaning over the railing of the pier, waving.

"Yoo-hoo. Wait until you see what we bought."

"Come on up. Let's watch the sunset. Where's Bridgy?"

Through the openings in the pier's wooden side slats, I could see large shopping bags resting at the moms' feet. They were certainly doing their part to support

317

the economy of our little town.

I pointed down the beach to Bridgy, who was doing stretching exercises. The moms called louder, and Bridgy turned and began walking back. When she reached me, I said, "It's great to see them having so much fun."

Bridgy laughed. "It's hard to believe they are here to support me if I got arrested for murder. They seem to have forgotten all about Oscar." Her blue eyes darkened. "But I haven't forgotten."

"Don't worry, sweetie, neither have I. Now let's go show the moms how fabulous the sunset is from the far end of the pier. It will be a colorful end to a fabulous evening."

The moms insisted on coming to the café with us the next morning. Bridgy and I were dreading the interruptions and confusion, but having them around was surprisingly easy. They took turns walking among the tables, offering refills of coffee and tea. At one point Emelia introduced herself to two regulars sitting at Robert Frost, and when they asked if she was related to Ophie, Emelia stood up straight and answered with gusto, "I sure am. She's my favorite sister. Of course, she's my only sister." And she laughed, delighted that she could finally joke about her sister.

I had a moment of panic when I went into the kitchen and found Sage hovering around Miguel's workstation. Then I realized Miguel was laughing and chatting while he rolled dough for piecrusts. Sage was looking through the photo album Miguel kept on a shelf in the office. The album was filled with dozens of pictures of Bow, his black Maine Coon, who, true to her name, wore a different-colored neck bow every day.

"She is adorable. Her personality shines right through. It's like she's standing in front of us."

"*Sí,* she is quite a character. I have some newer pictures on my phone. I will show them to you when we have time." Miguel looked at me. "Sassy, your mother has offered to bake some healthy treats for my sweet Bow. Isn't that so generous?" I lavished praise on Sage as I began hurrying her out of the kitchen. "Time to go. Today is your visit to the herb garden, remember?"

I invited Emelia but she said she would rather stay and help Bridgy. Fine with me as long as I was able to get Sage out of Miguel's kitchen.

When I pulled the Heap-a-Jeep into the church parking lot, Tom Smallwood and Pastor John were repositioning a high-backed bench.

Sage was enthralled. "What are those lovely fan-shaped bushes?"

Sage might be in her earth phase, but I was the one who could name a saw palmetto. When she heard the name, Sage turned gleeful. "An excellent source of support for men's health."

"Shush. This isn't the herb garden. This is the church lawn. You can talk herbs with Hector when you meet him. Don't bother Pastor John with your . . . your voodoo."

As soon as the word was out of my mouth, I knew I was in trouble.

"Mary Sassafras Cabot. Voodoo represents spiritual folkways. Herbs are tangible. They grow in the earth and sustain other life-forms. I'm shocked you don't know the difference."

I was saved from answering by Pastor John, who walked across the grass to meet us. I introduced him to my mother, and he was kind enough to tell her what a joy it was to know Bridgy and me. He talked about how we added pleasure and enjoyment to the community with what he called our "story-themed" café. "I only wish my wife, Jocelyn, was here to meet you. She always says that Sassy's book clubs are a wonderful source of what Jocelyn likes to call 'cerebral exercise.' "

I was thanking my lucky stars that Jocelyn was nowhere to be seen. I was sure she'd have a much different speech to make about the book clubs now that she was on her language tear.

"Little Miss, is this your mama?"

I reached out an arm to the weathered man in overalls. "Sage, this is my friend Tom Smallwood."

He stuck out a hand. "Honored to meet you, ma'am. Please, call me Skully. Just about everyone around these parts does."

Sage warmed to Skully instantly. "Your aura is amazing. Greens, blues and yellows all swirling around one another. You're self-sufficient but rely on nature. It looks like . . . perhaps the sea?"

If I could have dropped right through a hole in the ground and been covered with daisies, that would have been fine with me. I never knew when Sage would recite one of her aura interpretations, but surely even she should know that the church lawn was not the best place to go into her psychic energy routine.

I was totally surprised when Pastor John laughed and slapped Skully on the back. "She certainly has your number." He turned to Sage. "Self-sufficient doesn't even begin to describe Tom. He's an indispensable part of the barrier island community. He can fix anything whether need be for himself or for others. Without his help, my church would be tumbling down. As to the sea, he travels by canoe from island to island."

Sage looked exceptionally pleased with herself while I breathed a sigh of relief that we had avoided calamity. I moved the conversation along.

"We better get going. I need to be back at the café before the lunch crowd." I hustled Sage and Skully into the Heap-a-Jeep.

Sage pulled out her finest manners. "I can't thank you enough for arranging for me to visit a real herb farm. Florida weather has such a grand ability to grow so many crops."

"My pal Hector's been planting and experimenting 'round these parts since he was a lad. He'll be happy to have a visitor who takes an interest in his work. Sage, Hector will want to know how you got that name."

I nearly drove off the road when Sage answered, "And I'd like to know why you told me to call you Skully. Is it Skully or is it Tom?"

I hadn't heard it often, but I recognized his good-natured laugh. There was nothing artificial about Tom Smallwood. "Baptized

Thomas, mostly called Tom until a few years back I found a human skull over on Mound Island. Looked to be ancient. I carried it in my duffel for a few months while I decided what to do about it. Talked to Sassy's friend Ryan. You know, the deputy? Anyway, he said there was a rightful place for it, and some professor agreed. Now it sits in a museum up at the state capital, and there is a little sign saying I discovered it. Since then most folks call me Skully, and I'm right proud of the name."

By the time I dropped them off, Sage and Skully were chatting and laughing like old friends, and I could see a fun afternoon ahead.

I waved good-bye. "Call me when you're ready to be picked up."

When I pulled into the parking lot, a couple of people were standing by the bench outside the Read 'Em and Eat. That usually meant there were no tables available inside. Of course Emelia was there to help Bridgy, but how much help could she really be?

I raced toward the café with the words, "Thank you for waiting, I'm sure we'll have a table for you soon," on the tip of my tongue. As I got closer, I recognized Maggie Latimer talking to a man who looked vaguely familiar.

When she saw me, Maggie hurried forward and grabbed me by both arms. "They found Tammy Rushing. She's under arrest somewhere up north."

CHAPTER THIRTY

I came to a full stop, one foot resting on the curb, and Maggie was shaking me so vehemently that my falling on the ground was not outside the realm of possibility. She was super excited.

"Say something." Then she remembered her manners. "You remember Jake Gilman." The older man dressed in jeans and a denim work shirt gave me a brief nod.

Maggie finally released my arms. "Ryan Mantoni showed up at Jake's house this morning with a picture of Tammy that had been sent along by some sheriff in South Carolina. Jake identified her."

Poor Jake. He was usually so blustery, and now his cheeks colored at every mention of his name. I got the feeling he'd rather not be the center of attention even in our tiny group of three.

"We came to tell you and Bridgy the news, but with her mother inside, we asked for you. Bridgy said you'd be right back. We thought it best to wait out here."

I was still reeling. "Tammy seemed so nice. So normal. I can't imagine her killing anyone."

Maggie patted my arm. "I know. Think about the movies on the Hallmark Movies and Mysteries channel. The killer is never the person you would think. It's always some nice, unimportant character with a really weird motive. You'll tell Bridgy, won't you? I have a class to teach. C'mon, Jake, I'll drop you at home."

They took a few steps across the parking lot, and then Jake turned back to me. "I'm really sorry that my rental caused you all this trouble. Tell your friend. Apologies."

No wonder he was so awkward. In his mind, if he hadn't rented to Tammy, Oscar would still be alive and Bridgy wouldn't have been under suspicion. Poor Jake.

There was a small crowd of customers in the café, but Bridgy and Emelia didn't seem harried, so I was right on time. I signaled Bridgy to meet me in the kitchen, but Emelia grabbed my attention first. She was bubbling with excitement and half pushed me behind the counter.

"I've been dying to show you what I bought. Bridgy loves it."

Next to our electric teakettle I saw a shiny new gadget, about two feet high. Emelia picked up a tall stainless steel cup and pushed it over the spindle on the machine. The whir of the malted mixer brought back childhood memories of going to the local ice cream parlor on Saturday afternoons.

"I couldn't believe that you had this great restaurant but no malteds on the menu, so right before I left home I emailed Miguel and he ordered the malted milk machine and a case of malted milk powder. It arrived in this morning's delivery from the restaurant supply house." She stopped the machine, poured the thick, creamy chocolate malt into a tall glass and handed it to me. "Drink up. I even have a name for the drinks. Are you ready?"

Desperate as I was to talk to Bridgy about Tammy's arrest, I couldn't stomp on Emelia's sheer joy. And the malted did look delicious. I took a sip.

"*Maltese Falcon.* Get it? MALT-ese. And you have the Dashiell Hammett table right over there. He wrote the book." Emelia stopped, waiting for applause, and I gave it, loudly. She flushed with pleasure.

Bridgy came over and put an arm around her mom. "Isn't she the best? Why didn't we think of . . ." Her face grew serious.

"Excuse me."

Owen Reston was in the open doorway waving Bridgy outside.

I hoped he had good news. "Tammy Rushing was arrested" kind of good news. I set my malted on the countertop and went from table to table to ask if our customers needed anything, all the while keeping my eye on the front door.

Two fishermen came in and ordered four breakfasts for takeout the next morning. I marked the order "paid" and put it on Miguel's tracking board.

When Bridgy came into the kitchen, Miguel was at the stove and I was putting two grungy mustard jars in a soak pail to get them clean enough for the recycling bin.

"Before I talk to Mom, I want to tell the two of you. Tammy Rushing was arrested somewhere called Manning, South Carolina. She was pulled over for speeding, and there was a warrant out for her. So they arrested her."

"A warrant? For killing Oscar? Then why are we still answering questions at every turn?" I was hoping to finally get the full story.

Bridgy gave me that famous look of hers, the one that said, "Wait for it."

Fortunately, she didn't make us wait long.

"No. The warrant was issued in the state of Alabama."

Then she stopped talking. I was used to her antics, and given what she'd been through, I was willing to let her play, but Miguel was having no part of it.

"*Ay, chica.* Tell us the whole story. We have lunches to serve."

"Well, Tammy Rushing's real name is Tammy Rushing Lynn. Did you know she's a trust fund baby?"

I shook my head while Miguel motioned for her to speed up by rotating his hand in an ever-faster circle.

"It seems that she married Mr. Lynn, whoever he may be, and it didn't work out. Well, I know a lot about that, don't I? Anyway, Tammy got hit with a large settlement and has to pay heavy-duty alimony. It looks like she got tired of supporting him, so she skipped more than a year ago. She was happy enough to be here for the winter, but with the murder . . ."

". . . she didn't want anyone looking at her too closely." I finished her sentence. "You got all this from Owen?"

"Yes, Frank Anthony called him. He wanted Owen, and by extension me, to know the straight scoop before it got all over the island that Tammy Rushing Lynn was arrested for Oscar's murder. It's alimony court for her and a 'NUMBER ONE SUSPECT' sign still hanging around my neck."

The kitchen door opened, and a stressed Emelia stuck her head around the door. "Need a little help here, girls."

The lunch rush was on.

Halfway through the most crowded hour, Bridgy and I pushed the Barbara Cartland and Dashiell Hammett tables together for a family group. The parents each held a toddler, one grandma carried an infant and the other three grandparents carried assorted toys or baby paraphernalia. I offered high chairs for the toddlers. At first the mom said "no," but then she changed her mind. "We may as well try. They really are getting too big to sit on our laps at the table."

As I went to get the chairs, I heard one of the grandfathers say sotto voce, "That's what you been telling her, Ethel. She don't listen."

Apparently, he wasn't as soft voiced as he thought he was, because the toddlers' dad said, "Pop, we'll raise our kids our way. Okay?"

I brought two toddler chairs along with some plain paper and crayons. I put one chair on each side of the parents and placed the paper and crayons in front of the mother.

I left them with menus and grabbed a pitcher of sweet tea to offer refills. Emelia was just ahead of me with coffee and decaf. It was nice to have an extra set of hands during the busy hours.

The toddlers were happily scribbling with their crayons when I went back to take the family's order. Then the grandmother, whom I assumed was Ethel, said, "Take those crayons away. She's drawing on the chair."

Pandemonium. They were all talking at once. Accusations of bad parenting flew back and forth. Finally, the toddlers' father stood up. "Mom, you have got to stop telling us how to raise our kids."

I couldn't help but notice that the grandmother who was rocking the sleeping baby had a bit of a smirk, as though she was pleased that the other grandma had started the brouhaha.

I took a step back from the table until they quieted down. Then I asked the mother, "Do you want anything for the children? I can put their orders in while the rest of you are deciding."

Both sets of grandparents immediately began studying the menu. The mother asked for chicken fingers and applesauce for the toddlers. "And a small glass of milk for James. Janey is lactose intolerant, so we brought lactose-free milk for her. She'll need a glass, if that's okay."

I gave her a wide smile and held it for a few extra seconds until I was sure the grandparents saw it. Then, louder than I needed to, I said, "Sure, that's great. You're a smart mom."

When I placed the children's order on the pass-through, I nearly bumped into Emelia, who was filling the teakettle. I gave her a kiss on the cheek. "Bridgy and I are lucky to have you and Sage as moms."

She smiled her thanks. I was feeling so lucky to have such great "mom support" at our time of crisis that I couldn't wait to drive down island to pick up Sage and Skully.

The entire time they ordered and then ate their food, the family group continued to bicker, but it didn't bother me at all. Their nonsense reminded me how great my own family is. Sage might move through her different "phases" and be obsessed with auras, or aurae, as she liked to call them, but she was always in my corner. Proof positive? She was here. Even when I didn't ask, she knew I needed my mom. As soon as the café crowd dwindled, I took off to see my mom. I wasn't going to wait for her to call.

Hector Clifford's place was tucked in a corner of the island so far south that I was almost at Lovers Key when I started to think I might have missed the turnoff. Then I saw the neat hand-painted sign, green letters on a worn slab of wood, "FLOWERS and HERBS" hanging from a shepherd's crook light pole.

I made a quick left. Too quick. Gravel scattered from under all four tires. I wished I'd paid more attention when I dropped them off. Then I remembered. I was in such a hurry to get back to the café, I made a U-turn and barely slowed down to drop them off. Is that any way to treat a mother who loves you? I promised myself that I would be the perfect daughter forever more, or at least for the next little while.

I parked the Heap-a-Jeep next to a dust-covered Silverado that had once been dark blue by the look of it but now had a black fender and a lot of rusted scrapes. I heard voices behind the house. I found Sage surrounded by plants, some in clay pots, some in rectangular baskets.

Hector Clifford, a thickset African American man, was explaining something about a plant Sage was holding. He leaned over to show her the leaves, and his wide-brimmed straw hat slid down on his forehead. When he straightened and pushed the hat to the back of his head, he noticed me.

"Be right with you."

Skully came out of a shed carrying a pretty plant, green stems, bluish green leaves with a touch of mauve. "Hey, Little Miss. Hector, this is Sage's daughter."

Hector gave me a broad grin. "You the one named Sassafras?"

I laughed. "That would be me."

"Shucks, Tom here's got your plant. Momma wanted to surprise you but too late for that."

Sage took the plant from Skully's hand. "Oh my." She slowly moved the plant from right to left and back again. "It is absolutely perfect. I have never seen a sassafras plant so lush. I can't imagine how gorgeous it will be in full flower."

"It's a mite young, yet. Probably won't bloom this season. This type will grow to shrub not to tree." Hector turned to me. "Momma said you live in an apartment. Not much use for a tree, I suppose."

"Oh, but a shrub could live forever on my patio. I have just the spot in mind." I grabbed Sage and gave her a big ole bear hug, the kind I'd watched Bridgy give her

334

mom and aunt for years. "I love you, Mom." Sage squeezed me as hard as I squeezed her. Then she laughed. "I am thrilled the plant makes you so happy. Your aura is glowing."

Sage and Hector talked a bit more about south Florida horticulture and what's edible and what's not. She promised to come back again before she left for Brooklyn. I felt a pang at the thought of her leaving.

I opened the jeep's tailgate. Judging by the pots and baskets, it seemed like Sage had overbought, but I didn't care. In fact, I couldn't remember the last time I was this carefree. The moms were here. Everything would be okay.

CHAPTER THIRTY-ONE

We dropped Skully back at Pastor John's church. I got out and helped him unload some beautyberry plants that Hector had sent along as a gift to the church. As I was closing the tailgate I lowered my voice so Sage wouldn't hear.

"Thanks for the tip about Oscar's boat. I found the *Jersey Girl* on Pine Island, just as you said, but before I could search it, a security guard chased me away. Do you have any idea how I could find out what's on the boat?"

"Little Miss, there is only one thing to be done . . ."

I waited for Skully's best idea.

"Tell those young fellers in the sheriff's office. Let them do the searching. Whatever they find will likely help get Bridgy out from under their watchful eyes. They are trained to find things. You're not."

Disappointed though I was, I had to admit

he was right.

When Sage and I got back to the Read 'Em and Eat, Bridgy and Emelia had finished the dining room cleanup. I could hear them in the kitchen. Ophie was sitting at Emily Dickinson with her cell phone to her ear. She touched her index finger to her lips in the universal "shush" sign. We froze for a moment and then tiptoed past her. In the kitchen Bridgy and Emelia were unloading the dishwasher while Miguel was hanging a sparkling-clean apron on a hook for the next day.

"How was your garden trip?"

Sage was so enthusiastic that she didn't realize Miguel was more polite than interested. She sprang into a long speech about elderberry wine and then moved on to ground nuts and potato beans, which may or may not have been the same thing. It was hard to tell, but it did sound like Sage was using the terms interchangeably.

By the time Sage moved on to the healing properties of echinacea, Bridgy was rolling her eyes at me and touching her hands in a prayerful pose as if begging me to make Sage stop. But I was newly appreciative of my mother's unswerving support and was perfectly content to let her babble along.

Fortunately, Ophie burst into the room,

337

just ending her phone call.

"Thank y'all so kindly." She clicked off the phone and did a little dance, scary to watch with those mile-high sandals on her feet. She waited, an expectant smile on her face. When no one asked why she was so excited, she caved.

"Emy, darlin', yesterday y'all asked me about the shrimping history of Fort Myers Beach. Told me Bridgy mentioned the Working Waterfront Tour run by our local chamber of commerce. I called the chamber office and, being an active member" — Ophie raised a hand and waved at us as though she were the Queen of England — "I have, this very minute, arranged for a private tour for the three of us, first thing tomorrow. Sage, y'all coming with?"

Sage said, "Absolutely, I wouldn't miss a chance to study the waterfront up close and personal. Ophie, you're sweet as a hyacinth. Thanks ever so much for arranging the tour."

"*Señoras,* you will enjoy yourselves immensely. Did you know Lee County is one of the most important counties in Florida when it comes to harvesting seafood? And the shrimp that comes in on San Carlos Island is so fine, so fresh.

"I have an idea. Before you leave, I will

order pounds and pounds of shrimp and we will have our own shrimp festival. *La fiesta* will be at my house. And you can meet my sweet Bow. She will eat one boiled shrimp, chopped very fine. We'll all eat dozens of shrimp cooked in a variety of ways."

We were all clapping and cheering when the kitchen door pushed open. "How many times do I have to tell you to lock the front door when everyone is in the kitchen?" Ryan Mantoni stood in the doorway. "And what's this about a *fiesta*? Who's having a party?"

"You are invited, *mi amigo,* and bring the lieutenant. We need to pick a date and make a list of friends . . ." Miguel trailed off when he realized Ryan was wearing his well-pressed dark green uniform. "You're here officially, aren't you?"

" 'Fraid so. I need to talk to Sassy for a minute. Don't mind us. You go right on planning the party." He waved me into the dining room.

"I know the lieutenant called Owen to let him know that Tammy Rushing had turned up in South Carolina. I figured you'd be disappointed that we didn't arrest her straightaway."

"I was at first, but then I realized if her reason for running had to do with money and her ex, she likely had nothing to do with

339

Oscar's murder."

"That's why you shouldn't run for sheriff in the next election. Never bet on the 'likely.' I'm here, off the record, to let you know that while South Carolina and Alabama are getting their paperwork done, we are sending Tina Wei and another deputy to interview Tammy one more time. Maybe there is something that connects her to Oscar. Something we missed the first time around."

My heart soared. "Thanks for telling me." I head-butted toward the kitchen. "I won't say anything. It wouldn't do to get Bridgy's hopes up that this mess will be over sooner rather than later."

The kitchen door opened, and Ophie came out with a piece of buttermilk pie and set it down in front of Ryan.

He jumped up and gave her a kiss on the cheek. "Miss Ophelia, you do know the way to a man's heart. I will always bless the day that you brought your buttermilk pie recipe to the Read 'Em and Eat, and your lovely self along with it."

Ophie fluttered her eyelashes and gave Ryan a gentle pat. "Aren't y'all a handsome, sweet-talking man, and couldn't y'all charm the eagles right out of the sky?"

When she offered coffee, I smiled and,

hoping she'd take the hint, said, "Ryan is in a hurry and barely has time to eat your luscious pie."

"Well, okay, then. Holler if you need anything." And she sashayed back into the kitchen.

Before we were interrupted again I asked, "And Lolly? Any word about Lolly?"

Ryan swallowed a huge chunk of pie before he answered. "Lolly's name is Conrad Lolis. All anyone seems to know is that he went off to look for a job on the mainland. That could mean anywhere in Lee County or the entire state of Florida or all of North America, who knows?"

I gave him a withering look, and he lost his flippant tone.

"Unless we get lucky like we did with Tammy, it could take a good long while before we find Lolly and can question him. We've interviewed all his friends, called the one out-of-state relative that we know of, a sister out in west Texas, but all she could say is that he was looking to change jobs. He never told her he was fired from the *Fisherman's Dream,* and she had never heard of Oscar."

The laughter and chatter in the kitchen sounded so normal, and yet here I sat with Ryan, talking about murder.

I took a deep breath. "Have you searched Oscar's boat, the *Jersey Girl,* yet?"

Ryan gave me a sharp look. "Oscar's boat? How do you know Oscar had a boat? No, don't tell me." For a second I thought he was going to cover his ears in "hear no evil" monkey style, but then he continued. "You better tell me. The lieutenant is going to want to know."

When I mentioned Skully and Tony, Ryan chuckled. "Should have known. Nothing floats on these waters that one or the other of those two don't know all about, including the size of the engine or the manufacturer of the paddles."

"There is one other thing."

Ryan turned serious. "Go ahead."

"A security guard at the repair shop found me on the boat, and I, ah, pretended to be Oscar's niece."

"Good to know. This way when the security team gives us the information, we won't go to wherever and back looking for a niece who doesn't exist." There was no chuckle left in his voice. "So, did you remove anything from the boat? Steal a clue or two?"

I tried to muster up some indignation, but we both knew I was capable of being "helpful," and if I'd seen anything that I considered suspicious, I'd have picked it up.

"No. I wasn't on the boat long enough. It's a thirty-footer with a decent-sized cabin. I didn't have enough time."

"Don't look so disappointed. We'll give it a good going-over. If there is anything there, we'll find it." He looked at the clock over the door, grabbed his napkin and ran it across his mouth. "Got to run. Thanks for the info, and tell Miss Ophelia the pie was lip-smackin' good."

I locked the door behind Ryan and brought his plate into the kitchen where the party-planning committee was in full swing.

Sage said she would dress up as Madam Dora the Aura Reader and entertain the guests. Normally, I blanched when she volunteered to show her wacky side beyond family gatherings, but today I just beamed.

Bridgy elbowed me in the ribs. "What is wrong with you? You are glowing as if we found a new kitten and your mother said you could keep it."

"That actually happened. Third grade, remember? Black-and-white little fuzz ball. I named her Oreo." And I blew a kiss to Sage, who caught it with her left hand, pasted it to her lips and blew one back to me.

Miguel was busy taking notes as Ophie

343

and the moms were throwing suggestions at him.

"We have to have pie."

"What about music? Is there room to dance?"

"Oh, and lots of young men. We need young men to dance with our daughters." That one certainly proved that Emelia was related to Ophie.

Finally, Bridgy clapped her hands like a kindergarten teacher. "Enough party planning for today. If you ladies want to stop at Times Square to do more shopping, we better get to it. Let Miguel get out of here. Bow will be wondering where he is."

"*Ay, sí,* she will be looking for her treat. Each day after work I give her a tasty treat, to let her know I did not forget about her while I was gone. You will finish here?"

I nodded. "Of course. Come, I'll lock the door behind you." At the door I said, "I think the party will cheer Bridgy no end. Thank you for thinking of it."

Miguel smiled. *"Mañana,"* he said, and he left, but not before clanging the ship's bell in farewell.

When I went back into the kitchen everyone was in such a festive mood that I made a mental note that we should have parties more often.

"I wish I could go to Times Square with y'all, but I have a late appointment at the Treasure Trove. A decorator from Sanibel looking for special items for a fussy client. *Ca-ching.*" And Ophie was out the door.

Sage wanted to go back to the Turret to stash her plants and seedlings. It took two trips on the elevator to get them all upstairs. With piles of palm fronds stashed on one end of the patio and the potted plants, flats of seedlings and baskets of herbs spread around on tables and the floor, there was barely room to move.

Were it not for my newfound appreciation of her motherly love, I would have been counting the days until Sage flew home so I could get rid of all this greenery and make the patio livable again. But for now, patio or no patio, being with Sage gave me the warm fuzzies. We decided to walk along the beach to Times Square. Sage looped her arm through mine. "You know, my sweet hydrangea, Emelia and I are onto your tricks."

I did some mental gymnastics, trying to figure out where Sage was heading. Which of my tricks had she caught on to? I decided silence was my best option, although I knew I wouldn't get away with it for long.

CHAPTER THIRTY-TWO

For a while we were distracted by the beauty of strolling along the water's edge. It was very late in the afternoon, and we watched a mellow sun move toward the horizon. The beachgoers were beginning to head home for dinner, and the seabirds were flapping around, looking for a snack.

We were nearly at the pier when Sage broke the silence. "Emelia and I are not stupid, you know. We only had to be here for a few hours to see what's really going on; to understand why we never get invited here together. Bridgy's family and your family. We're always forced to take turns visiting."

Okay, so I was mystified. Where was she going with this? I couldn't think of a "trick" I'd ever pulled that would lead to this conversation. I decided to remain quiet until I could figure out where this was going.

"The two of you are super busy all the

time. Between the café and the book clubs, when do you take time for yourselves? Never, that's when."

I was getting a glimmer of where she was headed, and it wasn't anywhere I wanted to go. I tried to distract Sage by pointing out an exceptionally pretty seashell half hidden by seafoam, but it didn't work.

She refused to so much as look at the water's edge. "There will be plenty of time for seashells. Right now I want you and Bridgy to commit to a vacation. Not just a few hours for one of you to do something while the other one does the work of two. That is no way for young girls to live. A few days off will put some sparkle in your aura, and it will dust off Bridgy's, for sure."

"Sage . . . Mom . . ."

"Don't 'Mom' me. It's already settled. Emelia and I are sending you and Bridgy for some definite R and R. Did you think we were kidding when we talked about Key West? We are perfectly capable of taking your place in the café. Done deal."

"We can't burden Miguel that way . . ." As soon as the words were out of my mouth, I knew a colossal blunder when I uttered one.

"Burden?"

If I believed in auras, at that moment I

was sure Sage's aura was thundercloud black. I braced myself.

"Burden," Sage repeated. "Is that what you and Bridgy think of your mothers? We are a *burden* to you? We would be a huge help. You don't expect Miguel to cook *and* to serve, do you? The man only has two hands."

I was losing patience. "We appreciate the offer. We really do, but . . ."

"Don't 'but' me. You're moving right into your favorite trick. You and Bridgy can't possibly leave the Read 'Em and Eat at the same time. The sky will indeed fall in! Ha."

I hadn't seen Sage so worked up since a family wedding about five years ago when my father's aunt Cecily insisted that there was no such thing as auras. I decided to just let Sage ramble. Any interruption was sure to excite her further.

"Everything has to be scheduled around you. When you were a child we used to take shared vacations with Bridgy's family, but now Emelia and I can never plan a vacation for both families. Our daughters are too busy. Too busy, you call it. But that's not it. The problem is that you treat the Read 'Em and Eat like a new puppy that can't be left alone just yet."

Never was I so grateful to hear Ophie yoo-

348

hooing at me. She was standing at the entrance to the pier and waving a paisley scarf with drops of lemon sprinkled on swaths of pink, blue and green.

"Have you seen Bridgy and Emy? I thought every one of y'all was coming over here to Times Square, so I rushed my new client out the door and hurried down to join the fun, and here I stand all by my lonesome."

"We went home to drop off Sage's plants," I explained. "They know we're meeting here. Perhaps they're in one of the shops."

"No, there they are." Sage pointed, and I saw Bridgy and Emelia walking across the plaza. They stopped to watch a busker juggling three colorfully striped beach balls. He spun the small and large balls one on each of his index fingers. The medium ball bobbled on his forehead. The busker wiggled slightly to the left, and suddenly, the balls changed places. The large ball landed on his nose, and he flipped it back and forth from his nose to the crown of his head, still spinning the other two on his fingers. Just one more reason to love hanging out in Times Square anytime of the day or night.

Bridgy linked her arm through Emelia's, and they strolled over to join us.

Emelia said, "We just took a walk

along . . . what is that street?"

"Old San Carlos Boulevard," Bridgy answered.

"There are so many lovely shops. Sage, after we finish scouring the stores here on the square for every little treasure, we'll have to spend some time over there." Emelia waved across Estero Boulevard.

"Wait until you hear which shop really caught Mom's eye. I had to drag her away."

"I'll bet she wanted to try on every single dress in the cute little boutique up by Second Street. Emy was always one to fall in love with chic dresses."

Bridgy laughed. "Not even close, Aunt Ophie."

I saw Emelia give Bridgy a small elbow nudge, which sent Bridgy's laugh into a full-on giggle. Finally, she controlled herself enough to say, "The tattoo parlor. Mom *loved* the tattoo parlor. I had to drag her out."

Ophie's eyes popped. "What on earth were you doing inside? Did you get a tattoo?"

"Don't look so alarmed. I was only looking around. They do tattooing and piercing. The store is immaculate and decorated with beautifully framed pictures of tattoo work. It's art, pure and simple. And the jewelry they sell to go with the piercings, why some of the pieces were exceptional." Emelia watched Ophie's face change and continued on before her sister got miffed. "Not as exquisite as the items you have in the Treasure Trove, of course."

Ophie accepted the compliment with a shout. "Let the shopping begin."

I pointed to the tables in front of the ice cream store. "Let's meet back here for cones and cups in an hour. Agreed?"

Ophie and the moms nodded, waved and, anxious to browse every store imaginable, disappeared into the crowd.

Bridgy looked at me. "Do you want to walk the pier or would you rather hit the beach and meditate?"

"I need the walk, especially if we are going to have dessert later. Is it my imagination or are we eating way too much in the way of treats since the moms came to town?"

Bridgy mulled that over. "It could be the moms. I'm inclined to think it's our reaction to Oscar's murder."

We walked silently along the pier, watching tourists taking pictures from every possible angle. Someone yelled, "Oh look, a parasail." And a dozen people rushed to the railing, holding up cameras and cell phones.

A small boy in a blue and green tee shirt

with the Seattle Seahawks emblem on the front pushed past me. "Where?"

A teenager wearing the exact same shirt grabbed him by the arm. "This way, pipsqueak. You can see it better from this side."

"Got it."

I smiled at their enthusiasm for things we see every day. In fact, it wasn't so long ago that Bridgy treated me to a parasail ride for my make-believe birthday. It was quite an adventure. I looked up at the sail, a bright orange puff gliding past even puffier white clouds.

"We should go parasailing again sometime soon."

Bridgy agreed. "But not with Tony the Boatman's cousin Darrin. He's too touchy-feely for me. Imagine if Tony hadn't gone on the boat with us. Trapped with Darrin." She shuddered.

We ambled past the bait shop and headed for the covered seating area near the end of the pier. We took two seats and watched a fisherman cast off. We were facing Sanibel Island and could see house lights begin to twinkle. Another gorgeous sunset would be ours to view soon.

"Is your mom bugging you about sending us to Key West?"

"Yep. And Sage, is she pushing you to go?"

"Ordering me is more like it. She seems to think that the café is coming between us and our families, and not just by geography." I shrugged my shoulders. "They think work keeps us too busy to enjoy life."

"Why can't they understand how really happy we are. Our lives are perfect. Or, at least, we'll be back to perfect as soon as Oscar's killer is caught." Bridgy looked at her phone. "We better start back. It is almost ice cream time."

We stepped off the pier just as Ophie and the moms came around the corner from the shopping strip. They were carrying lots of bags and packages. Sage was particularly weighed down.

Before we could ask how the shopping went, Ophie said, "Y'all will never guess who we met and what *she* didn't know."

We knew better than to speculate. Ophie could play "guess what" for hours. Both Bridgy and I raised our hands as if caught in the cookie jar and surrendered instantly.

"It was that woman from the book club. The one with the superior attitude."

Emelia helped her sister. "You know, the one we met with her husband when we went to visit Randy Wayne White."

Ophie chuffed at her sister. "You visited Randy Wayne White without me?"

I interceded before the bickering got out of hand. "Ophie, you know we had dinner at Doc Ford's the other night. Randy Wayne wasn't there." Hopefully that ended that. I moved on. "So what you're saying is you met Margo Wellington?"

Three heads nodded in unison.

"She was quick to tell us that Tammy Rushing had been arrested. Seemed almost gleeful." I could see that Margo's elation annoyed Ophie no end.

Emelia chimed in. "I think she is one of those people who is proud to be the first one to announce the local gossip. She was just hoping we didn't know. She turned dejected the minute Ophie told her that the person she was talking about was arrested for alimony, not murder. Annoyed her that Ophie was higher on the gossip chain than she was."

Sage agreed. "Definitely. I told you before that woman has a difficult aura, but when Ophie out-gossiped her, well all I can say is that her aura turned mean. I've never seen anything like it. All cloudy dark green and murky brown woven through wide streaks of black. Negativity galore, and her energy centers are totally blocked. She is suffering from envy and misery. I bet the poor lamb doesn't even know why."

Again, it was my job to change the topic before we had to listen to lengthy descriptions of the muddy auras Sage has known.

"Let's find a table and buy some sweet treats. Then you can show us what you bought." I tried to move them in the direction of several empty tables, but Ophie held out her hand and circled her wrist to show off a wide silver bangle bracelet. She raised her arm high. "Emy bought it for me. Read what it says."

I read aloud. "#1 SISTER."

Ophie beamed. Emy gave her a quick hug. Bridgy, Sage and I clapped. As I looked at the laughing faces around me, I could only hope that the cloud of Oscar's murder that hung over us would be lifted soon.

CHAPTER THIRTY-THREE

Early the next morning everyone was flying around the Turret at warp speed. Bridgy and I needed to get to the café, Sage wanted to get her tai chi finished early and Emelia was determined to change all the bed linens before Ophie came to take the moms to the Working Waterfront Tour on San Carlos Island.

As soon as we got into the elevator, Bridgy half whispered, "Thank goodness Mom and Aunt Ophie are back to being bestie sisters. Ophie should be able to keep them out of our hair all day."

"You don't have to whisper. The moms can't hear us in here."

"Remember what they used to tell us?"

Together we bellowed, "A MOTHER'S EYES AND EARS ARE EVERYWHERE."

Of course that was the exact moment the elevator door opened and nearly everyone in the Beausoleil lobby turned to see what the uproar was all about. Blushing, we scurried out to the parking lot, climbed into the Heap-a-Jeep and headed off to work.

We took it as an omen when Sister Sledge came on the radio singing "He's the Greatest Dancer." As soon as the song stopped, Bridgy turned the radio off and we both began to sing "We Are Family." Every time we got to the word "sisters," we blasted a major shout-out in honor of lasting peace between the Brice babes.

As always, Miguel had the kitchen up and running by the time Bridgy and I arrived at the Read 'Em and Eat. He looked past us at the kitchen door as it swung shut.

"Where are the moms? I was getting used to them."

"Be grateful for a day without Emelia double scrubbing every possible surface and Sage trying to inspire you to cook with fresh herbs, while deciding what customers should and shouldn't eat based entirely on an aura that only she can see."

Miguel asked Bridgy to check the buttermilk pies in the oven and then looked at me. "*Chica,* the moms are trying to help you and to render support in this crisis. Be grateful for that. The rest, it is not so bad."

I knew he was right and said so. Then I heard the insistent gong of the brass ship's bell that hung outside our front door. Customers. The day had officially begun.

Toward the end of the breakfast rush, Tina Wei came in for a to-go cup of sweet tea. She looked very professional in her dark green sheriff's deputy uniform. I noticed her pants had a sharp crease straight down each leg.

As I was filling the container, I asked if she wanted a pastry. She leaned over the counter and said, "Ryan sent a message."

Knowing Ryan, I predicted, "He wants to know if Miguel has made any of those double chocolate chip mini muffins that were such a hit on the specials board last month."

Tina smiled and then turned serious. "I'm sure he'll want to know about the muffins, but he wanted me to tell you, with the lieutenant's permission, that interviewing Tammy Rushing was a big old wash. There was no Oscar Frieland in her past, no intersecting geography whatsoever, and when pressed, she claimed that she dropped her things in the trunk of her car and hurried into the café to use the restroom. When she came out of the restroom, Blondie Quinlin was standing in the alcove waiting her turn. Blondie verified the story, as did Augusta Maddox, who was sitting at one of the front tables waiting for Blondie so they could get seats next to each other at the book club meeting. Would have been less stress for all concerned if Tammy had mentioned that in her first interview."

I guess my disappointment showed, because Tina patted my hand and said, "Don't worry. Everyone knows Bridgy could never . . ."

Bridgy swung out of the kitchen with a plate in each hand. Tina faked quickly. "So what do you want me to tell Ryan about those muffins?"

I appreciated her change of topic. "Tell him I'll check with Miguel and let him know."

I offered drink refills to the lingering customers and then began wiping down the empty tables and chairs, getting ready for the lunch rush.

Three ladies came in and asked for a table. The one with the beet red, day-old sunburn said they needed to sit where they could have what she called a "protracted, talky meal," because they hadn't seen one another in a while.

I'd barely got them settled at Barbara Cartland when Ophie came through the door. She was both alone and breathless.

A man on a gray walker with yellow tennis balls on two tips and a fragile birdlike woman signaled from the Robert Louis Stevenson table that they were ready to pay their bill. By the time I brought back their change, she'd opened his walker and helped him stand. The gentleman left a generous tip on the table and told me that they'd be back before they went home to Maine. "The missus likes your breakfast better than anyone's 'cept maybe her own." And he pointed his walker toward the door. Ophie rushed to open it, and I walked alongside his purposeful steps until they were outside.

As the door swung shut behind them, Ophie grabbed my arm. "Where's Bridgy?"

"Kitchen. Why? And how was the tour? Where are the moms?"

Ophie ignored my questions. She looked around the room and nodded to herself. Apparently, she was content with what she saw, only three occupied tables each with customers that were keeping themselves busy. Ophie pushed me ahead of her into the kitchen.

Inexplicably, she burst out laughing. "Y'all should have been there. We had a fine time. The tour started at the Marine Science Center, where they taught us more than I ever wanted to know about the fish around here."

"Aunt Ophie." There was an edge of impatience in Bridgy's voice. "Where are the moms?"

"Oh, they'll be along directly. Wanted to stop at the Turret to buff up a bit. I suppose I could use a bit of cleaning up myself." She flicked an imaginary speck off the bodice of her cherry red surplice dress, cinched with a wide black patent leather belt that matched her spiky sandals. How she trotted all over San Carlos Island from shrimp boats to packing houses to the processing plant in those shoes amazed me.

"But I needed to tell y'all . . ."

Ophie turned her head until she had all three of us in her sights. "At the end of the tour we were walking back to my car, parked in that big lot behind the Marine Science Center, and who comes a-clumping across the parking lot? None other than the witchy pastor's wife."

"Jocelyn? What was she doing there?"

"Poor put-upon thing. She was picking up some pamphlets about an event geared for middle school kids. Said Pastor John wanted the information for the parish youth program. Don't think she didn't complain. Talked about how Pastor John could never get anything done if it wasn't for her. It was her usual patter until . . ."

Ophie waited long enough to get us on the verge of asking, "And then?"

"Until she asked if there was any news about Oscar's murder. 'Course, even if I had news, I'd never give it to her. Anyway, I said I hadn't heard a peep. And I was about to introduce her to your mothers, when Jocelyn said that she was truly and deeply shocked that the meddlesome Sassy and Bridgy hadn't stuck their noses into the investigation. And she prodded me to search my memory for incidents of all the worry the 'meddlesome twosome' had caused in the past.

"I give your mothers credit. They stood silently by, waiting for me to drop a rock on Jocelyn's toe, so to speak. And drop it I did."

"How did she respond when you told her that she was complaining about us to our very own moms?"

Ophie stretched her neck like a proud peacock. "I am gratified to report that Jocelyn had the good grace to turn green and to change the subject right back to the parish youth program."

Bridgy asked, "And the moms didn't smack her?"

"No, they thought it was hilarious that Jocelyn mistook your innate kindness and called it meddling. Emy said she felt sorry for Pastor John, and that was after spending less than ten minutes with Jocelyn."

Miguel interrupted our laughter. "You remind me. The shrimp *fiesta* is set for my house tomorrow evening. I ordered the shrimp and will pick it up right after work. Please come around six."

"Now that sounds grand. Y'all can count on me. I'm not one to miss a party. Well, I'd best get over to the Treasure Trove and pick up my messages. I have an appointment in . . . oh, in ten minutes. Bye now."

I was cheered and considerably energized by Ophie's Jocelyn story and Miguel's invitation. I could see that Bridgy was, too, which was a good thing, because the lunch crowd swamped us. When the lunch hour began, every table was filled within minutes. Soon we had a large crowd waiting outside. The day was unseasonably hot for March, so I set up a pitcher of iced lemon water alongside a sleeve of paper cups on the outside table.

Finally, the tide of diners dwindled. I was serving two orders of *Green Eggs and Ham* when Emelia opened the front door and held it for Sage, who was carrying a huge box. Ignoring the fact that I had a plate filled with food in each hand, Sage called, "Oh, my little hibiscus, could you help me?"

I set the plates in front of two surfer dudes sitting at Robert Frost and rushed to the doorway. By the time I got there, Emelia had put a hand under the box to steady it.

"Sage, what on earth?"

"Just set this box in a corner somewhere. Careful, it is fragile. I'll be right back with the rest." With Emelia at her heels, Sage turned and disappeared into the parking lot.

I pushed the box behind the counter and noticed a package on the shelf under the register. I'd forgotten about the copy of *The Florida Life of Thomas Edison* that Sonja had left for Margo. I made a mental note about the book, pushed the box in the corner and turned to find a customer at the register, a twenty-dollar bill in his hand. "Keep the change. We really enjoyed lunch. Great service, too."

Sage came in carrying a flat box filled with a half dozen large conch shells. She set the box down on the counter. "Where is my other box? Oh, I see it. And I need to talk to Miguel. He and I are going to help these shells support life once again."

And she gave me a thousand-watt smile while I was busy trying to think of a way to protect Miguel from Sage's enthusiasm for whatever the project might be.

CHAPTER THIRTY-FOUR

I tried to distract Sage by offering her a glass of sweet tea. I needed a plan to keep her away from Miguel, which didn't seem possible, since they were about twelve feet apart with only the kitchen door between them.

And of course, Miguel picked that exact moment to come through that very door.

"Sassy, about tomorrow night, I thought I might . . . *Hola* Sage, I didn't know you were back. And Emelia. Did you enjoy your tour? I hope it put you in the mood for the shrimp *fiesta* at my house tomorrow night."

The moms raved about the tour and practically squealed with delight at the news of the party. But then Sage ruined it all. "I have a surprise for you, Miguel." And she pointed to the box of shells.

Muddled for an instant, Miguel gave some version of "thank you, they're lovely," but Sage wasn't having it.

She pointed to the large box I had stashed behind the counter. "There's so much more."

More shells?

The final customer of the day, a mother with two small children, interrupted to pay for their meal. Bridgy took her money and said she hoped to see them again soon, while I mentally wished the kids well and hoped their mother was a bit easier to understand than Sage. Through all this, Emelia stood off to the side, her face filled with the expectant excitement of someone who was watching the birthday child open the best present ever.

I could see that Miguel was puzzled, but I was in no position to help. Sage began to tell him that basil is the easiest herb to grow and maintain. She opened the box that I'd set on the floor and pulled out some newspapers and spread them on the counter. Whatever she was up to, I realized this would be a great time to lock the door. We didn't need customers at this moment.

Sage removed two disposable bowls covered with plastic lids from the big box and set them on the newspapers. When she popped the lid on one, dirt spilled out onto the newspaper.

"Miguel, pass your favorite shell to me."

He stood rooted to the spot, so Sage elbowed him into action. "They are all so lovely, I know it is hard to decide, but, well, why not take the large one in the center."

Obediently, Miguel handed the tan and white shell to Sage, who placed it in the center of the newspaper. "Now watch. I am filling the shell with rich compost soil." She opened the second bowl and took out a few tiny rocks. "Aeration."

Sage mixed the rocks into the soil and bent down into the big box. This time she came up with two seedlings. "Basil, lovely and green."

Sage went on, blissfully unaware that she was the only one happy and excited about this project. When she finished securing the basil seedling in the shell, she held it up for all to see. "Thank goodness I didn't buy that other seashell. It was completely wrong. How nice of your friend to point that out to me."

As is often the case, I had no idea who Sage was talking about. I asked which friend, but Sage ignored me and continued. "I was standing in the shop with a gorgeous shell in my hand. Next thing your friend came along and said hello. When I told her about Miguel's herb garden . . ."

Miguel blanched more than a little.

"Well, as soon as I mentioned the garden, she pointed to this shell. She told me the one I had was a knobby, no, a knobbed whelk, but she said I needed this one because the horse conch is the Florida state shell. She saw it in a guidebook."

Sage placed a rock at each end of the conch shell opening and stepped back to admire her handiwork. Experience taught me that she was capable of puttering forever. Both Miguel and Bridgy were drilling me with their eyes, silently demanding that I make this end and fast. I decided to ask Sage the name of the woman she met in the shell shop. Maybe I could get Sage to focus on the woman's aura or clothes or something, anything to distract her from the plan of forcing Miguel to have an herb garden planted in seashells.

I was about to ask if Sage knew the woman's name, when Sage said, "Oh, and she said if I am ever in New Jersey, that is where I should look for a knobbed whelk because it is the New Jersey state shell. And, as foodies, you will love this. She said the Italian word for the marine snail inside the knobbed whelk is *scungilli*. As if I hadn't eaten that a hundred times at my aunt Loretta's house complete with vinegar and oil, peppers and tomato."

Together, Bridgy and I nearly shouted, "Who? Who talked to you about the shells?"

"You don't have to yell. Didn't I mention? It was your friend, the one with the husband. You remember, we met them at Doc Ford's. We told you we met her when we were shopping in Times Square."

Bridgy and I exchanged looks. Margo, the one person who said she'd never been to the northeast, and yet she knew the state shell for New Jersey. Something was wrong.

I motioned Bridgy into the kitchen, leaving poor Miguel to fend for himself.

I may have been a little overexcited, because Bridgy felt compelled to remind me that I'd warned her about jumping to wrong conclusions. "Maybe Margo just loves seashells."

She had no chance of convincing me. I was determined to talk to Margo.

"Sassy, stop. We don't even know where she lives. Can't we wait until she drops in again and casually thank her for helping Sage?"

Bridgy's words flew right by me. I already had my cell phone out, grateful that I had Maggie Latimer on speed dial. Since she knew where Tammy rented for the winter, she could probably lead us to Margo as well. And she did.

I thanked Maggie and punched the "Off" button on my phone. Then it hit me. What do we do with the moms? I knew I couldn't leave Sage here tormenting Miguel. That would almost certainly lead to our having no chef tomorrow morning.

I hit another speed dial button. "Ophie, do you have a reason to need the moms right away?"

"Y'all are the answer to my prayers. I just got a jewelry delivery, and I am having a problem deciding on my display space. I could use some extra eyes."

I pushed through the kitchen door. Miguel was as frozen as a deer caught in a Chevy Silverado's headlights. When I announced that Ophie had an emergency and needed the moms right away, I could swear I heard Miguel mumble, "*Gracias,* Ophie."

Sage protested. "What about my seedlings?"

Miguel diverted the potential catastrophe. "No problem, I will set them up on a rack in the slop sink. Nice, moist atmosphere, and we will take care of them *mañana.*"

Once Miguel convinced Sage he'd take excellent care of her seedlings, she was quite willing to leave the shell and basil garden until the morning in order to check out Ophie's emergency. The moms began to gather their things. I took the opportunity to slip behind the counter and pick up the bag with Margo's copy of *The Florida Life of Thomas Edison*.

We left Miguel to take care of the seedlings and walked over to the Treasure Trove with the moms, who were so delighted that Ophie's "emergency" involved jewelry that they barely heard us say good-bye.

We were halfway to the Heap-a-Jeep when Cady pulled into the parking lot.

"I guess I'm too late for coffee and pie."

For a minute I was tempted to tell him to knock on the door of the café and Miguel would give him a slice on the house, but I'd already burdened Miguel with shells and basil plants. I didn't think I should push it.

I held up Sonja's bag with the book in it. "We have to return this book to Margo Wellington." It sounded lame to me, but only because I knew my real intent. I owned a bookstore and I organized book clubs. What would be more normal than returning a clubbie's book?

"It's our cover." Bridgy sounded like a crook in a heist movie.

I rolled my eyes, but Cady took no notice of me. He sounded baffled. "Her book wound up in your book jacket?"

Bridgy grew frustrated. "No. It's our

371

cover, you know, like our *reason* for visiting her."

I watched Cady get it. "Oh no. Whatever you two think you are doing, don't. Just don't."

"It's probably nothing, but . . ." We told him about the knobbed whelk and the horse conch shells. I finished with, "Now honestly, would you know which was which?"

Cady groaned. "You are going to accuse this woman of murder because she knows the name of the New Jersey state shell?"

I waved him off. "Don't be silly. We're just going to return her book and . . . and invite her to a party so we can talk to her some more."

"What party? And why would she want to come?"

Bridgy chimed in, "Because Miguel is the best chef on the island, and we're all invited to his house tomorrow night for shrimp prepared a dozen different ways."

Cady waggled a finger between us. "Come on. Are you two making this up?"

I knew Miguel liked Cady and would text or email him an invitation, so I jumped the gun.

"No. There is a real party, and you are invited. If it makes you feel better, Ryan and Frank Anthony are invited, so we can all talk about Margo Wellington, Oscar and the seashells then. Unless she shows up, of course. In that case our own expert" — I pointed to Bridgy — "will start a conversation about some popular Florida seashells, and we can gauge Margo's level of enthusiasm."

Cady ran his hand over the top of his head, flattening his hair as he always did when making a decision. "If you are determined to see her, go ahead, but I am going to follow along behind you. If you are not out of her house within ten minutes after she opens the door, I am coming in."

CHAPTER THIRTY-FIVE

We drove south on Estero Boulevard and turned off on one of the canals south of the Matanzas Pass Preserve. The address Maggie gave me was a cheery pink bungalow with a white and black striped awning covering the front door. The driveway was extra wide, so I turned in, while Cady pulled up at the corner.

As if on cue, the front door opened and Margo's husband came out carrying suitcases, which he piled in the trunk. He had an iPad in his hand. He waved at us and yelled through the open door. "Margo, your friends are here to say good-bye."

Bridgy and I got out of the Heap-a-Jeep, but it was obvious Margo wasn't happy to see us. "Nice of you to stop by, but we are in a hurry to get on the road. We're planning to make Georgia by nightfall."

Her husband nipped that in the bud. "We'll be on the road for days, Margo. Why not spend a few minutes with your friends? You won't see them again until next winter." Then he sat sideways in the passenger seat of the car, stretched his legs out in the driveway and began to fiddle with his iPad. I glanced over at the street and saw that Cady was watching us intently. I wanted to tell him, "Nothing to see here."

I tried to give the book to Margo, but she pushed it back at me. "I have so many books. My shelves at home are stuffed. Do me a favor, please, and donate it to the library. We really have to go."

This was getting harder. I tried another tack. "It's too bad you can't stay another few days. We are having a shrimp *fiesta* tomorrow night."

Margo shook her head, but her husband's ears perked right up. He stepped out of the car. "Sweetie, the lease here isn't up until the weekend. If you want to stay . . ."

"I *told* you I have a medical appointment at home that I cannot miss. We have to leave today, right now."

Clearly trying to plot our next step, Bridgy made a long, drawn-out speech about how nice it was to meet Margo and that she hoped next year would find us all together again.

Margo began tapping her foot to an ever-increasing beat. Finally, she began massaging her temples and she leaned in toward Bridgy. "Honestly, it has been lovely, but I need to leave now, and you are holding us up."

I took one last stab. "Okay, but before we get out of your way, I want to thank you for helping my mother pick out the right shell."

A bit of confusion morphed into the palpable impatience in her face. Perfect.

"It would be a shame for her to go home from a trip to Florida with a shell that represents New Jersey."

It was as though a fire alarm sounded and we were trapped in a fifth-floor walk-up. Margo slammed the car trunk shut and yelled at her husband to get in the car. Uncertain, he obeyed. She jumped into the driver's seat, screamed at him to shut his door and then darn near hit Bridgy while trying to back out of the driveway. Cady ran across the street and stood at the bottom of the driveway, waving his arms to flag her down. Nothing was going to stop Margo. She aimed right for him. He was barely able to jump out of the way.

She was almost at the curb when a sheriff's department car screeched to a halt, blocking her exit. Frank Anthony and Ryan Mantoni jumped out of the car and ordered

Margo to stop. With their guns pointed directly at her, she didn't have much choice. She turned off the engine and began sobbing. Ryan opened her car door, and she slid out, her knees buckled and she had to grab on to the roof of the car in order to stand.

Her husband, completely bewildered, leaned across the seat and asked Ryan politely, "Should I get out, too?"

At the sound of his voice, Margo cracked completely. "This is all your fault. We should have gotten out of town when we had the chance." And she burst into tears.

Bridgy and I spent a long night at the sheriff's office explaining why we were at Margo's in the first place.

We sat alone in an interview room for hours. Finally, Ryan came in with Lieutenant Frank Anthony, who stood in the doorway, shaking his head. "You should thank your lucky stars that Cady didn't like Margo Wellington's attitude and called Ryan based on his newsman's intuition. Or you" — he pointed to Bridgy — "might be under the wheels of Margo Wellington's shiny silver BMW. It has all-wheel drive. She could have rolled back and forth a dozen times."

I was more used to being chastised by the

lieutenant than Bridgy was, but from the sound of it, this lecture was going to be one of the milder ones. We'd probably get out with our eardrums intact.

With our hands folded on the table like attentive kindergartners during story time, Bridgy and I exchanged a glance, but neither of us said a word.

Once Frank and Ryan sat down and turned on the tape recorder, the conversation began in earnest.

Frank made a little speech into the recorder, saying who we were and why he was taping the conversation. He used military language to state the time and ended with the date. Then the questions started. He wanted to know why we visited Margo. (Although I, for one, would hardly call it a visit.) He pressed us to go over what felt like every single minute of every single day from the time Bridgy discovered Oscar's body until Frank's sheriff's car screeched to a halt and blocked Margo's BMW in her driveway. Of course we had questions, too, but the lieutenant was not inclined to answer them.

It seemed like I'd only slept for about five minutes when Bridgy was pulling on my arm and whispering, "Time for work. The moms are still sleeping. Let's not wake them."

Groggy as I was, I knew waking the moms was the last thing I wanted to do. We got home mega late the night before. Aunt Ophie and the moms were waiting for us with more questions than even Frank Anthony. Although, in their favor, they served hot chocolate.

As had become our habit, I drove the Heap-a-Jeep, and we left Bridgy's shiny red Escort for the moms. I mused that we were up so late they would probably sleep until noon.

Bridgy laughed. "We'll be lucky if they are awake when we get home. Oh, and Miguel's party is tonight. At least we won't have to worry about dinner. Umm, shrimp."

We'd barely gotten out of the jeep when Miguel opened the café door. "*Chicas,* to think you had a gangster's girlfriend in your book club. *Ay,* and she's a multiple murderer."

"Miguel, all the deputies would tell us was that Margo confessed to killing Oscar because of something that happened in Atlantic City decades ago. How do you know . . . ?"

Miguel waved a copy of the *Fort Myers Beach News.* "I guess they told Cady a lot more than they told you. Freedom of the press. First Amendment to the Constitution. Read all about it. He has a right to know."

I snatched the paper from his hand. The front page headline read: "MOBSTER'S MOLL CAPTURED IN FORT MYERS BEACH." *Well,* I thought, *that will do wonders for the tourist trade.*

Bridgy stretched over my shoulder. She pointed to a paragraph just below the headline. "Look at this. She claims that back in the eighties her boyfriend beat her so she stabbed him in his sleep and made off with a pile of money he was supposed to deliver to his boss, a drug and gambling czar."

"I guess that proves stabbing is her murderous method of choice." I quivered at the thought. "But what does it have to do with Oscar?"

"Enough, *chicas.*" Miguel pulled the newspaper out of my hand. "Be grateful she is under lock and key and no longer coming here for sweet tea and pecan pie. Come see what I have done."

Miguel led us into the kitchen and pointed to the windowsill. "I came in early and planted basil seedlings in three shells, which is all that the windowsill will hold."

We smothered him with praise. I knew

that his effort would make Sage happy; I only hoped that it wouldn't lead her in new and more annoying directions.

Miguel was in the middle of telling us that he would put some shelves across the window so we could have more seashells filled with herb seedlings, when the ship's bell outside the front door began to gong insistently.

I slid my phone out of my pocket to check the time. It was much too early for customers. I went to see what all the commotion was about, and there were the moms.

Sage gave me a quick hug. "We know you and Bridgy have to be exhausted, so we've come to help."

Emelia chimed in, "And to prove to our little girls that we can handle this café." And the two of them marched into the kitchen.

Within seconds, we heard Sage exclaim, "Seedlings and horse conch shells. I knew they'd be perfect together."

I was grabbing another copy of the *Fort Myers Beach News* off the pile by the register when the ship's bell clanged again. Ophie!

She twirled in, rocking on gray patent leather high heels, which matched the belt cinching the waist of her black-and-white striped dress. "What do you think? Prison chic in honor of Margo, who'll be wearing stripes for the rest of her life."

I tossed the newspaper on the counter. Obviously, I was never going to be able to draw the direct line from Oscar to Margo. Usually oblivious to other people's frustration, Ophie was extremely considerate.

"Honey chile, y'all are upset. Not enough sleep, I'm guessin'."

"It's not that. Everyone seems to know what happened between Margo and Oscar except Bridgy and me." I shook the newspaper. "And I can't find a minute to read Cady's article."

"Y'all don't need a newspaper. Just remember the book club outing. Oscar was running his usual patter about knowing all us girls back when. He kept saying he remembered some of us from his Atlantic City days. Even said he thought he recognized a chorus girl or two."

"And that was enough for Margo to kill him? Oscar always joked around, he never meant anything by it." I was still stymied.

"We're all used to Oscar's clowning but a snowbird like Margo couldn't be sure. And she was a woman with secrets. She had no way of knowing Oscar's banter wasn't real. From what I read, she confronted him in the van, he kept up his teasing and out came the scissors. Both their fates were sealed over a bit of foolishness."

Ophie skipped a beat and pushed me toward the kitchen. "Emy called me to help run the café today. Now let's get Bridgy. Y'all are going home to rest up for Miguel's big shindig."

We resisted for a while, but with Ophie and the moms pushing and prodding, Bridgy and I went home to rest during the break between breakfast and lunch. It made sense. The five of us were tripping over one another, and I could see Miguel's frustration building. He liked a certain order in his kitchen, and the last thing anyone wanted was for him to be cranky at his shrimp *fiesta*.

CHAPTER THIRTY-SIX

Miguel had strung twinkling lights on the palm trees in front of his house and on the bushes along the bayside.

When Bridgy and I arrived with the moms, Miguel's yard was already filling up. Tina Wei looked adorable in shorts and an oversized baseball shirt that read "LEE COUNTY SHERIFF" in big letters. I reminded myself to congratulate her on the fabulous home run she'd hit in the softball game against Charlotte County.

Ophie, along with her friend Mark Clamenta, was serving *batidos* to Maggie Latimer and her daughter Holly.

Ryan, Cady and Owen Reston were grouped together, laughing like chums, which, now that Oscar's murder was solved, they were. I looked around for Skully, although I knew better than to expect him to show up at a social event.

Sage, dressed in a long, flowing rainbow

pastel caftan with matching turban, immediately began to go around the patio reading auras and telling everyone how fabulous it was that her daughter had so many friends. The screen door opened. Miguel and Cynthia Mays came outside each carrying a tray of finger foods.

"Come. Enjoy. *Tapas Cubana.*" Miguel held out his tray. "*Torta de frioles,* black bean casserole with homemade guacamole. Cynthia is serving chorizo with a nice sangria glaze."

I took a bite of the chorizo. It was heavenly. "Miguel, I think you have outdone yourself."

"This is only the beginning. I have made six shrimp dishes. No, no. I will not say. You must wait to eat until after the entertainment."

"Entertainment? Miguel you have gone all out."

"Not me. I have done nothing, but you remember my neighbor, Liam Gerrity, and his gorgeous Tess, *sí?* They are the entertainment."

I nodded politely. Since Tess was a beautiful snow-white bichon frise whose real name was Countess Aurelia, I suspected the entertainment would be of the sit, bark, roll over variety. "And what of Bow?" I asked about Miguel's high-gloss black Maine Coon. "Won't she play with us tonight?"

Miguel shook his head. "If you tread very lightly to the edge of the garden, you may see her. Bow is likely to be sitting on the roots of the red mangrove just past the saw palmetto bush. She does not like too much company."

I was about to go look for her when Frank Anthony, dressed in cutoffs and a surfer tee, came around the side of the house and used his lieutenant voice to command our attention. When he was sure he had all eyes and ears, he pulled out his phone and gave a quick look to his left as though waiting for someone or something.

Gray haired and balding, Liam Gerrity's protruding stomach came into view just before he did, with Tess at his heels. They turned to face the crowd on the patio, and Frank Anthony pushed a button on his phone.

As soon as we heard the first musical notes, there was a general uproar on the patio, and then we quieted down and listened to Silentó asking us to watch him whip and watch him nae nae. But it was Liam Gerrity and Tess who were putting on the show.

Mr. Gerrity was seriously getting his

groove on, and Tess was matching him step for step. When Tess extended her paw for the whip, we all cheered. She wiggled her cute little furry butt for the nae nae.

The music stopped, and Frank Anthony yelled, "Once again. Everybody." He pushed a button on the phone, and the patio turned into a dance hall. I almost doubled over watching the moms doing the stanky leg. When they got to the bop, Emelia said, "This part reminds me a little of the Charleston."

Ophie nearly exploded. "Emy, really, the Charleston? How old do you want these young'uns to think we are?"

After the third round of "Watch Me," I collapsed in a heap on a bench. "I need to rest."

Sage petted my head. "My sweet rosebud, your rest has been our goal. With Miguel's guidance, Emelia, Ophie and I can run the café for a few days. You and Bridgy need a break."

Bridgy plopped next to me. "If we could get away for a little R and R, where on earth would we go?"

Ophie joined the moms in shouting, "Key West."

AUTHOR'S NOTE

Tammy Rushing Lynn won a character naming in *Read to Death.* Her winning bid was used to support the Friends of the Wetumpka Library in Wetumpka, Alabama, a great town where I had tremendous fun at the 2015 library fund-raiser.

I am honored that artist Paula Eckerty allowed me to use her name and the name of her exquisite painting *Let the Fairy in You Fly,* which is part of an exhibit that celebrates the collaboration between the Southwest Florida International Airport and the Lee County Alliance for the Arts. The ongoing art exhibits have given hundreds of thousands of travelers, including me, much visual pleasure as we pass through the airport.

Finally, I'd like to thank Karen Owen for once again developing a tasty recipe that has quickly become a favorite for the Read 'Em and Eat gang.

RECIPES

OLD MAN AND THE SEA CHOWDER
2 tablespoons oil
2 small onions, chopped
1/2 cup sliced celery
1/2 cup sliced carrots
4 cups peeled, diced potato
4 cups chicken broth
3 tablespoons clam juice
1 1/2 cups water
1 1/2 teaspoons tarragon
2 teaspoons parsley flakes
1/2 teaspoon thyme
1/2 teaspoon paprika
2 pounds catfish fillets, cut into small pieces
1 dozen shrimp, cleaned, deveined and cut into two or three pieces each
3 tablespoons butter
1/2 cup flour
1 cup milk
Salt and pepper

Heat oil in large pot. Sauté onion and celery until tender. Add carrots, potato, chicken broth, clam juice, water and spices. Cover and simmer 15 minutes. Add catfish. Simmer 10 minutes. Add shrimp. Continue to simmer 5 to 10 minutes or until catfish flakes. Melt butter and mix with flour until smooth. Drop tiny dollops of flour mixture into chowder. Whisk each dollop gradually and thoroughly. Simmer 5 to 10 minutes. Lower heat, add milk, stir 3 to 5 minutes. Add salt and pepper to taste.

Serves 8-10

DRUNKEN RAISIN SCONES
by *Karen Owen*

Raisin Whiskey Reduction
1/4 cup raisins
1/4 cup whiskey
1/4 cup water
1 teaspoon cinnamon
2 teaspoons sugar

Place all ingredients in a small saucepan. Stir. Bring to a boil then simmer until the liquid is reduced by half. Remove from heat. Set aside two tablespoons of reduction liquid for the glaze. Set aside the raisins and the remainder of the liquid for the scones.

SCONES

2 cups flour
3 tablespoons sugar
3 teaspoons baking powder
1/2 cup soft butter
1/3 cup milk
1 egg
Raisin reduction minus 2 tablespoons liquid
  reserved for glaze

Preheat oven to 400 degrees.

Sift flour, sugar and baking powder in a bowl. Cut butter in small pieces and hand blend into the flour mixture until it resembles bread crumbs. Hand stir milk and egg into the flour mixture. Add raisin reduction to scone batter and mix. If dough is too wet, add a small amount of flour.

On a cutting board, shape dough into a mound. Cut into eight triangles and place on a cookie sheet without touching. Bake until the edges are golden brown. Remove from oven and let cool slightly before glazing.

WHISKEY ICING GLAZE

1/4 cup powdered sugar
2 tablespoons reserved reduced whiskey mixture (liquid only)
2 tablespoons milk

Place powdered sugar in a small bowl. Stir in liquid and milk. If glaze is too thick, thin to taste with a few drops of water.